Soulwalker
Erica Lawson

Soulwalker

Erica Lawson

Affinity
eBook Press
NZ
2015

Soulwalker
© by Erica Lawson 2012

Affinity E-Book Press NZ LTD.
Canterbury, New Zealand

2nd Edition

ISBN: 978-1-927328-76-7

Editor: Nann Dunne
Cover Design: Irish Dragon Designs

Dedication

To Em, Jane, Andi and Nann for being my guiding lights.

Table of Contents

Also by Erica Lawson

Chapter 1

It was a beast of a night.

The rain was incessant, the wind bitterly cold, and the darkness deep—a night best left to those creatures that thrived in the worst of weather, creatures that had no need for the light.

In the middle of the downpour strode a lone figure, head bent against the driving drops. The mysterious figure cast no shadow as it moved amid the puddles of water on the sidewalk. It appeared to be nothing more than a black shape in the muted shadows of the night. The shrouded head looked up for a moment, turned this way and that, and bowed its head again to continue the journey.

The streets were all but empty, except for this one soul who defied the fury of nature to venture out. But nature had little effect on this creature that wandered the streets with impunity. The figure, focused on its destination, barely acknowledged the maelstrom that raged around it.

No ordinary whim drove the shadow through this hell. It had a grave purpose that would brook no denial. Neither the elements nor the night would divert it from its course. It had only one mistress, and it was to her that it deferred its will. For without her it had no will, no thought, and no existence.

The storm showed no signs of abatement, instead it seemed a physical manifestation of the shadow that passed through it. But it had no emotional connection to this maelstrom. The shadow was a tool and nothing more.

The creature reached the building where the object of its purpose lay. With ghostly eyes it looked upward and studied the half dozen floors. It made its way toward the entrance, then changed direction at the last minute to find another, more shadowed, way in.

Instead of scaling the outside of the building, the shadow opted for the emergency exit. It slid up into the dimness near the ceiling to the fourth floor. It oozed along its path, found all the nooks and crannies that housed the night, and avoided the blinding flash of light: for that's where it existed... in the dark. It was a dark creature for a dark night.

Finally it reached its destination. It eased through a crack in the door and entered the darkened apartment. Hollow eyes scanned the blackness, easily seeing everything as if in the light of day.

Find him. Kill him.

The words resonated through its form. It had learned and memorized those words many times in the past and had carried out the order in the name of the government.

He was where it had expected to find him, asleep in bed. The creature stood over its intended victim for a moment before it extended an invisible hand slowly toward the man's chest. The hand continued through skin, muscle, and bone until it rested under the heart. Its almost nonexistent palm could feel the steady pumping action as the muscle expanded and contracted. Slowly and steadily the hand closed, putting pressure on the heart to stop. The man didn't stir from his sleep as the assassin's ghostly hand continued to squeeze, tightening until the heart could no longer function.

The shadow confirmed the kill. The victim lay there as if peacefully asleep. No one would ever know how he died.

The shadow retreated. It was time to return to its mistress, answering the lonely call of its sister's soul.

Covered in sweat, the trooper tossed and turned, her mind working frantically to bring her warrior home. She could see, feel, and hear every move it made in her mind's eye; it was part of her. Her inner warrior had performed its task and was now returning to rest until next time. Next time... how many times would she be called upon to carry out this duty?

When she had joined the Special Black Shadow Corps, little did Tarris Waite suspect that she would effectively be a shadow assassin. "Serve your country," the Council said. "You have a special gift that no one appreciates," they said. What a sap she had been. If she refused, she would be the next victim of one of her fellow warriors. Serve or die. She was trapped.

When it all began, she had little choice about what her vocation would be. Her special abilities had drawn the attention of the Union, as their reigning government was called, and opened doors that were firmly closed for everyone else. Of course, she had one physical attribute that earmarked her for the SBSC. She was an albino.

Tarris soon found out why only an albino could serve in the Corps. Her kind nurtured the inner shadow, expelling the soul to carry out the wishes of its master or, in her case, its mistress. From what she could tell, only a few albinos served the Council and even fewer female albinos. What had started as a glorious career in the service of the law had turned into something more sinister; something she no longer wanted to be part of.

Her shadow crept toward her, and Tarris prepared to accept it back into her body. The transfer took place as the dark shape seeped through pale skin and bone to reside in a disabled body that could no longer walk. How ironic was that? Tarris had a mind that could command an assassin, yet she couldn't move her own legs.

"Rya…" she whispered. Tarris was born a twin, though she never had the chance to know her sister who died at birth. But she could always feel her sister's spirit inside her. She was a friend when needed and a shoulder to cry on. The child had been named Ryalla at her burial because no child should be sent on to the afterlife without a name. So Tarris called her shadow Rya, in place of the twin she had never gotten to know.

Tarris opened her almost colorless eyes, and her pupils contracted in the light from the bedside lamp. She was drained and in pain. Pushing Rya through the heavy rain took more energy than she had imagined. Her fingers went to her wrist, and she gently rubbed the area over the pulse point. She closed her eyes, not bothering to move, and allowed the medicated patch sitting under her skin to do its work. She put aside all her concerns and would worry about it tomorrow.

†

Tarris blinked. The sun was out. It had been so long since it had graced the city that she had forgotten what it looked like. Gentle rays lay over her bedcover and showed how old the coverlet was. As much as she wanted to stay put, dismiss the day, and drown in a sea of medicated sleep, she had a meeting to go to this morning. She reached overhead to the wall to find the familiar button. A gentle whirr tilted the bed and allowed her to slide into the waiting wheelchair.

Some days she hated life. On those days, depression hung around her like a bad smell. The bad thoughts were just there, always reminding her of her disability. What she wouldn't give to be able to walk unaided, to run, and just to be like everyone else out in the street. Quickly and efficiently the motorized chair moved around, while electronic aids helped her dress, bathe, and eat. Nothing was simple anymore. Hands were only useful these days for pushing buttons.

As much as she dreaded it, she donned her disguise. As she stood in the metal body harness, she changed her hair color and eyes. Dark replaced light in an effort to blend in. She hated this, she really did, but society feared who she was. While her fellow Corps members revelled in their identity, she did not. If she wanted to move about freely it was necessary.

As she stepped out into the sunlight, Tarris pushed her temple to darken the lenses in her eyes. Sensitive to the point of pain, her pale eyes needed to be shielded from the glare, and she used the sun-protective lenses to compensate. Because she used the body suit only when she had to, it took a number of steps before she became accustomed to it once more. One of the older models, it caused her some pain, but its use was the price she paid not to be heckled.

She moved steadily through the crowded streets and

made her way downtown to an unremarkable building. Gray, metallic and windowless, it screamed of mystery, but very few approached it like she was doing now. A small glass panel appeared in the wall, and she had to touch her temple to show her true eye color. Her iris was scanned, and the nearly invisible door slid silently aside to permit her entrance.

Inside the walls, she dropped her disguise. Dark hair became light once more, allowing her long blonde locks to flow freely over her black-leather overcoat. Her pale eyes looked into the darkness and sought out the exit at the other end of the shadowed corridor. Barely a whisper could be heard from her body suit as servos and gears worked seamlessly to mechanically walk her down the passageway. Powered by two small atomic battery packs, the suit was surprisingly effective despite being nearly an antique. But the newer models had their problems, and she was happy to stay with the old suit and its little quirks, much to the derision of the other members of the group.

"It took you long enough." Her main competitor, Alix Corman, made a quick comment on her arrival. "Did you have to crawl all the way?" The two troopers seated next to him snickered loudly.

Tarris noted his negligent disregard of her and how his lips curled in a sneer. He was tall, thin, and arrogant, although the arrogance was his primary characteristic. Apparently Corman wore his dark clothes as a visual deterrent; the blackness drew attention to his white hair and pale skin and showed everyone how dangerous he was.

Tarris's blonde eyebrows met in a scowl, and she took a step forward. She looked down into Corman's eyes, but he wasn't intimidated. "Shut your mouth, Corman."

"Did you hear a squeak?" he asked his cohorts. "It sounded like a mouse."

Tarris bunched her hands into fists and felt Rya stir within her. The hair on Corman's skin stood up on end. Assuming Corman saw the stirring, Tarris didn't stop it. Rya took exception to her treatment at the hands of the egotistical blowhard facing her.

Corman's eyes widened and he closed his mouth. He lounged lazily over the chair, however, and refused to move his feet to let Tarris pass. He gazed at her and smirked. He was daring her to step over.

She touched her belt, and her leg shot out and connected with his ankle. As she passed, she shoved him and his chair rocked back. He regained his balance and tangled his foot with hers. Tarris sprawled on the ground, and there was a collective gasp. Each trooper looked from one to the other, but no one moved.

Finally, Shark stepped forward and placed his hands under her armpits. He lifted gently, and when she had gained her balance, he let go and backed away. Corman gave her a sly grin. "Can't lift your leg on your own? Maybe you should get yourself one of those gravity pods. It's got to be quicker than that clumsy thing you wear. No wonder you're always late." He flicked his hand in the air as though to dismiss her. He always wanted to have the final word, but one day she hoped to collect every nasty word he uttered and ram them down his throat.

He, and many like him, looked down on her because she wasn't, as they called it, "purebred" albino. The faint bluish tinge in her eyes attested to that fact. But what they considered a fault, she considered an asset.

Despite her tainted blood, she was considered the most

powerful in the group and none would openly challenge her. Whether or not that was actually true had never been tested, but Tarris herself didn't believe it. In her adolescence, Rya had responded to her anger and pain. Her shadow was seen by those who were supposed to rein her in as an almost primal force. Rumor and innuendo of her antics at school had elevated her status to that of "freak," not that anyone except Corman ever called her that to her face. That didn't stop the snide remarks though, and she was tired of them.

"I'm not always late. It was a nice day for walking. The sun's out for Christ's sake. When was the last time you saw that?"

"Why bother? It's our enemy, remember?"

"Whatever," she mumbled. Preaching was pointless. They weren't going to convert.

"Why do you continue to try to fit in? We're above all that."

"Because whether you like it or not, we all live on this speck of dust."

"Not for long…" Corman muttered, and a murmur of approval spread around the assembled group. Tarris held her tongue for now; she needed to keep silent. Making enemies of those in front of her was very dangerous indeed.

"Report!" a voice called from speakers set in the walls. The group sat round the table in a huddle, their attention turned to the small screen in front of them.

"One, go," Tarris said. Because of her perceived power, she always answered first. How many times had she said that? Another life snuffed out in the name of government security.

"Two, go."

"Three, go." All reported successful missions. Just once she wished it was for something other than death. When she first started in the group, their missions comprised stealth and covert operations, spying on their enemies, collecting secret information and sabotage. Now... now it was only assassination. One by one, anyone who opposed the government came to their attention.

Tarris kept her mind firmly closed to wall off any errant thoughts that might be picked up by someone in the room. She kept everything about herself to herself.

Rule One in her Survival Handbook: Never reveal anything that could be used against you.

Her survival handbook had been her bible. She had compiled it in her head over the years, and each rule had been a hard-won lesson in her life.

"Your next assignment will be in two days' time. It's a group operation." A metal microchip rose up through the desktop. She picked it up between her finger and thumb and stared at it. The chip was such a small thing, and yet it held so much power, the power of life and death. She placed it in her wrist computer to read their next assignment. It seemed simple enough.

What worried her was the frequency of these missions, which occurred on a nearly daily basis. They needed downtime to recharge. She suspected that the powers that be didn't understand the need for rest. She didn't have an unlimited power supply like her atomic batteries. If she didn't rest her mind, things could go wrong.

"Sir." She didn't want to be the one to bring it up, but no one else looked like they would do it. "We need rest.

This is the fourth operation in as many days."

"You don't think you can do it, soldier?" The intonation set off alarm bells in her head.

"Of course, sir. But lack of rest could result in mistakes." She vainly looked around to the others for support. She was on her own, as she suspected she would be.

"We don't make mistakes here, soldier." There was an unspoken message there. Make a mistake and you're dead. She could feel hostility from the others, like a pack of wolves circling a downed deer, ready to pounce for the kill. She had revealed herself, and now she was a marked woman.

Her ice-blue eyes swept the room, taking and holding each set of white eyes in turn. She let them know that she was still the leader and that they would suffer if they tried anything. However, she was not so sure she could hold them all off if they ever tried to fight as one. So far they hadn't figured that out.

"As you say, sir, but our minds need time to recover. Optimum performance comes from a rested mind." She didn't mind quoting back their rules.

"Well met, soldier. Very well, the operation will be postponed one solar day." Tarris breathed a sigh of relief. She had stood her ground and won. The wolves backed down and cowered away. "Dismissed." The troopers stood and moved away from the table as the meeting was concluded.

Tarris could feel the discrimination. The purebreds found one another and huddled together in one corner of the room, periodically eyeing her. They were narrow-minded fools who looked down on all those who didn't have the telltale white eyes. And yet she ruled, and it galled them that a pretender outranked them.

Tarris left her underlings to plot and plan and hurried outside to take refuge in the sunlight. She tapped her temple to increase the intensity of her lenses to turn her eyes dark. Her full-length, faux leather coat flapped open as she strode along, and her fingers deftly found the hidden pressure points in the body suit to increase her momentum.

Black hair swirled around the serious face deep in thought. Normally Tarris would return home after the meeting, but anger and concern occupied her. She took comfort from the warming rays; the bright light uplifted her depressed state. She cast her gaze around and observed an easy atmosphere. The sun, especially after such a long spell of constant rain, brought out smiles that hadn't been around since the last sunny day.

She stripped off her coat, slung it over her shoulder, and allowed the warmth to filter through her long-sleeved shirt and pants. Her legs felt nothing of it, but she knew it was there. Her fellow albinos were horrified that she worshipped the sun so readily, one more thing that separated her from her kind.

Tarris looked up. The onset of clouds already stained the sky. She sighed. Rain was on its way again, thanks to the chemical impact of the gasoline cars of eighty years ago on the environment. Well, that was what the politicians said. Gas had been banned from use years ago when the air became too polluted to breathe. Time had healed the damage to the air and yet pollution was still to blame. So rain and cloud blotted out the sun, perpetual rain the only survivor of the atmosphere. But sometimes Tarris wondered who ruled the planet, the Union or the albinos, because darkened skies were the friends of the white eyes.

Electric cars now prowled the cities, run by the same types of batteries that powered her suit. They weren't as efficient or as long lasting as what she had, but she knew people in high places, and it always paid to know people in the right places.

The rain returned as she stepped through the front door of her building. She was tired, not only from last night's activity but also from moving the body suit around the city. The Monitor had given her one extra solar day, so she would make the most of it.

She stripped off her clothes with the aid of her mechanical "helper" and sighed with relief when she was finally out of the power-driven suit. Her body slumped after being held up for so long by metal and wires. Once more in her bed, she stimulated the medication tag in her wrist, feeling the drowsiness grab her and drag her down to sleep.

✝

Fleeting shadows disturbed the night. Tarris awoke to the whispers of shifting air. Helpless to fight effectively despite the body suit, she sought out her shadow warrior to defend her. With great difficulty she calmed her mind, drew up the assassin, and felt the familiar rush as Rya left her.

Blackness became light as ghostly eyes surveyed the room. Two of Rya's kind were in the room and shifted in concert toward her reclining body. Tarris knew Rya had never been in this position before. How could she find weaknesses in ghostly forms that had none?

Tarris did not back down. She blocked the simmering anxiety of her own imminent death and didn't allow her actions to falter. How dare they even try to take her down! Though she was impure of blood and body, Tarris was pure of mind and spirit. She didn't fight with deceit or dishonor like they did. She was an assassin, but she had a soul.

The larger of the two warriors feinted toward Tarris's warrior and drew her off. Rya always attacked her enemies without fear, and a shadow warrior was no different to her. This, Tarris thought, was why she would always succeed. The two of them fought as one, one lending strength to the other when the need arose. Tarris knew this one truth that the rest of them would never understand.

Tarris realized the error almost a moment too late. She sensed the swift movement behind her as Rya faced her enemy. Rya moved with great speed to cover her unprotected body and took the brunt of the attack on its shadowy form. With a strength unknown to Tarris, Rya lifted her useless body and moved it out of the way as the two specters increased the attack. There was nowhere to run.

Darkness became bright light as they passed across a portal that had not been there before. Rya struggled to hold form under the harsh light of day. Tarris was placed in the shadow of a great rock and felt her ghost warrior lose her battle with the light. She was safe, but at what cost?

Exhaustion lapped at Tarris's reserves as she floundered in the shade. She closed her eyes and rested. She would worry about her future later.

Tarris woke to someone hovering over her. There was no strength left to fight it off, so she quietly accepted that this was the end of the line. A hand reached down to help her to her feet.

She was a striking woman, with short, dark hair and

rich blue eyes. "Arrloovarite?"

†

Tarris awoke with a jerk. What was that? She was not a Seeker of Truth, prone to premonitions, but could she deny what had transpired in her dream? Or was it her anxious mind playing out what she was afraid of? Either way, could she afford to ignore it?

"Light on." Too wound up to sleep, she tapped the button above her bed and slid easily into the waiting wheelchair. The muted brightness of the light forced her to touch her temple to darken the implanted lenses to a tolerable level. She had never regretted having the operation, because it made her life easier. Of course, her fellow assassins saw it as a betrayal to the cause and another wedge between them. They, and especially Corman, were proud to be albino, so any enhancement to their appearance was considered a betrayal of their heritage. She could never understand their position to stay "pure" and give up the comfort the lenses provided.

She touched the buttons on the chair to move smoothly to the kitchen, barely an alcove in these times. She punched in her order and waited moments for the food to be reconstituted and heated automatically. Tarris wondered what it would have been like before all the automation, to survive on her own skills, her courage, her guile, and her instincts. It was but a pipe dream. She would never be allowed to travel outside the metropolis to find out.

She had heard of wild adventure holidays that did just that. They would take you to a barely habitable piece of the planet and leave you there for several solar days to scratch around in the dirt. You never knew where they were going to take you; if you were lucky, you ended up in an area with vegetation. If you pissed them off, might as well kiss your ass goodbye. It was a highly regulated industry because of the risks involved, but it was extremely popular among the naturalists who found the environmentally controlled parks not enough for their adventurous spirits.

The food was tasteless in her mouth. Its only redeeming factor was that it had all the nutrients she needed. Of late, everything was not as satisfying as it used to be. The food was a little blander, sleep a little less restful, and her job a little less appealing. Life was missing something, and she didn't know how to change that. She grabbed what was left of her meal and moved her chair over to her computer that sat on a desk in the far corner of the room. While she ate, she tapped away on the computer monitor to check her mail. Several messages beeped at her, and she knew she couldn't avoid calling her mother. No time like the present...

"Hello?"

"Hey, Mom, just returning your calls." Tarris thought she looked a little worn out.

"How are you, Tarris?"

"I'm fine."

"You look a little tired, honey." Tarris couldn't help but smile. "What's wrong?"

"I was just thinking the same thing, Mom. Are you working too hard?"

"Don't you worry about me. I just wanted to see your face again. I... I miss you."

She didn't want to hear it because it would be the final straw to her day. "Me, too, Mom. Me, too. How is it at the commune?"

"The same. Nothing ever changes here, you know that." Yeah, she knew that. The government communes were nothing more than free labor in exchange for a bed and food. Many times she had tried to get her mother to move into the metropolis, but the older woman was set in her ways and didn't want to change. Maybe it was better that way; it avoided any explanations.

"So, how's work going?" Her mother's voice cut through her thoughts.

"Fine. The same as usual."

"You know, Tarris, you should find something more exciting than computer work." They had the same conversation every time they talked.

"What else am I good for, Mom? Bound to a wheelchair limits my options." No way in hell was she going to tell her own mother what she really did for a living.

"Still, you don't get to meet people, hon. You need to get out more."

Tarris mentally rolled her eyes. Get out more. Sure. Like that was possible. "I tried, you know that. It was more trouble than it was worth. Now I just live my life free of the stares and sly remarks." All communications were monitored, so the talk with her mother was always superficial. Protect what is yours was her motto. "When are you coming next to visit?"

"I don't know…"

"Come on, Mom. I haven't seen you in ages. I'll send a hover out for you in a few weeks." Tarris was so lonely that even a visit from her mother would be welcome.

"Honey, I…" Tarris could see the indecision in her

mother's eyes. Something was going on. "I'll think about it, okay?"

"Sure. Fine."

"I'll get back to you sometime next week."

"Good." Tarris couldn't hide the disappointment in her voice.

"Honey, don't be like that. I will think about it... honest."

"Fine. I'll hear from you next week then." Tarris felt snubbed. She had an urge to see her mother in the flesh instead of on the videophone, but the woman balked at the invitation.

"Take care of yourself, Tarris."

"You, too, Mom." The screen went blank, and Tarris stared at it. Her mother, Clerek, was the only one who accepted everything that she was. Well, everything that she knew about. To her mother, it didn't matter that Tarris was albino. Her mother considered it just a matter of color and not class distinction.

Tarris had never known her father. Clerek was part of the artificial insemination program run by the Union, so the father's identity was never revealed. Still, she had been the only albino in a neighborhood of dark-haired children. Even her own twin was a dark-hair, or so she was told. Why was she so different? Didn't that go against the laws of science?

She wondered. Her naturally suspicious mind had always thought that strange. Was she genetically engineered or just part of the natural selection? She hoped to her god that she was a natural aberration and not part of some master plan by the people in power.

She smiled. The accident that resulted in her losing the

use of her legs would cripple their plans. *Serves you right, you bastards! Meddling in things that are better left alone.*

She steered the wheelchair back to the kitchen and reached for a caffeine pill and a bottle of what she thought of as water. Over the generations, the liquid had been tinkered with, manipulated, and altered at a microscopic level. Who knew what the liquid had first tasted like? Maybe it was like the rain that fell. She hoped not. The contaminants in that would slowly poison her.

Tarris returned to the computer screen, popped the lid on the bottle, dropped in the pill, and activated the heating pack on the side. She placed the bottle down on the table to allow the mixture to ferment.

An interesting article had been sent to her by one of her powerful friends, and she began to read it while sucking on her beverage. A mediprac had done some innovative research on nerve regeneration, and Tarris was eager to find out if it could help her. She wanted to get out of her chair any way she could.

It sounded promising. She looked for the mediprac's name. Asher Hyrea. Tarris moved her chair to a shadowed corner of her apartment. "Safe..." she murmured. A small block of the wall became transparent and revealed a metal box inside. Here she kept her secrets, the material and emotional ones. She extracted a small device, momentarily looking into the box and studying its contents. If they ever found out what she possessed, her life would be forfeit. It didn't worry her though. If they got that far, she'd be dead anyway.

She put the box back in the alcove and closed it "Stealth..." The cloaking device was the best she was able to obtain, just like her other little toys in the box. Not only did the field hide the box, but also it was resistant to all types of electronic probing. To those who searched, it was just another piece of wall.

Tarris plugged the tiny device into the computer port. The Silencer now made communication safe, setting up a ghost line that made it invisible to all but the sender and the receiver. It was worth its weight in crude oil. Touching the name, she waited momentarily for the person to answer. When the call remained unanswered, she left a message to try to arrange a meeting in a few solar days. By then her next assignment would be completed and she would be rested.

Tarris read the article again. To date no one had even come close to this kind of research, and if this person had any chance of getting her out of her chair, Tarris would call on every friend she had to make it happen.

She finally let her lethargy overcome her. She wheeled back to the bed and pulled her immobile lower half onto the platform. "Light off. Locks on." Her home now secure, Tarris touched the medicated patch, and as sleep slowly descended, her heart was a little lighter with the thought that she might have a chance to live a normal life again.

Chapter 2

The day had barely begun when Tarris woke. Rain continued to fall and settled a heavy gloom over the city. While she lay in bed and looked at the ceiling, she tried to decide whether to go back to sleep or try to make something of the day, because tonight... well, tonight was work.

She's just woken up from a dream, one that she hadn't had in quite a while. Why was she dreaming about Boothe now? So much had happened in her life since then. She had done so many vile, unspeakable things in the name of the Council that they had become a blur. Boothe was just a passing friend who died in suspicious circumstances...

"Why?" Tarris asked angrily.

"It was an accident, Tarris," the teacher said.

"But... but, Educator Charis, I don't understand. I know who did this, and you let him get away with it." She wanted justice, and she wanted it now.

"But you can't prove that. We can't just summarily punish him without proof."

"So Boothe dies without justice?" Tarris could feel her restless spirit squirming around inside her.

"Are you all right?" Charis looked at her with

concern. *"Tell me what you feel."*

"You know what I feel. Why do you ask me?" Tarris had learned that her ice-blue eyes slowly darkened to a cornflower blue when she experienced emotional turmoil. Of course Charis observed that.

"Because you need to vent these feelings. You need to let go."

"I don't want to let go. This is all so unfair." Tarris's anger rose.

"What about the power within you? What is it doing now?"

"She is crying out for revenge!" she screamed.

"She?" Tarris could see that Educator Charis was interested, and it annoyed her to no end that he was dealing with it in an almost clinical way.

"Yeah, she. She's churning away inside me, and she wants to come out."

"She's evolving like you are, Tarris," he explained patiently. *"Puberty is a turbulent time. Maybe she's reacting to what you feel."*

"I know that. Stop treating me like a child." Tarris paced angrily, like one of those caged lions she had seen on the archive discs. She had heard the rumors about her "potential," but she wasn't interested. She just wanted to be normal, to be invisible. The constant scrutiny upset her. She had been labeled "a freak of nature," because they had heard whisperings of secret experiments. Not that she believed it. Tarris was a breed apart, and she was suffering for it.

"Calm down. Breathe deeply like you've been taught."

Charis's efforts did nothing to help her. In fact, it only irritated her more. *"Why? Why am I different?"*

"I'm sorry, child, I can't answer that. All I know is that you, unlike the others, were one of twins, and a mixed union at that."

"No others?" Strange.

"No. Everyone who has passed through here was born as a single child. Maybe those blue eyes of yours are not so much an imperfection but a sign that you've been touched by your sister."

Tarris grabbed onto that explanation with both hands. She vainly tried to find some positive thing out of her birth. "What about what I feel inside? It... it's so strong... too strong."

"Then I will see to it that your training is accelerated so you can control her."

Control her? Did Tarris want to do that? In her younger years, Rya had been a comfort to her, a friend when she had none. Did she want to do anything as callous as control her like some object? "What about Boothe?"

"I'm sorry, Tarris, but the ruling has been made. It was an accidental death."

Tarris shook her head to dispel the image and the emotion the memory held. She was rested enough and was looking for some diversion from the job to come.

Work of late concerned her. In her mind she tried to justify what she did by claiming that if she didn't carry out the assassinations someone else would. It was a pretty poor excuse, even to her. Still, she made the deaths as quick and painless as possible, taking no joy in the kill.

She reached for the button and waited impatiently for mobility. The wheelchair moved over to her single window, and she looked out. Gray cloud obliterated the sun. She thought about what she wanted to do for a moment, and a slow smile crossed her face as she made her plans for the day. She knew exactly where to go.

A short time later she was on the street. The rain dripped down her damp hair into her eyes. When a taxi pulled up, she activated the hidden buttons on her belt to move the body suit to a seated position inside the cab. "Park Three." The low volume of her voice carried to the speaker that connected her to the driver. Smoothly, the electric car moved into the sparse traffic and headed toward the center of the huge city.

Tarris looked out the window and watched the world pass by. Despite the rain, life went on. While not many pedestrians stepped out into the foul weather, many took covered walkways or taxis. Private cars were for the rich, while the general populace was forced to find alternate transport.

The car pulled up in front of a massive block of metal. Conspicuous only by its size, inside it was a wonderland. Tarris placed her wrist against the scanner in the cab for the machine to access her tattooed barcode. The amount of credits for the trip would be automatically deducted from her account. She studied the black ink on her arm. The small lines encoded everything that she was—her finances, her health, her status, everything, right down to the tiny mole on the bottom of her ass. Nothing escaped them.

It took a few moments for the servos to click into an upright position to enable her to walk, and waiting for them left her hunched over in the rain. Water droplets hit her hair and ran down inside the collar of her coat. "Damn it!" Impatiently, she kept tapping the servo buttons. "Come on... come on..." She felt like an idiot standing in the rain looking at the ground.

Finally, after interminable seconds, the suit responded and she moved swiftly to the sheltered doorway. Her barcode gave her entrance to the building, and she sighed deeply as she stepped through the door. Like that old, old movie, *The Wizard of Oz,* which was one of her favorites, she stepped over the doorway from black and white to living color.

Before her lay a massive park, filled with trees, grass, and birds—a little bit of the old world that she adored. She looked up to the sky, a holographic delight filled with fluffy white clouds and bright sunshine, and breathed in the fresh dry air. It was a beautiful piece of Old Earth in the midst of depression and bleakness.

Steam rose from her damp clothing as she wandered along the pathway, and warmth seeped into her cold bones. While no one in the park knew her true identity, Tarris was a walking contradiction to both white and dark eyes. She was a white eye who loved the light, and she did everything she could to keep that her secret.

Her hand rose to her temple and touched the skin to darken her eyes further. The suit ran smoothly in the warmth, apparently enjoying the dry air as much as she did. Why was it that everything worked better in the light?

"Tarris! Back again I see." A man, maybe in his seventies, sat on the grass under one large tree while he idly picked at the cloth on his pant leg.

"Darmen. Do you live here or something?"

Darmen casually leaned against the tree trunk and enjoyed the sunny day. "If I could, child, I would, but somehow I don't think the Park Service would let me."

"Child?" She was thirty-two years old, she was no

child.

"To me you are, Tarris." When he graced her with a genuine smile, age lines crinkled his skin. "Enjoy your youth, my friend."

"I'll try, but these days there's little to enjoy."

Darmen, a casual friend whom she met whenever she visited the park, didn't know of her disability or her origin. At moments like these, she wished for a friend who knew everything, someone she could let her façade drop in front of and be herself. It would never happen though. Having a friend like that was too dangerous, both for that person and herself.

Rule Two in her Survival Handbook: Don't cultivate friends to be used as hostages by your enemies.

While this rule led to a very lonely life, breaking it had dire consequences. Living alone never worried her excessively before, but of late, a lot of things in her life were becoming burdens. Everything had been fine up to the present. Why was she questioning her life now?

"Come... sit." Darmen patted the grass next to him.

"Not today, Darmen."

"It's a beautiful day, Tarris. Take a load off those feet of yours."

"You are living in a dream world, my friend. Have you seen outside?"

"Of course, but don't you agree this is much more pleasant?"

"I wouldn't be here otherwise." Tarris chuckled at his easygoing banter. Her friend was apparently letting his worries float past him, at least for a short while, as he enjoyed the respite in the sun.

"Come," he said, tantalizing her. "Come." He again patted the ground. She was so tempted to try, but her suit wouldn't allow such a maneuver and that would eventually lead to an explanation.

"As much as I'd like to, I can't."

"Can't, or won't?" The twinkle in his eye and the sly grin on his lips told her he wasn't taking any offense at her refusal.

"Can't." She quickly thought. "My hips won't flex that much. I'd get down there but never get up."

"Oh…" He hesitated. "I… I'm sorry to hear that, child. I hope it's not serious."

Damn… Now she had the old man worrying about her. "It's fine. I've lived with it all my life. I know my limitations, and that"—she pointed to the spot next to him—"is past it." The forlorn look on his face made her continue. "But if you would like to join me for a walk, I'd be grateful for your company." His aged features creased into a grin. She had appeased him, and somehow that made her happy. A few words, and she had made someone happy. Strange.

She reached down to him and felt the fragile strength in the hand at her wrist. Some power still existed in that ageing body. Tarris wondered what her body would be like at that age, if she lived that long. Science had extended human longevity to a ridiculous degree. Older ones, aged way past one hundred and twenty, still survived, the flesh far weaker than the mind that controlled it. But Tarris sincerely doubted she would ever reach such an age. The nature of her job would prevent that.

They strolled along one of the pathways that threaded

through the mammoth park. "So, Tarris, still have no one in your life?"

"Nope, and I doubt I ever will."

"Ahh, if I were forty years younger, girl, it wouldn't be a problem for you."

The heat from the faux sun beat down on them. Beads of sweat broke out on Tarris's brow and upper lip. That was about as much sun as she could tolerate on her white skin at any one time. "Darmen, could we move over to that pathway?" She pointed to another path that wound through the trees, where the overhanging branches broke the light into dappled patches.

"You're looking a little red-faced, Tarris. I was about to suggest that same thing."

"This damned skin of mine won't take too much sunlight."

"Say no more, little one."

Little one? One dark eyebrow rose at him in question. He looked down into her dark eyes and smiled. *Oh...*

"I'm not that small," she muttered. One of the advantages of living alone was that she didn't have to measure herself against anyone else. She was who she was, and that was all that mattered.

Darmen laughed loud. "Big of heart, my friend. Big of heart."

Tarris smiled back. *Yes, big of heart...*

Her mind returned to the past when one particular incident shaped who she was now. Big of heart. It was that big heart of hers that changed her comfortable life to living life on a knife-edge. She had no trouble remembering what the weather was like...

It was raining. Always raining. Rya shifted easily through the darkened side streets, a shadow within a shadow. It was all so easy then. Confidence and a sense of righteous indignation ruled Tarris's life. The victims were flaunters of the law and needed to be dealt with. Cold, efficient, and without feeling, she carried out hits with military precision.

This particular operation involved an Administrator. What had the man done? A hit on an Administrator was unheard of. He was one of the Council, one of those who had control over her unit. His crime against the Union must have been great indeed.

Tarris had been given the assignment because of her status and power. She knew where her strength lay, and she used it without prejudice. As Rya moved through the building that housed the Administrator, Tarris lay quietly and idly noted the abundance of wealth that was on display. So the rich get richer and the poor get poorer. Nothing had changed in the last few millennia.

Eerie white shapes filled her ghostly vision as Rya moved silently through the rooms to search for her targets. The first door didn't move when the shadowed form slid in between the cracks and returned to substance on the other side. Stealthily, she moved forward, the death of the humans inside already complete in Tarris's mind. Just as Rya was about to strike, Tarris stopped her. Confused, Rya sought out her twin. *Why?* The word was presented as a random thought, with no substance to the word, but Tarris understood it just the same

No! Tarris screamed in her head.

Why? Rya repeated.

Look. She is but a child... a baby. Her targets before

were men and an occasional woman, adults who had knowingly broken the law. But a baby was an innocent, and Tarris just couldn't take that innocent life. *Check the other rooms. Do not kill any of them yet.*

Rya did as she was commanded and slipped easily into each room in turn. This was the man's family: three small children and his wife. Tarris had been ordered to kill the man's family. Where was the justice in that?

Return... Tarris whispered. *Return.* Without question, Rya returned to Tarris.

What was going on? They had never targeted children before. Tarris had to know what the man had done to warrant such a harsh punishment. She dressed as quickly as she could and ventured out into the night. It had been a long time since she had tasted the night air. She took a weapon with her just in case of ambush. No matter when you lived, there were always those who prowled the streets at night in search of victims. She had seen them through Rya's eyes on many occasions.

She avoided using a taxi; no one could know what she was about to do. She needed to talk to the Administrator without arousing anyone else's suspicions. It took some effort to make her way to the front door of his building. Leaning heavily against the wall, Tarris sent Rya in search of her victim. *Find the Administrator. Bring him to me.*

There was never any doubt in her mind that her warrior would succeed. The door opened, and Rya held a middle-aged man who stared at Tarris. "We need to talk," she said as she pushed past him, "somewhere secure."

Maken Derille was in a daze, but Tarris knew he recognized who she was. "I think we do," he said.

Rya, put him down and return. Tarris closed her eyes

momentarily as she felt the shift along her skin. She nodded to the Administrator and silently followed him to what looked like a study. She closed the door and stood there while he took a seat.

"Administrator Derille. I assume you know who I am, or at least where I come from." He nodded but offered nothing more. "I do not kill children, sir. Why do they want your family dead?" she asked bluntly, not one to dance around the issue.

"I'm not sure."

"What have you been discussing recently that would give your fellow administrators cause for concern?"

"It's none of your business, soldier."

His effort to maintain some kind of control of the situation was all too late. That Tarris was there demanding an explanation had already stripped him of any power. "Sir, they want me to kill your children. It has now become my business. I want to know what you've done to deserve this."

"So you're going to be my judge and executioner, is that it?" He appeared angry at her impudence.

"That is what you do every day, sir. It seems it's now your turn."

"I don't have to answer to you."

"But you do, sir. I hold the future of your family in my hands. You know very well what I'm capable of, but I'm giving you a chance to plead your case."

He had nowhere to run. She had shown him her Shadow Warrior and what she was capable of. He had no choice. "We had recently been discussing extending the scope of your unit, soldier. I had some concerns about the change in policy."

"That's pretty vague, Administrator. You haven't

changed my mind yet."

He sighed deeply. "The Council is trying to increase its power. This was just the start. Your unit would eliminate the serious threats to society. They wanted to extend it to include political adversaries and threats to the Council."

Tarris was not a stupid woman. "I see."

"Can you see where this was heading? Soon the Council would be all-powerful, and the Union would become a dictatorial state."

"Why does it worry you? You're one of them." He was an administrator with a conscience? That was as absurd as... as a soldier with a soul.

"Yes... yes, I am. But a few in the Council really are working for the good of the people. Strange I know, but we do exist. We have to be the voice of reason and try to keep control of uncertain situations."

"You'll get no help from SBSC, you know that."

"Yes, I'm aware of the feelings of discontent within the ranks."

"It's a dangerous path you choose, Administrator."

"Please, call me Maken."

Tarris knew he wanted her to move her opinion a little toward the middle so they could find common ground.

"You obviously have some doubts, soldier. Otherwise, you wouldn't be here and my family would be dead."

"The only doubt I have, sir, is killing children. They have done nothing wrong but be born to you."

"True, but what future do they have if the Council instigates this action?"

Tarris could feel the beginnings of a headache. This was too much information to absorb in the middle of the night. She had no time; she knew that.

"I would say think on it, soldier, but I know you have to report tomorrow about the mission." He paused. "What is your decision?" he asked almost hesitantly.

"Are you so quick to know your fate?" Tarris snapped. Her hand rose to her brow, and she rubbed frantically across the skin in frustration. "This is a dangerous road you've put me on, Administrator Derille."

"You've put yourself on that road, soldier. I've only shown you what's up ahead."

"Don't use your political oratory on me, sir." Angrily, Tarris paced the floor. Why had she been put into this situation? Was it a test of her loyalty, or was it nothing more than another assignment? She was being forced to make a decision she didn't want to make, and yet she couldn't bring herself to kill the children. "All right! All right. Get your family out of here tonight. Tell no one. You hear me? No one! Not even the house staff. To you, and the world, they are dead."

She turned away, to be stopped by a large hand. "Thank you."

"Let's hope it doesn't kill us all."

"Your name," he asked.

"It's better not to know."

"Please... your name," he asked again.

"Tarris... Tarris Waite." She didn't look back as she left the room, mentally preparing for her death even then. This was going to have ramifications, she just knew it.

†

Tarris's walk to the meeting the next morning was long and arduous, both physically and mentally. Her moment of truth had arrived. Would the deception hold, or would she be facing her death? Her heart beat wildly as she stepped down the dark corridor toward the conference room.

"So, blue eyes, how's your sex life going?" Corman taunted. Raucous chuckles filled the air as Tarris walked into the room. She was close to adding one more kill to her list.

"Probably better than yours, Corman." The tall, thin albino turned to face his cohorts, his angry look silencing their laughter.

"No one could have a worse sex life than you, Tarris, unless they were dead."

Rule Three in her Survival Handbook: Don't go into a battle angry.

She tried to hold onto that rule in her head, but Corman had a way of circumventing all her good intentions. She stepped up to her adversary, the force of her personality making up for her lack of height. She was upset with herself because she was about to break one of her life rules. "What is your problem, Corman? My death not coming soon enough for you?"

"Can't you take a joke, woman? Sheesh." Somehow he made it sound like it was Tarris who had the problem.

"Certainly, if it's a good one. This one has gone way past tasteless to downright sick."

"Hey! I'm not the one who's a cripple." He stared angrily down at her.

"Listen, you sick bastard, that has to be the lowest thing you've said to me. When I get my legs back…"

"Get your legs back?" He laughed loudly, and those

around him joined in the joke. "You were a cripple, you are a cripple, and you always will be a cripple."

"And yet I'm still the leader of this group." Tarris felt a tingle along her skin; Rya was also feeling anger at the slur. Corman took a step back and lowered his gaze to the floor. Tarris could make him feel her power when he stood so close to her. He couldn't defeat her fair and square, so he attacked her psychological weakness.

"Corman," the Monitor said, "please stay behind after the meeting." Tarris knew Corman hadn't expected to be overheard, but it seemed that he had. Now he would have to grovel.

"Take your seats, soldiers." After several moments, the meeting began. "Tarris, report."

"Four hits accomplished, Monitor." It took all her strength to keep her composure. It was foreign to her to tell a lie, and yet here she was doing just that. This was one time where Rule Four didn't apply.

Rule Four in her Survival Handbook: Lie as little as possible so you won't get caught later on.

"The Administrator has already released a statement. It seems he has arranged a private disposal of the bodies."

Bodies. That sounded so… cold, coming from Derille. Not even "dearly departed" or "his family." Bodies. Nothing more than immobile flesh and bone. She only hoped when her time came that she was more than just a body to those left behind. Tarris looked around those seated at the table. Maybe not.

She tried to appear unconcerned about the turn of events, because she knew very well that she was being scrutinized for her reaction. To overcome her anxiety, she glared at her fellow soldiers, turning her passive stance to one of aggression. "What are you looking at?" she growled.

"Iddy biddy kids, eh, Tarris?" Corman said.

"Yeah, not even a real quarry."

"Silence! It was a special assignment from the Council itself." Corman was suitably shamed. A special assignment was only for the elite, a class he had not yet reached. Tarris had been blessed by the Council with a rare honor.

"Sorry, Monitor," Corman mumbled.

"She had four targets, and you had but one. You have a lot to learn yet, soldier." The disembodied voice expressed some anger, something it had not had to do in a long, long time. "Everyone dismissed. Tarris, you will be contacted when the next meeting is."

"What about us?" Corman asked

"What?" The Monitor sounded displeased.

"What about us... errr, sir," Corman said.

"Better. Assignments will be given out tomorrow. Tarris, because of the four kills, will have a while longer to recover. Dismissed."

Corman still grumbled as the troopers exited the room. "Who did you have to sleep with to get that job? Must have been someone who didn't have any expectations, huh?" He chuckled to himself.

Tarris snapped. She grabbed his shirt and shoved him up against the wall. "You son of a whore! Enough of this, or I'll let someone else do the talking. You understand me?"

"I'm not afraid of her." He sounded unconcerned, but Tarris knew better.

"Well, you should be." Tarris let Rya seep to the

surface and allowed her menace to ripple along her skin. "Feel that?" she whispered. "This is her nice mood. You don't want to see her pissed."

"Enough!" the Monitor announced forcefully. "Corman, return now. Waite, go home."

Tarris left the room, donned her disguise, and exited the building into the light rain. The weather perfectly matched her emotions: angry and depressed. She didn't take cover as she walked home, and the body suit stiffened. The damp cloth stuck to her, wrapped around the mechanical legs, and slowed her momentum. When would the day end?

✝

To her surprise, the next morning Administrator Derille managed to convince everyone that his family members were indeed dead. It must have been his political experience in bald-face lying that helped him.

A day later, Tarris received a mysterious package and inside was a small electronic device. That night, she took a call from the Administrator who explained the function of the device and that he was using one on his phone line to talk to her. He told her six of these devices had been made before production had been closed down by the Council. After all, it did them no good for people to be able to block their monitoring of all communication.

So in her hand she held the Silencer, the first of many such small gifts from Maken Derille. The meeting after the supposed kills went as well as she could have expected, but she knew the lack of bodies would cause some concern despite Derille's explanations on that point. Government departments, and especially the Council, liked to have evidence of anything they had asked for, even if it was a body or two in the closet. Maybe it originated a hundred years ago when bureaucratic red tape ran riot through the government. Gradually, they tried to reverse the trend by making paperwork disappear into thin air. Still, there were some things that could never be taken on the word of a politician, not even one as highly ranked as Administrator Derille.

From that moment on, Tarris suspected she was being watched, her total loyalty now in question. She knew the Council members were content to use her power while it suited them, but she also knew her actions were under scrutiny. Her only sanctuary now was within the four walls of her apartment.

Whether she liked it or not her actions had forced her to take sides.

"Tarris? Hello?" Darmen said.

"Huh?" Tarris blinked rapidly as her mind returned to the present.

"Watch it there, child. You nearly walked into a tree."

"Oh, sorry." She tried to push the memory back into its compartment. She could see that Darmen was curious, but she couldn't divulge what her thoughts were about.

"Too much serious thought for such a nice day." He chuckled at her incredulous look. "It was all there on your face, dear. It wasn't too hard to figure out."

"So much for hiding my feelings," she muttered.

In a mock whisper he replied, "Don't worry, Tarris, I won't tell anyone."

She seriously doubted that he really had any idea what

she had been thinking, but she was content to let the matter rest. She sighed deeply as she tried to marshal her rampaging thoughts. What had brought this up now? Today was for enjoying the warmth of the holographic sun and leaving her troubles behind her for a few hours.

She detoured to a small metallic receptacle on the grass verge. She scanned her wrist and waited for the dispenser to give her two metallic flasks. She shook them gently before she activated the button on the side. "There you go." She handed one over to Darmen while she drank from the second container.

"Thank you, child."

The flask went cold as the chemical reaction in the reservoir lining had the desired effect. The cool liquid was welcome as their walk continued along the shaded pathway. Birdsong could be heard from a nearby tree. Of course, it wasn't a real bird but an animatronic one. No one was allowed to keep live pets anymore. There was so little left of the old days after the Food Riots of fifty-three and the Oxygen War of sixty-seven, even affecting nature and the environment. Thousands of species had been starved into extinction, while many thousands more struggled to gain a foothold and flourish. It was happening even now, but it was a slow process.

That was when the world stood at the brink and stepped back. A world governing body, the Union, was formed to repair the damage done. Massive tree planting took place as they tried to replace the earth's lungs. It took many years before they could finally breathe a sigh of relief but it had been done. In the meantime, scientists manipulated the atmosphere to bring rain to regions that had none. Large tracts of land were converted for planting food and raising animals. It had taken near extermination for the world to realize what was really important. Tarris hoped they didn't forget that lesson too soon.

"So, Tarris, what sort of work do you do that allows you to go for an idle walk?"

"Computer input, what else?" she lied.

"I'm sure you could find something else if you wish to change your profession." Darmen seemed genuinely interested in her welfare.

"I don't really care one way or the other. It's a job and it pays the bills." She looked at her friend walking beside her. "And what about you?"

"Me? Well, as luck would have it, I repair them, my dear."

"Then what are you doing here?" She gave him a friendly smile as she asked the question to take the sting out of the inquiry.

"Sometimes I just appreciate here more than my job."

"And you still have a job? You have a very understanding boss." Tarris wished for a boss like that.

"You're looking at him," he said straight-faced.

"You're the boss?"

"Don't believe everything you see, Tarris." She looked at him with new eyes. He certainly didn't look like an executive. Then again, she didn't look like an assassin either.

"Amazing. Do I know the company?"

"Computronics. But shhh, don't tell anyone." He grinned at her.

"Holy hell!" She was standing next to the boss of one of the largest computer companies in the world. "I... I..."

"Tarris, now listen to me." Darmen stopped and put his

hands on her shoulders. "I'm still the same man as I was last week. I don't want to lose the friendship we have. It's nice to be treated as a man and not an icon."

Tarris looked into those eyes of gray to see the old man from the park. She really did like him. He was a free spirit who sought freedom in a city, and a job, that allowed very little. "Darmen, I couldn't care less if you were from the Council itself or a lowly rubbish collector. You're a nice man, and I'm glad to call you friend." Friend... yeah, he was a nice friend.

"I feel the same, my dear. I always look forward to your visits. I hope that won't change." Uncertainty filled those eyes, and she could see that he was wondering if he had driven her away with his revelation.

She lifted her hand to touch his cheek. "No it won't... my friend." She had a friend, and a friend who wanted nothing from her but her company. For all of her life everyone she came in contact with wanted something, all except him.

"I wanted to give you something, but I wasn't sure how to do it. Now you know who I am, and it'll be easier."

"I don't want anything from you—"

Darmen held up his hand to stop her words. "It's something we've been working on, and I'd like you to have it. If it will make it easier to accept, think of it as an experiment. You're testing out a new piece of equipment for us. How about that?"

"Testing new technology, huh?" One dark eyebrow rose as Darmen presented a brightly wrapped box to her. "Funny looking official red tape," she said. He stood idly by as she unwrapped the present and opened the box. "Errr... okay." She had no idea what the small electronic box was.

"It's for finding bugs, monitoring devices, homing signals, and such. The ultimate bug detector."

Tarris laughed. "A bug detector? I hope you're not going to call it that."

"Well, its official title is SFGD-13279A, but somehow I don't think that will convince people to buy it, do you?"

"Errr... I don't think so."

"We're working on something a bit more... snappy."

"I don't know what to say, Darmen." Tarris looked at him. "Darmen? Is that your real name?"

"No, but I'd like you to call me that. It's a name especially for you."

"For me?" Tarris could see he was smitten with her. "You're not making a pass at me are you?"

Shyly, he looked at her. "Maybe."

"Look, Darmen..."

"Okay, enough said."

She reached for him. "You are a very special man, Darmen, but it would never work. I think you know that."

"Yeah I know, dammit."

"We have a very special friendship, and I will work very hard at protecting that." She meant that, especially considering he was the only real friend she had. The crestfallen look on his face tore at her. "Tell you what. How about we meet back here in a few days, and we'll organize dinner. Does that sound good?"

Darmen smiled. "Yes... yes it does. I'm sorry, Tarris. It was just a foolish old man's dream, you know?"

"I'm flattered, Darmen, I really am. And I don't think you're foolish. My life is sort of... complicated at the moment, so I don't have much of a social life. I do look forward to these walks though. Why do you think I come here so often?"

"Oh… ohhh."

She knew she had said something right when his smile widened to a grin. They were two lonely people in search of company for a short while.

"Now, tell me about this box," she said.

☦

Tarris hadn't intended to be in the park for such a long time, but she and Darmen got talking and the hours had flown by. Now at home, she was paying for it. Her upper back was sore from supporting the body suit, and she was sunburned. Not only did the holographic sun give light and warmth, but it also delivered those ultraviolet rays that her skin had an aversion to.

She found a small aerosol bottle and sprayed herself with it. The chemical mist solidified into a fine layer over her skin. By tomorrow morning, the sunburn would be a distant memory.

She gave the medipatch under her skin a gentle tap to release enough painkiller to dull the nagging ache. It was so easy these days to dull whatever ailed you. One patch to sleep, one patch to kill the pain, one patch for this and one patch for that. All of life's challenges were solved with a touch of the skin.

She studied the small present from Darmen. It was such a sweet thought, given without expectation of receiving something in return. She didn't have the heart to tell him that she already had one, courtesy of Administrator Derille, so a second one was superfluous. Maybe she would take it with her when she visited this mediprac, then she could say she had used it without feeling guilty.

She placed the electronic bug in her hiding place, along with the other devices, while she contemplated what the meeting with the mediprac would reveal. Would there be a chance of recovery? Would there even be a chance to try? Would she give up her dream to walk again if this avenue failed? The last question was something she really didn't want to face. To accept that this was how she would be for the rest of her life was depressing, and as long as she didn't make that decision, there was always hope. So she made none, as usual, and convinced herself that it was not time to give up just yet. She always reached that conclusion, because without hope, she was lost.

However, the mediprac was going to have to wait. The big operation tomorrow night took precedence over her life, and she had a feeling she was going to need all her wits about her for this one. She sighed as she wheeled herself into her bathroom to perform one of life's major obstacles, at least for her.

Chapter 3

Tarris stared off into space while her dinner reconstituted itself. Her skin had been dutifully scrubbed clean, and her damp hair hung limply down her back. It had been a long day, and she was bone tired. Despite her apartment being full of things to keep her occupied, none of them appealed to her. In resignation she retired for the night right after dinner and let the medicated drug claim her and drag her down to somnolence.

"Tarris! Stop! Stop it! You're killing him!"

The words barely touched her consciousness as Rya pounded in her head. Waves of energy sprung from her and spread out like rippled water. Parson was within the grip of her power, and she wasn't letting him go anytime soon.

"Tarris!" She no longer feared her educator. Tarris had been growing away from the Institute, and her departure was imminent. They had tried everything to entice her to stay, but as far as she was concerned, all they were worried about was their loss of control of their most precious asset. There was no fairness here, so she had no choice but to dispense her own brand of justice. Parson was slowly losing his battle with her and was within seconds of losing his life.

One moment Tarris had been consumed by the anger and need for revenge that she and Rya had for this boy. She fed Rya's need just as Rya fed hers, leaving her a nuclear explosion waiting to happen. Her next recollection was the fall down the stairs, her body twisted, broken, and in pain with each collision of flesh against rock. The agony was slowly swallowing her whole as it tore away every defense she had to protect herself. When blessed unconsciousness came, she was grateful.

The darkness of her room held little comfort as Tarris awoke with a start. Her heart pounded, and a light sheen of sweat covered her skin. "Light... low," she murmured. She waited for the overhead glow to dim to an acceptable level. Tonight it was no help, and she was forced to darken her eyes. The headache that was pounding in her head was probably causing her intolerance to the light. Her limbs remembered the pain of that fall, the excruciating agony as muscle was torn from bone, the snapping of bones in her legs, and skin being ripped off her body.

A shudder flowed through her as her mind refused to let the past go. She tapped her wrist for the meds and prayed for relief. As the drug flowed through her body, she relaxed and allowed it to work. Why was she bringing all this up now? It had taken her quite a few years to put the accident behind her, but now her memory decided to punish her some more.

Life was hell in the ensuing months after the fall, and many times she wished for a quick death. The medipracs lost count of the number of broken bones she had, so instead concentrated their efforts on her broken back. What should have been a simple spinal fusion turned out to be a never-ending series of failing operations, each one trying to correct the mistakes of the one before it. It was at that point that the medipatches were inserted, and she was taught the dangers and benefits of self-medication. Finally, she gave up and just asked to be left alone.

Her mother had been by her side through it all, and it took its toll on her. She aged before her daughter's eyes. Tarris knew she had worried her, but she was not in a position to change anything. Tarris was helpless in the hospital until such time as the medipracs would release her. In a way, it was probably better that she was there and not at home. At least she wasn't a physical burden on her mother.

What had surprised her was that her mother left not long after her discharge, placing her care in the hands of the Institute. Numerous explanations were made, and while she understood some of them, it didn't take away the pain that her mother would give up her child. There was no way the woman could afford to attend to her "special needs," as the people at the Institute had called it, whereas they felt an obligation to look after her. Their obligation didn't keep her warm at night.

Now, sixteen years later, she had located her mother, but they still weren't together. Many times she wondered whether her mother's presence at the small working community was in exchange for the Institute paying for her medical care, but no amount of encouragement would bring her mother to the metropolis. And she was still alone.

Tarris lifted her arms and put her hands behind her head. She gazed at the ceiling while she contemplated her life. By the time they had given her the means to end her life, she no longer seriously considered it. There were the bad times, of course, where the thought passed fleetingly across her mind, but even in the worst circumstances, she willed herself to continue on. She was a fighter, she knew that, and her fighter's spirit, Rya, wouldn't let her take the easy way out. She'd been determined to prove she was still a valuable addition to the community.

When she was able, the Institute intensified her training, not only to build her shadow's ability but her own body as well. The power suit she wore was one of many gifts that made her life easier. In fact, now that she thought about it, the Institute's generosity was more than acceptable; it was an overabundance. Why was that? Tarris didn't consider herself anything special. Maybe it was a guilty conscience. While they constantly denied it was anything but an accident, maybe they were trying to make up for what was taken away on their premises. Not that they would ever admit it.

She turned her attention to the dream and tried to figure out why she was taunting herself with it now. The thought of this mediprac being able to help her had brought this all about. Yes, that was it. Her subconscious was making the connection between the fall and the researcher.

Tarris moved her hand to her face so her wrist was in her line of sight. The patch formed a faint lump where it sat under her skin. It had been there so long she didn't notice it anymore. The tattooed barcode, however, had been a recent improvement. Well, in her lifetime and since her accident. There had been a hue and cry about its introduction, freedom lobbyists bemoaning the possible abuse of the system. Considering what was happening now, they were very insightful indeed. That barcode was used to track suspected troublemakers. The "big brother syndrome," as it had been nicknamed about a century ago, had come to be. Those freedom lobbyists were the first ones to be silenced in the name of unity and cohesion. If they were to survive against the other mega-dominions, there could be no dissension, or so the governing party told them.

As much as Tarris felt uneasy about the government control, she wasn't stupid enough to say anything.

Rule Five in her Survival Handbook: Never reveal your political leanings... to anyone.

That rule was a big one as far as she was concerned, and it was one that could see her on the hit list that was so judiciously kept by the Prime, Roden Sholter. She wasn't part of the cause; she was part of the solution.

When had the government converted from democracy to totalitarianism? It had been a subtle and well-crafted move on the part of the Prime and his ministers. World politics had been favorable, and the Prime used the excuse of defense and unity to slowly shift power. Before anyone realized what had happened, new laws had been passed and put in place. Some of the opposition still believed they had a say in the running of the state. Not that Tarris was privy to such information. Much of it was hearsay. Whatever the government had in mind was a well-guarded secret.

All this deep thought was feeding her headache, and precious sleep was eluding her. Tarris looked at her wrist again. She knew very well that she was addicted to the drugs, but she was not going to sleep on her own. She rubbed her wrist gently, slowly releasing the sedative into her system. As her eyelids began their descent, she murmured "Light off." She hoped she would be allowed some peace of mind.

†

The next afternoon, Tarris found herself standing in front of the Archive building. She had spent many hours here immersed in the past, which seemed a much nicer place than the present.

"Ah, Trooper Waite. Back again so soon?" The plexiglass screen was blank, as it always was with its greeting.

"Yes, Archiver. What's showing today?"

"One of the classics from a hundred years ago. We had a number of requests for a re-screening."

Don't say it. Don't say it. Tarris cringed as she awaited the words she had come to abhor.

"Bill and Ted's Excellent Adventure!" the robot announced.

Damn... and the day had started so promisingly.

"Not to your liking, Trooper?"

"I was in the mood for one of the older ones."

"How old?"

"Fifty years before that. Something like... like...." She hadn't come to the Archive with any specific film in mind, just something to remove her thoughts from the mission ahead. "How about *The Wizard of Oz?*" Her trip to the park yesterday had brought the film to mind.

"That one is out on loan." The words came out flat, as if expressing an opinion.

"Damn, I was in the mood for that."

"There is a screening of *The African Queen* in Room 32-908."

49

"Fine. And I would like to book *The Maltese Falcon* and… and… *Gigi.*" She rather liked the musicals, much to the disgust of the Archiver. Maybe she did it just to annoy the grumpy piece of circuitry who tried to discourage her taste in such films.

"It will be ready for pickup when you emerge, Trooper."

"Thank you." She had been here often enough to know her way around the myriad of floors and doors quite comfortably and found the room she wanted at the far end of corridor 32. Barely a handful of people were present for the screening, all sitting and waiting for the film to start. As always, Tarris took a seat at the back.

Rule Six in her Survival Handbook: Always keep your enemies in front of you to avoid getting stabbed in the back.

No one stabbed anymore. More efficient ways of doing that were available. Still, the sentiment was the same. The holoscreen went black as the titles came up, and Tarris lost herself in the fantasy for a while. She enjoyed watching the old color 3-D films in their natural state. It made her feel more human.

The film was barely halfway through when her wrist computer tapped her. The tiny illuminated screen delivered its message and switched off, returning the room to semidarkness. Tarris frowned. She really hated leaving in the middle of a screening, but she had no choice. The Monitor had called an emergency meeting.

†

She arrived at the monotone building with little trouble. The sun had finally been given a reprieve and was valiantly trying to dry out the mass of puddles that dotted the city. The cool air hit her as she walked through the front door, and she sighed in relief. Her leather coat was not the best piece of clothing to wear when the sun was out.

Tarris looked around the conference room. Three seats were conspicuously vacant, not that it surprised her. Corman always did like to make an entrance.

"Let us begin," the Monitor announced.

"But, sir—" One of the younger troopers, Shark, tried to intercede but was cut off.

"I know, Trooper. We will begin."

At that moment, the door slid open to reveal three albinos negligently standing there. Corman sauntered in. He cast his eyes over the seated group majestically, while his two "lieutenants" eyeballed anyone who dared look back.

"You are late, Troopers."

"I am," the lean man said and made a point of looking at his chronometer, "on time, Monitor." His disdain dripped from the words like the eternal rain that cursed the metropolis. Corman slumped into his chair, as if already bored with the proceedings. Jackton and Luton followed suit, albeit a little more respectfully.

"I wish to stress the importance of tonight's mission, Troopers. This is a multi-target contact, and I... the Council... want no mistakes." The voice hardened. "There is to be no bloodbath. Do I make myself clear?"

"Yes, Monitor." All but one answered until Corman grudgingly muttered the two words.

"Deadly. Silent. Mysterious. It is to appear as an enigma. No cause of death but heart failure."

Tarris watched her nemesis as the Monitor made clear what the Council wanted. She was the Group Leader, but she knew her authority would be ignored. As the sly smile crossed Corman's lips, she wondered how she was going to maintain control. It seemed what the Council wanted and what Corman wanted were two different things. Tarris had a bad feeling about this.

†

Shadow infiltrated shadow in the stillness of the night. The moon rarely showed its face, but it did so tonight. Maybe it was a bad omen. Tarris watched Rya move through the deserted streets with purpose toward the outskirts of the city where their current mission was to take place.

Tarris felt that her spirit was restless, as was she, even though Rya held little emotion of her own. But Tarris suspected it was her own disquiet that Rya was expressing, the calm long forgotten and replaced with the apprehension of the coming events.

Tarris lay on her back and stared at the darkened ceiling. Even though she had sent her shadowed assassin on her way, her concentration was not what it should be. Corman had planted the seed of doubt in her, and she questioned her ability to keep him from doing something stupid. Either he was very ignorant or very arrogant. She suspected it was the latter, but wouldn't rule out the former either. The Council wanted to come out of this mission with their hands clean. A bloodbath would only fuel the accusations of the opposition in parliament.

Tarris tried again. She closed her eyes and sought out

the deep part of her that resided in Rya. Tonight, most of all, she needed every ounce of concentration she had.

Rya gazed at the small compound that was their target. Two guards stood at the gate, talking to one another. She sensed the arrival of the other members of her group, their emitted auras easily read by her own senses. This was their first mission as a team, and one that would test Tarris's ability to lead.

Waves of energy spread out from Rya's ghostly form to instruct the others to find their assigned targets and reinforce the need for stealth. Tarris smiled as Rya competently organized the attack.

Rya took up position on a nearby vantage point. She watched the white auras of her team spread out around the compound. Corman's shadow, Gareth, hovered by her side. It was the calm before the mayhem.

No bloodshed, Corman. Tarris projected the order to her counterpart and tried to put as much threat as she could in her command.

Yeah yeah. Whatever you want. Corman expressed it not so much as a respect for authority but as a lazy admission and then an instant dismissal. Gareth casually swept forward toward the gate. Apparently Corman didn't even care that the guards could see his shadowed avenger. And so it began.

Tarris watched Rya carry out her duty. She slid around the perimeter of the courtyard and through the shadowed crevices not illuminated by the floodlights. The residence was not in complete darkness as it should have been. It was as if they were expected. There could be more to worry about than a mere hiccup in their timetable.

Rya circled the outside of the building and sought out

the darkened places that resided there. Finally she found her access point. A small vent had been left open. It was all too easy... and too convenient.

Tarris voiced caution as her warrior contemplated the tiny hatch. Shark's shadow joined her and did not hesitate to enter, his caution dissolving like the harsh light in the dark of night. Before Rya could react, the vent closed with a bang to imprison the assassin inside. There was a brief flash before silence. They had to assume Shark had been "blinded."

Ghostly eyes looked skyward to study the outside of the building. Rya had no choice but to go up, and Tarris sighed. Things were never easy. So far the mission had gone from bad to worse, so this turn of events, while unexpected, wasn't out of the realm of her worst nightmare. Whoever had betrayed them would pay.

Slowly Rya climbed the wall. She reached for minute crevices to aid her ascent. From her vantage point outside a window on the second floor, she looked out over the illuminated courtyard and was able to easily pick out the members of her group. Efficiently, her unit moved to their assigned targets, easily silencing their breaths with the twist of a shadowed hand. Her vision found the heated aura of Gareth as he stealthily crept up on his prey. A spike of fear pierced Rya from her connection with Tarris, both of them waiting to see if Corman would obey.

The silence could nearly be tasted as time seemed to stand still. Nothing. An eerie quiet before the storm. A piercing scream broke through the darkness. Tarris pursed her lips as the screaming deteriorated into an agonized gargle. Was Corman doing this to make her look bad? Knowing him as she did, he would do it just to piss her off.

She had no time to hesitate. Tarris gave whatever strength Rya needed to complete the mission and encouraged her to hasten. Rya crept past the window on the second floor and headed for the roof. To gain access meant having to cut the power supply situated on top of the building.

Rya wasted no time locating the microwave dish and disabling it. Moments later, the roof access door opened and two armed guards nervously paced across the flat top toward their target. Arcs of light shakily broke the darkness as they scanned for their enemy. Little did they suspect that she had been behind them all the way across the expanse of rooftop.

"Hurry up, will you?" The young man's gaze swept the darkened area in front of him.

"Hang on. I've still got to check it out." The older guard magnetically attached his maxi-torch to his torso. He felt around the box containing the circuitry illuminated by his torch. "Damn. It looks like we're going to need some replacement stuff. You stay here, and I'll be right back." He removed three circuit boards and walked away. The beam of light slowly faded as he found the door and disappeared inside.

The young guard hummed to himself as he waited.

Rya's shadowed head shifted to one side as if studying the young guard in front of her. As quick as a viper, she struck. Her hand slid through the guard's back and spine, all the way to his heart. His body jerked as the invisible hand squeezed tightly.

"I've got the..." The second guard arrived just in time to see his compatriot slump to the ground dead. "Holy—" His eyes swiveled around hurriedly. "Who... who's there? I know you're there."

Tarris knew he had no knowledge of who, or what, was there, but he had surely heard stories. Gruesome, supernatural stories that were meant to scare children and old women.

Another scream could be heard from the compound, and Tarris muttered "Shit!" from her apartment. Panicked voices shouted at each other as they tried to make sense of the terror that sat over the courtyard like a cloud heavy with rain. The mission had gone to hell, and Rya was stuck on the roof.

"You're stuck here, you know." The guard tried to sound confident, but the timbre in his voice rose and fell. Tarris didn't need to see his face to know he was probably peeing in his pants right about now.

Through Rya's eyes, Tarris watched him as he moved around nervously while he prepared to make his move. His heat signature was different from her unit. His nervousness elevated his body heat and made him an easy target.

She understood the need for darkness to try to complete her mission and to achieve Rya's escape. Another gargled scream echoed across the night air. It seemed Corman had lost his senses and was having Gareth kill indiscriminately. He had finally stepped over a line he couldn't return from.

Rya shifted through the deepening shadows and found her target. Her hand slipped though skin, muscle, and bone to his heart. His ragged breathing became more labored as her fist tightened, ending in an agonized sigh as the guard's last breath left his slumped body. This was not good. Their work was meant to be done by stealth and in sleep, not in the heat of battle. This was supposed to be a simple elimination of enemies of the state, not a wholesale slaughter.

While Rya didn't express an emotion, Tarris knew her warrior didn't like change and she could only agree with it. If not for Corman, they would have been in and out of the house before anyone knew something had happened. Now the compound was wide-awake. At least they were in darkness for now.

The warrior oozed down the stairwell wall like dark oil, until she reconstituted herself at the bottom of the stairs. She could be any shape she wanted to be, but she took comfort in the shape of her friend, her home...Tarris. It seemed a practical shape, one that moved her swiftly and silently, one that connected her to her unit.

Her blank eyes searched the darkness room by room for her original targets. The bedrooms on the top floor appeared empty, the beds not slept in. The occasional guard rushed by her as beams of light tried to find the intruder, but she paid them no mind. Too many had already died this night.

But her search couldn't find her quarry. Tarris instructed her to return without completing their mission. It was a disaster, and they would all have to face the consequences at the meeting tomorrow. Rya dodged in and out of the shifting shadows to seek solace in the blackness that was her friend. It was only by the width of a finger that she escaped the compound before light was restored. She glanced down at one of Gareth's victims, his flesh torn apart and scattered haphazardly across the ground. This was no subtle killing, but one to demonstrate what they were capable of.

Pretty, isn't it?

Rya stared at the aura that had crept up next to her. Gareth.

Are you mad, Corman? Tarris asked. When he was like this, trying to speak with him rationally was useless. The power he possessed was like a drug, and he was addicted to it.

Maybe you should watch your back, freak.

And what was the point of all this?

This is who I am. Unlike you, I say kill them all.

Rya shifted away, intent on returning home.

Too much for you, Tarris? Then maybe you should leave the unit to those who can do the job.

This had been their first failure, and the mixture of emotions roiling around in Tarris made her twitchy. She had to get Rya home immediately, so any care she might have taken through the streets was forgotten. She needed Rya, and Rya needed her as well.

Tarris lay in her bed and cursed at the ceiling. This particular mission had taken a lot out of her, as much from Corman's insubordination as from the mission itself. The man was an arrogant shit hole. Man? Corman himself denied such a label. He thought himself God's gift to the masses. Maybe that was his game. But it raised an interesting question. Could one member of the Special Black Shadow Corps overthrow a government? She doubted it. While each shadow warrior was virtually indestructible, the same could not be said for its host. And that's where Corman's plan would let him down. Kill the man to kill the shadow...

Rya slid effortlessly into Tarris's apartment and settled

like a well-worn blanket over the top of her. The familiar rush filled Tarris as the shadow melted away through skin and muscle to find her home deep within Tarris's body.

Tarris blew out a breath slowly and allowed the sensations to die down to normal. How many more times would she let Rya roam the streets? Automatically, she reached for her wrist and briskly rubbed the patch, ready to seek respite from the worries flooding her brain. Tomorrow was going to be stressful enough without lack of sleep on top of it.

†

Tarris opted to walk to the meeting the next morning, so she had to tolerate the escalating discomfort from walking so far. Maybe it was a way to prolong the inevitable. The cloudy sky seemed to reflect her current life perfectly. Slowly building storm clouds gathered around her, and she was helpless to stop them.

She leaned against a wall outside the nondescript building and contemplated what was about to take place. She knew she would be dealt some sort of punishment. After all, she was the leader of the unit and therefore the responsibility of the mission ultimately lay with her. Suspension? Incarceration? Death?

She shivered at the last thought. Would it come down to that final of all punishments? Would she fight the sentence? Would it matter if she did? She checked her chronometer several times and wished it was all over, one way or the other.

She pushed off from the wall and traversed the final few yards to the front door. She touched her temple to clear the lens for scanning. The door slid silently aside. She took a deep breath and stepped across the portal to her future.

She felt a coldness in the room, and it wasn't from the air. Corman and his two cohorts had already arrived, and by the frigid reception she got, they had already convinced the others that this disaster was all her fault.

Tarris was content to occupy one corner. She leaned against the wall so she could face all her enemies at once. One of the younger members approached her and took his place alongside her.

"How are you feeling today, Shark?" The question was more one of courtesy than one of concern. She knew exactly how he felt.

"Like shit," he muttered. The others were studying the two of them keenly.

"Happens."

"Does it get any easier?"

"Not really, no." She smiled as his head dropped. "But it doesn't come as a shock anymore. You just learn to be more careful." Her pale eyes caught his. At least he had the good sense to feel berated. "Now you know."

"Yeah, now I know."

She remembered the first time Rya was blinded. It felt like her insides had been ripped out. Terror flowed through her tired body like a tide, the missing entity leaving a hollowness that threatened to swallow her whole. The experience was sobering, one that brought her mortality into sharp focus. Rya did return, and for that she was forever grateful.

"So what have they been up to?" Tarris nodded slightly in the direction of her nemesis.

"The usual." Shark's voice remained low; his words

wouldn't carry the length of the room. "Corman's trying to convince us that it's all your fault."

"So what else is new? He's a dick."

The young man didn't reply, but it did bring a hint of a smile to his face.

"And?"

"And?" Shark didn't understand.

"And what's the verdict?"

"I don't know."

"Oh, come on, Shark. You must know what's going on." Despite the cold shoulder, she felt she knew the members of her team. Tarris's eyes met each person in the room as she tried to gauge their reactions. Apart from the open hostility of Corman and his followers, emotions seemed to range from mild interest to mild disinterest. No one would let her know where their loyalty lay.

The door slid open. The meeting was about to begin, and her fate was in the hands of the man who filled the doorway.

"Everyone, be seated." The Monitor's voice remained emotionless.

Everyone tried to sit as far away from the aggressive rogue as possible, leaving just a few seats available. Tarris had no choice but to sit next to him. When she reached for the chair, Corman lifted his feet and placed them on the cushion. She was tempted to smack the smile off his face, but she settled for leaning against the wall. No way in hell was she going to beg.

"Well, that was a massive cock up," the Monitor said.

Tarris blinked once... then blinked again. Did he say what she thought he said? Or was it the fact that he said it so calmly that startled her?

"Don't all answer me at once."

"As far as I'm concerned"—Corman jumped in before Tarris had a chance to air her grievances—"the blame lies with the leader."

"True…"

Tarris could feel her chances of survival drop at the word.

"But she wasn't the one who openly disobeyed orders, was she, Corman?" The Monitor leaned forward and rested his arms on the conference table. "Oh, that doesn't mean Tarris will escape unpunished for this… but you, Corman, deliberately screwed this mission up." The Monitor wasn't intimidated by Corman's hard stare. In fact, he returned the look with one of his own. "Don't you try that with me, soldier," he growled menacingly.

"It's her job—"

"I know what her job is!" he bellowed, "The least of which is to put up with your crap." The Monitor leaned back heavily in his chair. "And thanks to you, the unit has been put on notice. One more screw-up and we're all out of a job."

While the conversation transpired, Tarris watched her enemy carefully. Corman didn't seem surprised by the news. In fact, he nearly seemed pleased.

"Luckily it will be on full pay."

Corman grinned.

"Except for Corman and Tarris. Corman, you're suspended for four weeks without pay."

His grin disappeared. "Four weeks! But—"

"Tarris, you're suspended for two weeks without pay and loss of rank. You should have seen this coming."

She did see this coming. She just couldn't stop him.

"Yes, Monitor." In a way, it was a relief not to be unit leader anymore. Her only fears were who would replace her and would he be strong enough to resist Corman's influence.

"Dismissed. You will be contacted when the backlash of this mess has blown over."

The room emptied quickly, with Corman and his men near the last to leave. Corman looked over his shoulder at Tarris and mumbled, "Pathetic." He sauntered arrogantly out the door as if the world were his for the taking.

Maybe she was pathetic. The blame ultimately rested on her shoulders for Corman's actions.

"Get that thought out of your head, soldier."

Tarris looked up from her musings. The Monitor stood a couple of feet away from her. "Pardon?"

"We both know Corman. What Corman wants, Corman gets."

"True. I think he did it just to piss me off. He succeeded."

"What happened?" The Monitor called up the official report on his computer screen.

"They knew we were coming. The compound was lit up like the Council building. Shark got blinded, and I had to shut down the power on the roof. The targets were gone, Monitor. The rooms were empty. Of course, Corman's victims were screaming like banshees as he ripped them apart. And it wasn't one or two, Monitor. He was going through the guards at will." She didn't like laying blame, instead content to let the cards fall as they will, but it was good to let off some steam. And the Monitor needed to know they had been betrayed.

"I don't know what's going on," the Monitor said, "but

I'll look into it. In the meantime, take some time off and rest up. It's been a hell of a couple of weeks."

"Yes, Monitor." She pushed off from the wall toward the door.

"Oh, and Tarris? If it's worth anything, you did a hell of a job getting everyone out of there."

"Thanks." She left the room, and the door silently closed behind her.

The meeting had gone better than she could ever have hoped for. While it meant two weeks without pay, her head was still on her shoulders and that was of utmost importance. As she strolled toward her apartment, other matters surfaced. Maybe she could arrange a meeting with the mediprac who she hoped would help her walk again. She wanted her legs back.

Chapter 4

Tarris sought out the one place where she felt relaxed. At the park, she found the familiar form of her friend, Darmen, in his usual position under a tree. Here was a bright spot in an otherwise awful day.

"So you do live here! I knew it…" Tarris couldn't help but smile.

"I'm here often enough, my friend. Maybe I do."

"Either that, or you're spying on me."

"Would that be a bad thing?" When the smile slid off Tarris's face, Darmen added, "It was a joke, Tarris. Not in a good mood?"

"Sorry. No, I'm not in a good mood."

"Do you want to talk about it, or do you want me to leave you alone?" Concern etched his wrinkled face.

It didn't take much thought to answer the question. "I could use some company. Maybe we can plan this dinner you seem so keen to have." Tarris felt the tension leave her as the old man smiled at her.

"Where would you like to go?"

"I don't know. I don't go out much."

Darmen laughed. "Me, either, except when I have to. You know… for work."

"Ah yes, those kinds of dinners."

"Boorrrriing," he said with a moan.

"What makes you think this one won't be the same?" Tarris's communication skills were pretty bare, to say the least. "I haven't had a lot of practice at making polite conversation."

"You seem to be doing fine with me."

"I suppose you're right." And he was right. She had to remind herself that she was going out for a meal with her friend. She shouldn't make more out of it than needed to be.

"Of course I'm right." Darmen shook his head. "Now can you please help an old man up?" He extended his arm for Tarris to grab.

"You know very well you can get up on your own." But that didn't stop her obliging him.

"How many times do I have a beautiful young woman to come to my aid?" His words made her blush.

"Plenty of times, I'm sure." She clicked her tongue. "You are incorrigible, old man. Preying on my good nature like that." The light banter eased her concern.

"Feeling better now?" It was as if Darmen could read her thoughts.

"Yes, and thank you."

"For what, my dear?" His eyes twinkled in mischief.

"You know very well what, you old scallywag!"

"Now there's a word I haven't heard in a long time. That's the problem with this world... trying to replace the old with the new."

"And not all of it is good," Tarris added.

"You like some of the old things?" Darmen asked.

"I like the old movies. You know, like the olden days."

"Bill and Ted—"

"No, not that crap! The real ones like"—she scanned her memory—"*The Godfather* and *Ben-Hur.*"

"The Archives have screenings of all the good ones."

"I watched part of *African Queen* yesterday." She had so wanted to know how that one ended. "I like them in their disc format."

"You mean on DVD?"

"That's the one. It's much better than the hologram copies. Sometimes I just want to be an outsider looking in, so I can get lost in the story and characters and not get distracted by the technology."

"Ahhh, a woman after my own heart." Darmen smiled. "But they allow you to go to these screenings? You must have an understanding boss."

Shit. She had missed that. "I work nights."

"Then maybe you should be home asleep." He looked at his chronometer. "If you hurry, you could still get a few hours' rest."

Tarris had to admit that the morning's meeting had taken its toll on her. Besides the emotional upheaval, the body suit began to annoy her. "Maybe you're right. I better go." She took a step toward the entrance. "About dinner..."

"Go on. We can do this some other time." He gave her a wink. "Rest well, my friend."

"Until next time, Darmen." She was about to walk away when he stopped her.

"Oh, by the way. Have you tried the scanner yet?"

"I'm sorry, no. I've been really busy." That sounded hollow, especially after mentioning her visit to the Archives yesterday. "I will, I promise."

"I'm sure you will, my dear. When you get around to it." He waved her off with his hand before he returned his attention to the small screen he had been studying when she arrived.

✝

Tarris resorted to a medicated sleep when she finally settled on her bed. She was exhausted and needed some downtime.

The room swam with phantoms, swooping and diving at her in an attempt to get to her. They had changed to floating phantasms to negotiate the obstacles. Rya would protect her friend for as long as Tarris's mental strength held out.

This was her moment of truth. The unit had turned on her, and she was on her own. Tarris was strong, but was she strong enough to defeat them all? The group split to approach from opposite sides to force their leader to choose.

Tarris was cornered, trapped in a body that wouldn't do her bidding. Malevolent forces circled ominously, and her only defenses were her soul and her courage. Rya enveloped her and lifted her broken body with ease.

A light suddenly appeared in the room and seemed to be the only avenue open to her. Rya stepped toward the light even though it would "blind" her. She placed Tarris down carefully before her form dissolved away to nothingness. Rya had been blinded, and now Tarris was completely helpless...

"Arrloovarite?"

"Huh?" The word didn't make sense.

"Are... you... all right?" The words were enunciated

68

crisply, and their meaning now understood, but Tarris didn't pay heed to them. She was struck by the beautiful woman hovering over her. Those eyes—rich sapphires that glistened in the harsh light— burrowed into her like twin needles. She could feel the pain, but she couldn't turn away.

"Errr... yeah. I suppose. Where am I?"

"Home... you are home." The voice was low and seductive, uttered by a woman Tarris estimated to be in her mid to late thirties. Short, black locks framed her oval face, the ragged fringe touching the dark elegant eyebrows. She took Tarris's breath away.

Tarris woke up drenched in sweat. What did it all mean? This was her second such dream. Was it a portent or wishful thinking? Her hand crossed her brow. Life was too much today, and so she sought solace in sleep as the drug flowed through her tired body.

Some hours later, the sedative wore off and left her with that familiar lethargy "hangover," She rubbed her face with her hands. What was she going to do for two weeks? Lying around looking at the ceiling was a recipe for weight gain.

She suspected she would be a frequent visitor to the Archives and the park, both of which gave her much pleasure, but she couldn't spend two solid weeks there. Even that was a waste for her enforced holiday. No, she would save those delights as rewards for accomplishing something more mundane. But the unit was her life. Nothing else existed for her. No hobbies, no distractions... no partner. She was alone. She had no one to blame but herself for her enforced celibacy, but she wasn't going to be pitied for the sake of a little companionship. Rule Seven in her handbook was one she steadfastly stuck to.

Rule Seven in her Survival Handbook: Never start anything you can't finish.

She rose slowly from the bed. Some days her patience was tested by the slow, deliberate nature of her home aids. This was one of those days. She moved the wheelchair quietly across the carpet to her computer and booted it up. She tried to remember the article she had read the other night. It had been put off while her attention had been focused on her work. Now that wasn't a problem. In fact, it was the ideal opportunity to follow up on it without the distraction of her profession to interrupt her.

Tarris wheeled over to the far corner and withdrew her Silencer for the conversation to come. She had to know, but the few intervening days to see the practitioner were going to be unbearable. "Hello?" a voice said. The screen was blank but the computer confirmed the connection.

"Hello? Who is this?" The voice was low and hypnotic and triggered a response in Tarris.

"This is Tarris Waite. I called you the other night and left a message. Is there something wrong with your monitor?"

"I'm sorry, the screen has shorted out. How can I help you?"

"As I mentioned earlier, I was interested in your work on nerve regeneration."

"Are you from the Council?" Tarris could hear the suspicion in the tantalizing voice.

"No. I'm a private citizen."

"How did you get hold of my paper then? As far as I'm aware, such research is not available to the common citizen."

"I have a friend or two in high places," Tarris said.

"But you said you weren't from the Council."

"And I'm not. Why is it so important that I'm not from the Council?"

"I usually don't discuss my work with anybody. I'm sorry but I can't help you."

"Please! Please, wait. Can we meet? Just once?"

"Why should I?"

"Because…" How much should she reveal to a perfect stranger? Normally she would reveal nothing, even to close acquaintances, but her life was dependent on this conversation. "Because I'm in need of your treatment."

"And you are a mediprac, are you?" The voice was openly hostile. Tarris could see that this woman jealously guarded her privacy nearly as much as she did.

"No, but I've seen enough of them to know I need one." She bit back an acerbic remark. She couldn't afford to alienate the one person who might be able to do something for her.

"And you think I'm the one who will help you, do you?"

"I would have thought you would leap at the opportunity to try out your theories on a live donor." Tarris was getting seriously pissed off at the woman.

"I will when I'm ready, not because you're in a hurry to be healed." Annoyance laced the words.

"Why are you being so hostile?" All thought of supplication to get what she wanted was washed away by the negative words coming from the blank screen.

"I don't like people sticking their noses into my business. I'm a private person, and I like to keep it that way. Goodbye."

Stunned, Tarris stared at the screen. She had a mind to report the mediprac to her governing body for such rudeness and refusal to help. Didn't these practitioners have some sort of obligation to help other people?

The screen on her wall erupted with the news of the botched assignment.

"... here is a statement by the Prime concerning the rebel attack on the home of the Opposition Leader."

The announcement made Tarris sit up. She ignored her computer for the news. The familiar face of the Roden Sholter filled the large screen.

"Citizens. Last night the home of Opposition Leader Regis was brutally attacked by the cowardly forces of the resistance. While Administrator Regis and his family escaped unharmed, a number of his staff were murdered while defending his property." The old man paused. He turned his head from side to side as if he were addressing a rally. "This has forced the Council to enforce a curfew from sundown to sunup. Protectors will be stationed around the metropolis for the safety of the citizens."

Tarris's mouth fell open. It was all a setup. They were deliberately sent on a mission that was bound to fail from the very beginning. It was an excuse to establish martial law. She felt betrayed. She had given them everything, and they used her. "Protectors... pah!" It was a fancy word for soldiers.

The Prime continued his political rhetoric, but she paid it no heed. She had heard enough. Her belief in the government had been severely shaken, and it left her empty. No one had ever used her like that before. She wasn't naïve or stupid. After all, she had to put up with jerks like Corman for most of her life, but to actively use her loyalty and expertise to undermine the very fabric of society... that was unforgivable.

The wheelchair was too slow for what she wanted to do, so she exchanged it for her body frame. Once it had settled in place, she left to walk the streets. Her anger pushed her on to look for something, someone to ease the turmoil within her. Without conscious purpose, her rambling delivered her to an address that she had only just discovered. She looked up at the low-rise building and knew the person she wanted to see was inside. After all she had just spoken to her. Maybe if she saw the woman face-to-face it would help. If not, then she would just slug the woman in the jaw to ease her frustration.

Her visit to the mediprac was just plain reckless, but she didn't care. Why couldn't common sense override her anger? Tarris knew she was being watched, so visiting this scientist was going to put them both in danger. Suspicion and paranoia ruled the metropolis these days, and anything out of the ordinary like this visit would be interpreted as a dangerous move.

She had presented all these arguments to herself, but she ignored them. Maybe Rya would see reason and stop her. Not that she would listen. After all that had happened today, to be able to walk again was paramount. The whole world was kicking her in the teeth, and she wasn't going to take it anymore.

As she stood in the hall outside the woman's apartment, she chided her warrior. *Thanks very much, Rya.* Her hand passed over the beam to announce her presence.

"Yes?" The muffled voice was barely heard in the corridor.

"It's Tarris Waite." She tried to keep her voice low. She didn't want anyone to know who she was except the woman on the other side of the door.

"Who?"

Had she made so little an impression on the mediprac? "Tarris Waite. The woman you hung up on earlier today."

"I told you before, I'm not interested."

"And I'm not leaving until I talk to you." Tarris's voice hardened as she spoke, a touch of menace seeping into the words.

"Go away, or I'll call the enforcement agency."

She was so close to saying "I *am* the enforcement agency," but she knew this wouldn't help her case. "Please, a couple of minutes of your time and then I'll leave you alone."

The door slid open with a gentle whoosh to reveal a woman of short to middling height and straight, black, cropped hair. Tarris stumbled back against the far wall, her heart beating at a blistering pace.

"Are you all right?" Bright blue eyes looked on in concern as the young woman's hand reached out to help her.

"Ah... ah... err." Tarris stammered like an idiot. This was the woman in her dreams. Was she going mad?

"Come on. It looks like you need to sit down." The woman moved to Tarris's side, put her shoulder under Tarris's armpit, and helped her into the apartment. Gently Tarris lowered herself into a waiting chair. Her fingers swiftly moved to the hidden pads in her belt to adjust the suit to a seated position.

The woman disappeared and returned with a glass of water. Who the hell was this woman? More important, why was she dreaming about her?

"Now, what's wrong?" Tarris saw concern in those eyes intently watching her, but she couldn't tell her of the dream, at least not yet.

"Sorry. You reminded me of someone so much, I thought I was seeing a twin."

"Why do you want to see me?" The wall of mistrust had risen once more, and Tarris was back to where she had started. So much for medical care.

"I wanted to see if your research could help me to walk again."

"You seem to be walking just fine."

Now Tarris would have to show her. Sighing deeply, she rose unsteadily and adjusted the suit to a stand position. She reached for the Velcro on her pants.

"Just what do you think you're doing?"

"You believe I can walk? Fine." She dropped her pants to show the mechanical frame that helped her walk.

"Hmmm." The woman crouched down to study the metal. Tarris's heart ached as she watched the woman move around. She so wanted to be able to do that again. To be able to walk, run, crouch, and just feel. "Interesting." Intent eyes looked up at her. "Come with me."

"Hang on, errr... Mediprac, Doctor, errr...."

"Don't sprain your tongue there. Call me Asher."

"I'm Tarris."

"So you keep telling me. Come this way."

Tarris fumbled with her pants while she tried to keep the young woman in her sights as she disappeared farther into the apartment. She looked around and took in the surroundings. While it was a lot smaller than her own dwelling, it was comfortable but didn't reek of wealth. Asher was not among the Council's favored. Maybe that was why she was so hostile.

One of the rooms had been converted into a laboratory filled with equipment. "Now…"

Tarris held up her hand. She reached into her pocket and extracted Darmen's bug detector. She activated the device and wandered around the walls. The silent alarm triggered off, and she went in search of the source.

"What…?"

Tarris touched her lips with her finger for silence. Where was the thing? Every time she moved, it moved, too. There was some sort of bug in the room, but there wasn't. Did that make sense? She handed over the box. "You try it," she whispered.

Asher used the box as she was shown and came to the same conclusion. She was about to return the device when its signal increased. "What…?" She looked perplexed. "Turn around," she murmured. She waved the box over Tarris. Finally she stopped on a spot in the small of her back. "It's on you."

"Me? Impossible." Tarris grabbed back the detector and waved it frantically over her back. There it was, as surely as she was standing there. "How the…?" There was no way she could be bugged. She would know.

"Leave now. I told you—"

"Now wait a minute."

"You lied to me. I will not become the Council's lapdog. You hear me? Go back and tell them I'm not interested."

"I'm not from the Council. How many times do I have

76

to tell you that?"

"You can no longer be trusted." Tarris could hear the finality in Asher's voice.

"I didn't know about this, okay? I'm as surprised as you are." But Asher was unimpressed. Tarris again reached for the Velcro. "You don't believe me, huh? Fine." She clumsily lowered her pants, grateful for the help to step out of them from Asher. "Check it out." Asher waved the scanner over the cloth. "See? Nothing there."

She moved the scanner toward Tarris. "It only means it wasn't in your pants." The box still had a positive reading.

Down to her underwear and the metal frame, Tarris was going to need help to get them off.

Asher watched in fascination as Tarris manipulated the metal frame to walk herself over to the bench. Curious, she swept her eyes over Tarris's body and noted that her legs, while a little on the thin side, were not atrophied, while the white skin was probably from a lifetime indoors.

"Can you...?" Asher moved to stand in front of Tarris, nose to nose. Tarris began to undo the frame, and Asher bent down to assist once she had figured out how to unlatch it. Tarris shifted her weight to the bench as the frame slowly came free, until she finally ended up on her elbows to support her useless lower half.

Asher moved quickly to assist her and help lift the dead weight of her legs onto the table so Tarris could lie down.

Asher quickly scanned the frame but still nothing. And yet the scanner continued to register a bug in the room. She passed the box over Tarris and discovered a mild signal coming from her stomach.

"Let's turn you over," Asher said.

After much struggling and panting, Tarris lay facedown on the table, her nose ground into the Perspex top. This was ridiculous. She was almost down to bare skin, and yet there still seemed to be a signal. The cool metal slipped down her spine as the device searched her, until it stopped abruptly at the small of her back.

"You're not going to believe this, but the signal is coming from inside you," Asher said.

"No. No. It can't be. I'd know if they put something into me. They wouldn't dare..." Tarris closed her mouth so hard, her teeth crunched together.

"They? Just what is going on here?"

"Nothing you need to worry about. Now you have me in this position, is... is there any chance you can do something for me?"

"Why should I help you? You're carrying God knows what inside you, and you expect me to be happy about that?"

"You can see I'm helpless here. Are you even remotely interested in trying out your theories?" Tarris was getting desperate. She could feel the shift away from a positive reaction. She was losing Asher's interest.

"As I said, I'm in no hurry." Asher sounded too calm.

If Tarris had to guess, the woman was in a desperate hurry. She didn't have to be on the Council to know that, if Asher was doing research on a grant, she would be expected to have answers yesterday. No, Asher needed her help as much as she needed Asher's help. "What's it going to take for you to change your mind?"

"You tell me everything," Asher said. "No secrets,

hidden agendas, or lies."

"You want it all. You may not like what you get."

"That will be my decision then, won't it?"

"But if I reveal it all, I'm in a very vulnerable position. What guarantee do I have that you won't use what I show you?"

"It can't be that bad."

"Oh yes it can. You're asking me for everything without any strings attached."

"That's about it," Asher said.

"Well, I'm sorry. I can't do that." Tarris could feel her own disappointment as if it were a tangible thing. Rya stirred within her, also feeling her pain. *I'm sorry Rya. It looks like we're bound to this suit.* "If you'll help me with the suit, I'll leave you alone and not return." Tarris didn't know what to feel. Anger? Despair? Frustration? As she slapped the frame into place and reached for the familiar clasps, she couldn't look at the woman who had gutted her.

"Why should I trust you?" Asher's low melodious voice held a hint of confusion.

"Because I'm telling you the truth. But you don't want the truth, so just let me get out of here with at least a shred of my dignity intact." Tarris could feel her dream slowly die, withering away with each passing second. She looked at the hand on top of her own, and desperately decided to give it another try.

"All right, you want it all? Don't say I didn't warn you." Tarris reached around to the back of her neck and found the soft skin at the base of her scalp. As she tapped the skin, her hair color slowly faded, the deep brown melted away to the snow-white strands that were her natural coloring.

From beneath her lashes, she watched Asher and waited for the look of horror on Asher's face. Albinos were universally feared. To be albino meant that you were a member of the Special Black Shadow Corps. Concealed whispers and mutterings in the dark had told of what the troopers of the Corps did. Oh yes, she was to be feared.

She reached up to her temple and tapped it to remove her dark irises. Slowly the ice blue tinge emerged from the white, and it softened the otherwise sharp visage. Her angular features were now bordered in white, perfectly balancing the pale skin. Tonight her skin was pink-tinged, as she still felt the aftereffects of sunburn, but she knew the picture she presented to Asher.

"Well…"

"I told you so," Tarris said.

"I figure if you were here to kill me, I'd already be dead." Asher's response was not what Tarris expected. Terror, yes, but not mild interest.

"Yes, you would." She looked up into those rich eyes and saw a hint of fear but nothing stronger. "Maybe I should leave. I've probably put you in danger just by coming here." Her hand reached to the small of her back. "I can't believe this," she muttered. "Someone's going to pay."

"Stay." That was the last thing Tarris expected Asher to say. "You're already here, and the damage is done." Asher's smile took the sting out of the comment.

Tarris stopped strapping on her suit. "I don't understand."

"I don't either. Since you trusted me with your secret, I suppose I can at least look at you." Tarris's blonde eyebrow rose. "For scientific purposes, of course."

"Of course." *Well, well, well. What's going on, Rya?* "You'd better help me then." This time Tarris leaned back and allowed Asher free rein to remove the rig once more. She grinned impishly as Asher glanced at her from her position near her legs.

"Errr… yes. Give me a moment." Asher shook her head and focused on the clasps to complete the task. She finally put aside the cumbersome frame and helped Tarris to roll onto her front.

Tarris studied Asher's face as she examined her. She didn't need to look at her own body. She knew it intimately. She was more interested in seeing what the mediprac thought of her. Asher's medical eye took in the small bag attached to Tarris's lower stomach, artificially compensating for her lack of control of her urinary system

Asher's warm hands pushed and prodded down either side of Tarris's spine, but Tarris didn't mind. These hands were… well, they weren't like a mediprac at all. And she was an expert on mediprac hands. She had felt enough of them on her body to know medical interest and something else entirely. But what that something else was, she didn't know.

"What is this?" Asher asked.

"What?"

"This lump at the base of your spine."

Tarris reached around to feel for the spot. "That? It's scar tissue from the operation."

"What operation?"

"When they tried to repair the damage."

"How long ago was that?"

How long? A lifetime? An eternity? "Let's see. I was sixteen when the accident happened."

"Accident?" Asher said absently as she continued to examine Tarris's back.

"I fell down some stairs and broke my back. They tried to repair it but were unsuccessful."

Asher didn't express any opinions to Tarris, she just kept asking questions. "So how many years have you been like this?"

"Are you trying to find out my age, Doctor?"

"It's strictly professional interest."

"Uh-huh." Tarris liked this game. It allowed her a moment to be normal. Her social skills were sadly lacking, and the light banter put her at ease. "All right. Sixteen years ago."

"Let's take a look at this." Asher moved to a nearby shelf, sorted through the equipment there, and grabbed a hand-held box. "This won't hurt. I'm going to scan your spine to see what shape it's in." Tarris buried her head in her hands. "Move your arms to your sides, please."

"Tarris…" she mumbled.

"Sorry?"

"Move your arms to your sides, please, Tarris."

"Are you coming on to me, Trooper?"

"Ahhh, no…" Was she? After the accident, she became obsessed with sex. What would she miss out on? Would she ever find out? It took some self-realization on her part to understand that it was all rather pointless and a waste of time and energy. When she finally accepted her fate, she decided to funnel her curiosity and sexual energy into something more productive. Finally sex was no longer an issue. She couldn't feel anything, so why even bother? Tarris could sense the beginnings of a blush in reaction to the question. A gentle laugh could be heard, and she blushed even more.

"I was kidding, Trooper."

"Please don't call me that. I have a name."

"I know you have a name. All right I'll drop it. Now lie still." As Asher slowly ran the device down Tarris's back, a nearby monitor revealed her spine, nerves, and cord as an echogram. "So far, so good."

Tarris looked up at the screen and tried to take in that the image was her spine. "Wow!"

"Been awhile has it, Tarris?"

"Don't like medipracs. They never had anything good to tell me."

"Yeah, this sort of stuff is old news to me, but to the common citizen, it's still a source of amusement." The scanner continued to move down the white back. "Ahh, here's where you suffered the break." Asher's voice rose. "What is that?"

Tarris's pale eyes narrowed as the damaged site came into view. Indeed, what was that? "What's wrong?" There was almost a panicked edge to the question.

"You see this bit here?" Asher pointed to the bulged section of the spine. "That's really strange."

"Strange?" Tarris felt her heart thumping in her throat. Was this more bad news? She'd had just about all the bad news she could take about that back of hers.

"It looks..." Asher's eyes narrowed as she moved closer to the monitor. "Oh my God, that looks like a metal ring around your spine. Did anyone say something about repairing the damaged bone with a metal ring?"

"Ring?" At this point, Tarris could barely remember her name let alone what happened sixteen years ago. She could feel Rya trying to calm her so she could think straight. "No, I don't think so."

Asher continued to study the image. She shifted the scanner around to get different angles of the damaged site. An adjustment of the settings on the device allowed the rays to filter past the metal to the bone underneath. Asher blinked once then looked again. She adjusted the scanner to an even tighter field so the spinal cord slowly came into focus. "What the hell is going on?"

"What? What?" Tarris was nearly hysterical. Rya fought a losing battle to calm her host.

"If I didn't know better, it looks like there's nothing wrong with your spine. That can't be right," she muttered.

"I don't understand."

"It looks like the ring is designed to compress your nerves."

"You mean to say that they deliberately crippled me?" Tarris's voice slowly rose in volume until the last word shook the glassware that sat on the shelf.

"Now calm down."

"Don't tell me to calm down!" Tarris's voice was now at full volume. "Some bastard has deliberately ruined my life? What about the signal?"

"There's a tiny device attached to the ring. I'm sorry, but I'm not an electronics expert, so I don't know exactly what it does." Asher hesitated. "But it looks like someone wanted to keep track of you."

Keep track? Tarris thought for a moment about those early days when she was learning about her gift. Her teachers had told her she was one of the best they had ever seen, but she had always thought it was designed to make her feel good. What if that were true? Had she been crippled in an effort to control her? Was someone else involved that she didn't know about? What was she really capable of? Tarris had always thought she hadn't yet reached her full potential. Did they know what she suspected?

"Are you all right?" Asher asked gently. Her hand slowly drew circles around the damaged spine.

"Yeah. No. I don't know." Tarris turned her head to look at Asher. "What now?"

"Indeed. What now? What do you want to happen now?"

"That depends on you."

"Me?" Asher sounded surprised.

"I suppose I have two choices. Leave things as they are... or remove it."

"Remove it?" Asher's eyes widened in fear. "Oh no, no, no. That's a very risky operation."

"And you're not prepared to do it?" Tarris didn't want to beg, but if she had to she would.

"I didn't say that. That ring has been in there for sixteen years. Your body has accepted it, and tissue has grown around it. Removing it will not be without consequences."

"Asher, I am a paraplegic. How much worse can it be?"

"Infection, damage to your spine," Asher said as she counted the problems off on her fingers, "damage to blood vessels, and the list goes on. Let alone what removing the device will do to your life."

"Our lives," Tarris corrected her.

"I beg your pardon?"

"Removing that device will affect us both. I suspect the Council is behind this. They'll know you did it."

"Another reason for me to tell you to get out."

"Look—" Tarris said.

"But it would be inhumane of me to let you continue like this."

"You're running a great risk here," Tarris said. "I've put you in an untenable position, and for that, I'm sorry." It was a little too late to say sorry, but she had no choice. If she wanted Asher's help it would take a few more "sorry"s before she was through.

"You didn't know it was there."

Tarris smiled up at Asher. "So now you believe me."

"I suppose I do, though heaven only knows why." Asher shook her head. "Give me tonight to think about it. I'll meet you tomorrow at the Citizens' Galleria in the Beverage Bar and let you know my decision."

"That's not wise. I'll probably be watched." Tarris suddenly felt guilty that she involved this stranger in her problems. Had she just sentenced the young mediprac to death?

"That's my decision. Take it or leave it."

"I don't think I can. I feel guilty enough for risking your anonymity now. Tomorrow will only make it worse."

"Take it or leave it," Asher repeated.

"Fine, it's your life. At noon then." Very little was said as Asher helped Tarris to dress. Both seemed lost deep in thought over what had transpired and what was about to come.

Chapter 5

Tarris sat and quietly sipped her coffee substitute from her temperature-controlled cup. Her dark-tinted eyes scanned the plaza to look for both Asher and her spy. She spotted Asher some distance away, walking determinedly toward her. Rya was restless, and Tarris was tempted to send her warrior in search of their quarry, but Rya didn't like the light. Somehow, these days, Rya's well-being was as important as her own.

Tarris's eyes fixed on Asher. Her mind scattered in all directions with random thoughts as she watched her approach. Tarris wasn't sure exactly what she felt about Asher. She was full of wary optimism, suspicion, guilt, and a warm fuzzy feeling that annoyed the hell out of her.

"Hello, sweetheart." If Tarris had made a bet with herself as to what Asher would say, that wouldn't have even been on her "just in case" list. Her jaw dropped open when Asher lowered her head and planted a kiss on her lips. The kiss was warm, wet, and tender, and fanned the flames of the warm fuzzies swirling in her stomach.

"Errr…" Tarris stumbled over the exclamation. She must have looked like an idiot. Judging by Asher's grin, she would have kissed Tarris anyway just to see her blush.

Asher leaned in farther and moved her lips to Tarris's

ear. "Just play along. I'll explain later." The whispered words were spoken quickly, followed by a kiss on the cheek. Asher's voice rose to normal pitch. "I'm sorry I'm late. I had trouble finding my underwear. I finally located it under the mattress. We sort of lost track of clothes last night, didn't we?"

Underwear? Clothes? What was the woman talking about... oohhh. "Errr... yeah." Tarris wasn't sure what game Asher was playing, but it bordered on the ludicrous.

"I've been thinking..."

In Tarris's mind, Asher had done too much thinking.

"I accept your offer to move in with you," Asher said.

Offer? There was an offer? Tarris battled on, completely ignorant of what was going on. "That's good to hear. When can you move in?"

"I have a few things to collect back at the apartment, but today if you want."

"Sure." What was Tarris getting herself into? All she wanted was an opinion on her back, and now Asher had plans to move in? It was bad enough to struggle in her apartment alone, but now she would have someone watching her every move. "This better be good," Tarris muttered under her breath.

"I have a plan," Asher muttered back.

"A plan." Tarris expressed in those two words what she thought of the plan so far.

Asher grabbed Tarris's hand and pulled her to her feet. "Come on then. I'm eager to move in." Asher slipped her arm around Tarris's waist to pull her closer so their bodies touched. She actively encouraged Tarris to slip her arm over her shoulder so they presented an enticing image of two lovers.

"I'm going to kill you for this," Tarris whispered.

"If this doesn't work, you'll be waiting in line to do that. Come on, let's get my things."

Despite the limitations caused by Tarris's suit, they made good time across the city to Asher's apartment. Once the front door had closed, Tarris disengaged herself from Asher's arm and moved farther into the living room. "Talk."

"You were worried about our lives being in danger, right?"

"Tell me something I don't know."

"Wouldn't two lovers be less suspicious than if you came to see me for professional reasons?" Asher said. "That's what they're going to see, you know."

Asher was right. Being lovers would be less likely to draw attention. "There's one big problem with that."

"Please don't. I thought long and hard about this."

"There…" This was all so embarrassing, and Tarris steeled herself for the revelation. "There hasn't been anyone in my life, and now you pop up? That's suspicious in itself."

"No one? Ever? I find that hard to believe."

Tarris's head dipped. She just couldn't say it. A lone finger touched her chin. Asher silently demanded that she look up into her eyes. "But why?"

"I thought that was rather obvious." Tarris spat out the words, anger mixing with frustration and sadness. "I'm of no use to anyone." Then, of course, there was Rule Seven.

"That is so sad. To have never experienced love."

"Love? Sex? It's all the same."

"No, it's not. They are as diametrically opposite as… as you and I."

"I don't need them." Then why did Tarris feel that was a lie? She quickly changed the subject. "What was all that play-acting in the plaza?"

"Didn't you say you were being watched by the Council? I was just adding credence to our story."

"Our story? You decided on this action before consulting me. Now you've put us both in a situation where we have to continue this charade or be unmasked."

"I didn't have time to discuss it with you. Didn't you do exactly the same thing last night by coming to my apartment?" Asher's eyes blazed. "You want my help or not? This is a solution to that problem so stop complaining."

Tarris couldn't believe it. Asher actually argued with her even though she knew who, and what, she was. "And what does moving in with me accomplish?"

"You can't go to a hospital for the operation, so I'm going to have to improvise. You won't be moving anywhere once it's done, and I need to keep an eye on you. Wouldn't it be more logical for me to move into your apartment rather than the other way around?"

Tarris raised her hand to her forehead and rubbed briskly in frustration. "All right! All right. How did I let you talk me into this?"

"If I remember rightly, it was because you were desperate for help. I should be offended, you know, because to you I've become an act of desperation. I've never had to work this hard to get a date."

"Let's get this over with then." Tarris admitted defeat.

"You're such a sweet-talker," Asher cooed.

"One more crack out of you, and you won't need to worry about the Council."

It took a couple of hours to pack Asher's equipment and clothes. It was really happening. In a matter of hours, she had gone from a single woman living alone to someone who wasn't going to be alone anymore, at least for the near future. Asher would know it all.

Tarris shuddered at the thought of tomorrow night when Asher would see Rya emerge, but there was no way she could avoid it. The plan was in motion, and she would to have to live with it… or, in this case, with her.

"Stop worrying. You haven't got anything that I haven't seen before." Could Asher sense her concern?

"Don't bet on it," Tarris mumbled. She still had one surprise to reveal to her, one that would probably send her running from the apartment.

"Come on. Let's get moving." Asher pulled the trolley that held her bags. The medical equipment was secreted inside the bags that looked to the world like she had a huge wardrobe. The ceramic wheels moved the platform easily, and Asher needed very little energy to pull it.

Outside, Tarris touched her wrist computer and sent out a signal for a taxi. Moments later, the checkered vehicle pulled up to the curb and waited for them. Asher went around to the back of the vehicle with her trolley while the baggage platform emerged from the bottom of the cab. She pushed the trolley onto it but didn't wait to see the platform disappear back up into the metal compartment.

Tarris got into the taxi. She smoothly touched the pads that would collapse the hydraulic joints to make it possible for her to sit. Was this foolhardy charade worth the risk of them both dying so she had a chance of walking again? Sadly, there was only one answer as far as she was concerned. Yes.

†

Tarris hesitated outside the door to her apartment.

"What's wrong?"

"Nothing… everything." How could she explain this? "I don't know if I can do this." She flinched when Asher's hand touched her own.

"What are you afraid of?"

"Nothing. Fear makes you weak, it makes you slow, and it will eventually kill you, so it's not a matter of being afraid." Tarris feared very little, of that she was sure. "It's more… more…" What did she want to say? "I suppose it's a matter of losing my independence." Did she truly believe that? Maybe she was a little afraid of letting someone in, and somehow she had a feeling this woman would be the one to do it.

Rule Eight in her Survival Handbook: Don't let your enemies see your emotion; it leaves you open to attack.

Asher gave her hand a pat. "I'll stay out of your way as much as possible. Okay?"

"Okay." But she would still be there. Watching her. Judging her. Tarris reminded herself why she was doing this. She would do what it took to walk again. She swiped her barcode over the infrared lock, and her gaze dropped to the floor as the door slid open.

"Well, here it is." She stood aside to allow Asher inside with her trolley. The clatter of the jostled bags disturbed the peace of the apartment. "Light," Tarris announced. She felt like her inner sanctum had been violated. "Coffee?"

"Sure," Asher answered as Tarris walked smoothly to the kitchen alcove. Tarris returned to where Asher was seated and handed over a thermal cup full of synth coffee. "Thanks."

Tarris reached to the nape of her neck. The color drained from her hair to return to her natural white.

"How do you do that?"

Instead of answering, Tarris put down her cup and flipped her hair forward to allow Asher access to her neck. Asher stood and circled her. "Just under the skin is a small tab." Asher felt around until she found the small circle of metal. "I just tap it…"

"Can I?"

"Sure." Tarris felt Asher's fingers brush her neck then tap the spot to switch on the current.

"That is so amazing," Asher said with enthusiasm

"It's pretty cool all right."

"How does it work?"

"The tab is connected to a tiny battery that sends a light electrical current over my skull. It conducts down the hair follicles and reacts with the chemically treated hair. While the current is on, the hair will remain dark."

"Don't you run the risk of giving yourself a shock?"

"The current is so low that wouldn't happen."

"How does it feel?"

Tarris felt Asher's fingers trail over the nape of her neck. "It tingles a little, that's all."

"And what about if it rains or when you wash it?"

"I get wet?" Tarris flipped her hair back and studied Asher's annoyed expression. "It's safe enough, believe me." She reached back and tapped her neck once more to return the color to white.

"And is it all worth it?"

"Yeah… yeah, it is." She had thought long and hard before she made the changes to her body. She hadn't gone into it blindly or lightly. Tarris really wanted to be invisible to those around her.

"Can I ask you something?" Asher waited for a nod before proceeding. "Why do you hide yourself? The others make no effort to blend in. In fact, they seem to take pride in who they are."

"They are also arrogant, self-absorbed pricks, but that's just my opinion." Tarris chuckled. Her definition didn't fit Corman anymore. His arrogance was so immense that he needed the entire planet just to house it.

"I don't understand." Asher looked at her quizzically. "Why aren't you like them?"

"I don't know. Maybe my legs remind me I'm human like everyone else."

"But you're not like everyone else. You should know that."

"Yeah… yeah, I do." Tarris picked up her cup and drank the hot beverage. She used the action to end the conversation.

Asher reached into her pocket and took out the small device Tarris had given her. She activated it and scanned the room, noting the signal emanating from Tarris.

Asher stood and wandered around the apartment. "Nice place you have here." With some amusement, Tarris watched her scan the room. She would find nothing. "A bed in the living room. Interesting choice."

"I think so. It's been very comfortable for me, and I have good access. The spare bedroom is too small."

The light on the box flashed. "Honey," Asher said, "do you want to show me around?"

"Wha…" A small hand quickly covered Tarris's mouth and stopped her from muttering anything more. Slowly, Asher's hand moved to her lips to show silence.

"What?" Tarris whispered. Asher showed the box to Tarris and let go as it was snatched away.

Tarris checked the settings and re-scanned the area. No, the first reading was correct. That couldn't be. She scanned her apartment regularly with the device from Derille. Not sure what she would find, Tarris moved along the wall and narrowed down her search with the aid of the device. Sure enough, she found a small hole in the wall, just above an abstract painting that hung there. Slowly she approached it, sliding along the wall to keep out of sight. She saw the reflection of a lens. She was being watched. Anger burned within her. She. Was. Being. Watched. First there was the betrayal of purposely damaging her spine, and now this.

A tap on her shoulder nearly sent her into action. Only her mental checking of herself stopped Tarris from slamming Asher against the wall. "What's going on?" Asher mouthed the words. Tarris wanted to hit something, and bad.

She motioned Asher toward the door and indicated she should keep to the walls as she did so. When they reached the hall, only then did Tarris speak in a low murmur. "I'm being watched. How the hell did I miss that? I can't believe it." She paced up and down the narrow corridor, agitated to the point of wanting to lash out. "All this time I've been watched. I just want to—"

"It could be a recent thing," Asher said.

"Maybe. But why didn't my own detector pick it up?" Now Tarris's suspicious mind began to see more conspiracies and betrayals.

"It could be faulty."

"It could be. It could also be deliberately meant not to work." Had Derille played her all along? What did he want from her? Had she jumped to conclusions? Whether it was all in her head or everyone was out to get her, life had just gotten infinitely more dangerous and complicated.

"So what do we do now?"

Indeed, what should they do? They? Tarris never had to consider anyone's actions but her own before. "Maybe you should go home. The rules of this particular game have just changed. I can't allow you to be hurt in this."

"I think that would be my decision not yours, Trooper."

"No, I forbid this."

"You forbid? Just who the hell do you think you are? My mother?"

Did Asher know whom she was speaking to?

"In this matter, yes," Tarris said. "I'm not going to be responsible for whatever might happen to you. I'm going to need all my wits about me to protect myself, without worrying about you."

"You would worry about me?"

"As I would about anyone else in your situation."

"Oh." Asher sounded disappointed. "But that still doesn't change my decision. I'm staying. It's got to be a hell of a lot safer with you than without you."

Tarris looked at her and saw that Asher had made her decision. For better or for worse, they were in this together. "All right. Don't say I didn't warn you. We've got two choices. We either use it or lose it."

"Huh?"

"We either use the camera to our advantage, and it means carrying on this stupid plan of yours, or we dig it out and wait for the consequences."

"You mean we carry on this romance thing for real?" Asher's voice nearly squeaked.

Tarris watched Asher's breathing hitch. Pretending they were lovers outside was one thing, but doing that in bed was another. Could she stop herself from getting involved? Somehow she doubted that. That fine line between make-believe and reality could be stepped over very easily.

"Errr... yeah." Though she had voiced it, Tarris had serious doubts about being able to do this. This would surely uncover a particular facet lacking in her life. She could handle being a fool in front of Asher, but what about those who watched them? No doubt Corman and his cohorts would have a good laugh at her expense. It galled her to think of him having this piece of information over her.

Now why did that come to mind? Actually, he seemed to know a lot about her personal life. Was he in on this conspiracy? Could she trust no one?

Could she trust Asher? She looked at her. Rich blue eyes returned her gaze and studied her in silence. Tarris was drawn into those depths and held there, bathed in a warming glow emanating from within. Trust was fleeting, or so she thought. Time would tell who was on her side.

Asher seemed to hesitate.

"Are you having second thoughts about this?" Tarris said.

"I... I..."

"We can go back in there and have a fight, and you can return home. I'll call for a taxi."

Asher lifted her chin. "No. No. I can do this."

Tarris could hear the resolve in her voice. "I'm not some charity case here. If it's going to be a chore, then don't worry about it. I've survived very well up to now without help—"

"Hey! Hey. Slow down." Asher placed her hand on Tarris's arm. "I didn't mean it to sound like that. It's just... I'm not the sort of person who jumps into bed with someone I've just met."

"Me, either." Tarris chuckled. What an understatement that was. Asher joined in the levity.

She looked shyly at Tarris. "So, what do we do?"

"I don't know. I really don't know." Tarris looked inside to Rya for help. *What do I do?* "If we do this, it won't be a matter of slowly easing into it. They think we're already lovers."

"I know. All right. Let's do this."

What Tarris wanted to do right now was shuffle her feet, but the frame couldn't perform such refined movements as that. "Err... one other thing. I... I've never done this before."

"I already know that."

"You do?"

"You already told me, remember?" Tarris stared at her blankly. "Don't worry about it, Tarris." Asher smiled. "I'll lead you." Her voice dropped to a whisper. "I won't let you fall."

"Are we doing it on the edge of a cliff or something?"

"No, silly." Asher leaned in closer, as if to reveal a

secret. "I'll make you look good."

Tarris just nodded. They re-entered the apartment and sidled along the wall toward the bathroom. Tarris spoke softly at first, getting louder and louder as if coming out of one of the other rooms. "So, that's it. I'll have to make some space for your things."

They moved into the center of the room, into the sight of the camera. Asher grabbed Tarris and pulled her toward her. "Come here. I don't bite," she whispered.

Tarris tried to watch as Asher kissed her, but the sensation drew her in and her eyes closed. Unconsciously, she wrapped her arms around the source of the warmth that filled her. She pulled Asher closer so that their bodies touched. Oh, what she made her feel. A moist tongue touched her lips. She drew back, and her pale eyes widened with surprise.

"It looks like it won't be so hard after all," Asher murmured, just before she drew in Tarris once more. This time there was no resistance. A tentative touch from Tarris elicited a moan that rumbled in Asher's throat. Tarris explored further, emboldened by Asher's frantic movements.

Asher pulled back. "Whoa there, tiger. Let's save something for tonight." Tarris felt disappointed, and Asher chuckled.

"Is… is it always like that?" Tarris asked.

Asher smiled sweetly. "Better."

"Will…" Tarris paused. Her naïveté showed, she knew that, but the anticipation of what she could feel was killing her. "Will I feel anything?" Her whisper was urgent.

"Maybe not here…" Asher said and slipped her hand down toward Tarris's crotch momentarily before she lifted it to rest on her forehead. "But you'll feel it here"—she tapped the skin with her fingers and then dropped them to Tarris's chest—"and here."

"And… and…" She just had to know.

"Shhh. You'll find out tonight, all right?" Asher stepped backwards and put some space between the two of them. Her voice rose for the benefit of the spy camera. "So what are we going to do this afternoon?"

Tarris reined in her rampaging thoughts and directed her attention to their plan. "First, let's find a home for all your belongings." She pointed to one of the bags that she knew held clothes. "Just bring the trolley into the spare room."

Only now she realized that her bed in the living room was in direct line with the hidden camera. She had never felt so violated in her life. Like peeping toms, they had watched her in all her acts of intimacy. Dressed, undressed, sleeping, or awake, they saw it all. Indignation burned brightly within her at the thought of such an invasion of privacy. They would pay for such a violation of trust.

Tarris scanned the rest of her apartment and took a small amount of pleasure in the fact that only her bed area was on view to whoever felt it necessary to watch her. "I'll clear a bit of space here for your stuff," Tarris said from the bathroom. She hoped she yelled loud enough to deafen those who listened. "Do you mind if I put on some music?"

"No problem," Asher replied from the spare room.

Tarris fetched her portable player, placed it on the vanity counter, and turned the sound up loud. "That okay?"

A mop of black hair appeared at the doorway. "Huh? I can't hear you over the noise." Tarris put her finger to her lips.

"Your medical stuff. Get it," Tarris muttered in a low tone. When Asher disappeared, Tarris activated an infrared scan with her barcode and watched with some satisfaction as a small platform descended from the roof. It had taken some doing to have this installed quietly, but right now it was worth its weight in oil. That is, if her enemies didn't know about it already. She hadn't used the hidden space for quite a while, so she held some hope that it had been installed before the hidden camera was there.

Asher returned with two large suitcases and placed them on the metal plate. The platform disappeared into the roof of the bathroom. The seams disappeared as the sheet locked into place.

"Thanks, sweetheart." Tarris raised her voice. She turned down the player. "Finished putting your things away?"

"Most of them. Just a couple of things need to find a home."

"Tell you what," Tarris said, "how about a nice walk in the park?"

"Sure. Do I need anything?"

"Just me." Tarris knew she had said something mushy when Asher gazed at her with her vibrant blue eyes in a way that tugged at her heart.

†

The afternoon walk had been surprisingly delightful, even though the conversation was stiff and formal at first, but the warming sun and companionship eased Tarris's troubled mind. Not since Boothe had she attempted to engage in any kind of friendly relationship. Well, except for

Darmen, but she saw him infrequently.

Now the time had come. The daylight had gone, and Tarris had no more excuses. Even dinner had passed far too quickly for her.

She opted to remove her suit and use the wheelchair, storing her precious walking aid in the spare bedroom. Removing the frame, in Tarris's mind, was not sexy and was something better out of the way before bed.

Tarris's heart was thumping wildly. What she had held in expectation from earlier in the day was now upon them, and she was more than a little nervous. She watched anxiously as Asher approached and stopped mere inches from her. "Take my clothes off," Asher murmured.

"Why?" Clear ice eyes widened.

"It's part of the seduction."

"It is?" Really? Maybe she should have paid more attention to the intricacies of the mating ritual.

Asher stepped into the space between Tarris's legs. Her hands grabbed the wheelchair armrests and pulled Tarris slowly forward.

From the moment Asher's lips touched hers, Tarris's emotions soared. It took only moments for her to pull Asher closer as she remembered the body-to-body sensation with relish.

Asher pulled away slightly. "Now, undress me." The low light of the room cast enticing shadows over Asher's face. Her eyes darkened from azure to a midnight blue in a matter of moments.

Tarris couldn't help but look over to the wall. "Now I wish the bed was in the spare room."

"Ignore them. It's only us, all right?"

For Tarris to convince herself of the mental deception

wasn't easy.

Asher wrapped a hand around Tarris's neck and pulled her in, her tongue demanding entrance and receiving it. Tarris's fingers touched her and slid slowly over her shirt to find entrance to the skin beneath. Asher whispered, "I have a feeling I don't have to show you anything."

Tarris could feel Rya shifting anxiously as curiosity and apprehension swirled around inside her. She was driven to know. Her fingers finally found the clasps and clumsily undid them to reveal shadowed terrain. As if outside herself, Tarris watched her hands slide past the material to Asher's pale skin. Her heated fingers burned a path across a patch of skin that was soft and enticing, unlike anything she had felt before. She wanted to convey all her emotions in that touch: innocence, curiosity, sensuality, and excitement to name a few.

A shaky sigh escaped Asher's lips at that first touch. The whisper of material sounded like an explosion in the silence of the room. Tarris had taken the first step down the road of discovery. Her eyes were at their strongest in the low light, and she used them to great advantage. Her gaze wandered down over the skin she had touched moments before. Rya shifted again. "Steady," she whispered.

"Did you say something?"

"Just talking to myself."

"Come…" Asher grasped Tarris's shaking hands and lifted them to the magnetic clasp on the front of her bra. Tarris's eyes remained fixed on her chest for long moments before they rose to meet her own. "You can do it." Asher's hands rested over Tarris's as the clasp came free. The moment Tarris cupped her breasts, a low moan escaped Asher's lips. "Oh God, honey." In a flurry of activity, she tore at Tarris's clothes, bringing skin against skin.

Tarris felt herself being steered toward the bed and helped to lower herself fully to the mattress. Her apprehension grew as her skin was slowly revealed. Her body trembled as her pants gave way to the colostomy bag lying against her skin

"You are beautiful," Asher murmured. Tarris looked into her eyes and knew in her heart that Asher meant it. She hadn't considered herself beautiful. She was well aware of how her body looked. Her muscular upper body was due to compensating for her paraplegia, and it made her lower half look emaciated. Yet, when she looked at her lower half alone, it wasn't wasted but merely thin. The suit she wore had exercised the muscles, thereby keeping them pliable and useful. All that was needed to make them work was the nerve conduction.

Tarris felt naked in more ways than one. Asher studied her, and Tarris didn't know whether she liked it or not. Was it the physician or the woman who looked at her? A lone hand traveled up her body, starting in territory where she felt nothing and crossing over the border to sensation. Her skin twitched before it instinctively withdrew. Asher continued the easy stroking of her skin, allowing Tarris to relax and welcome the new touch. Her eyes never left Asher's hand as it discovered her, even when she found her breast. It was… it was… A gentle sigh escaped her lips as Asher teased her nipple.

"Good, huh?" Asher chuckled. Her soft lips replaced the hand, and her moist tongue gently circled the rapidly responding nipple.

Tarris planted her hands in Asher's hair. She wanted more contact. "Please…"

"What do you want?"

"Come to me." When Asher made a move, she was stopped. "No, naked," Tarris said. "I want to feel you next to me."

Tarris watched Asher undress as she slowly removed her clothes one piece at a time. A sensual heat spread out over Tarris's skin and a smile touched her lips. What could have turned out as a disastrous event had turned into something wholly unexpected.

Asher moved to the other side of the bed and stripped the covering back before wrestling Tarris to the sheet underneath. "Now, where were we?" she asked in a sensual tone. She slid into welcoming arms, and Tarris felt the heat infuse into her skin. They touched, they tasted, and they teased, but kept the pace slow and easy as Tarris learned about love.

Tarris wished so much to be able to feel everything. She wanted to love, to live, and just to be happy. Could she ever have that? Random thoughts flew through her mind haphazardly, and she was unaware that she wasn't the only one thinking them. Rya absorbed her sister's wishes, intent on giving her what she wanted. After all, it was through her that Rya even existed at all.

Tarris just couldn't get enough of Asher. It was like a dam had burst. All her emotion and need exploded around her. She needed something, but she didn't know what. Asher had been right. It was in her heart and in her head.

Lost in the moment, Tarris wasn't wholly aware of Rya's movement from one body to another.

Asher sat up. "What… what's going on?"

"What's wrong?"

"I don't know. I feel weird. I don't know what it is."

Tarris had a moment to reflect on what was happening, and her mind settled a little away from the contact. Something was wrong. She searched herself for Rya but couldn't find any evidence of her. As she lay there she calmed herself, meditating until she found that state that would send Rya on her deadly journey. It was then that she sensed Asher. *What are you doing?*

Helping you.

Tarris rarely received clear words from her shadow warrior. Her communication usually consisted of images and emotions.

You're scaring her.

But this was a chance to feel what Asher felt. "Calm down," she said to Asher. She wrapped her hands around the metal bed frame to pull herself farther up the mattress. The mood was rapidly disappearing, and Tarris vainly tried to hold things together. She was close to what she had denied herself all these years. "Come here," she whispered gently. "Don't be afraid. It..." Oh God, the moment of truth. Will she run or will she stay? "It's me in you."

"It's you?"

Tarris watched intently as Asher thought it through. "My... my... shadow warrior." Tarris hadn't explained things very well.

"Okayyy." Asher made a move away.

"No!" Tarris wrapped her hand around Asher's wrist and held on. "Please. Please." She hesitated. "For want of a better word, it's my soul."

"Your soul."

Tarris sighed deeply. "You want to know what makes us different from you? Why we are feared so much? Well, this is it."

"Uh-huh."

"We're able to detach our souls from our bodies. Only albinos seem to be able to do this." Asher regarded her dubiously. "Fine." Tarris lay back and called Rya to emerge. Before the thought had finished, the black shadow seeped through the pores of Asher's skin. Asher gasped but was stilled by the hand holding onto her arm. Rya's dark shape lay gently over Tarris's prone form and slowly sank back into its host.

"That... that..."

"You can leave," Tarris murmured. Rya wrapped herself around Tarris's heart and helped take the pain. Tarris closed her eyes. She didn't want to see Asher leave. She just knew this was going to happen. She was destined to live her life alone. Time dragged on without a sound. Had she left so silently?

Rya could feel Tarris's sorrow and tried to comfort her. Tarris knew that Rya had good intentions, but Asher wasn't prepared to accept who she was. Tarris threw her arm across her eyes, as if physically blocking out the outside world for a while. The tears wouldn't come, and Tarris wouldn't allow them. It was not who she was.

At first she was only vaguely aware of the hand on her skin, slowly caressing its softness and warmth. Moments passed before she sensed Asher was still next to her. She could feel the warmth and smell of her. Tarris's turned to look at her. "Why?"

"It... it just took me by surprise, that's all. What was that?"

"She... she's a part of me. What is she? A manifestation of my mind? My soul? Who knows? I consider she's my twin that never lived. She has been a part of me all my life, and without her I'm not complete."

"She, huh? And does she have a name?" Asher's voice held a hint of curiosity.

"Of course." Tarris let a smile cross her lips at the question. Maybe things would be all right after all. "Rya."

"So was Rya being a busybody, or did you send her?"

"Me? Oh no, no, no. I would never do such a thing." Tarris's lips said one thing, but her hands told another story as they slowly caressed the skin still visible to her. Of course she wanted it all, but she wasn't going to admit that readily. "Rya was just helping by letting me feel what you feel."

"And you can sense what she senses? What about me? Can I feel you?"

"I have no idea. I would say by your reaction that you felt her there."

"You've never tried this before?"

"Errr… no." Tarris's voice became guarded because she was moving into territory where she didn't want to go. "Now…" She swooped down to kiss Asher and frantically tried to make her forget what the conversation was about.

"She wouldn't hurt me, would she?" Asher asked.

"Of course not." *Not unless I told her to.* "She was just curious, that's all."

Asher seemed to make some sort of decision. "If I asked her to leave, she would?"

"Of course. She means you no harm." Tarris couldn't believe that Asher would even consider allowing Rya inside her again. What would she get out of the connection? "You… you would do this for me?"

"For us, Tarris. I must admit that I'm curious also, but… but there's that element of fear that makes me hesitate."

"Then it won't be an issue."

"But here's your chance to feel it all."

"Not at the expense of you. It can wait until I can walk again." But both knew the likelihood of that was marginal at best. Too much time had passed, and it would take a miracle for it to happen.

Asher took a deep breath. "Oh boy. I can do this," she muttered.

Tarris touched a long tapered finger to her chin to ask for her attention. "It's not necessary, Asher. Just... love... me."

"Rya," Asher whispered, "come to me." She looked up. "Can she hear me?" Tarris nodded. "Come on then. I won't hurt you." Tarris tried very hard not to laugh. If only Asher knew what Rya was truly capable of.

Go on, but be gentle. Tarris felt the familiar rush as Rya left and watched as she momentarily hovered above Asher before she descended through her skin. It was strange to see it happen, and Tarris felt a twinge of jealousy. Rya had been hers and hers alone, a gift she had rigorously guarded. Now her twin was going to someone else, and Tarris wasn't sure she liked it. However, she did have that connection and keenly observed the interaction between the two of them.

Asher lay back as Rya moved from one body to another. "She tickles."

Tarris chuckled.

"All my nerve endings are jumping. I feel like I want to scratch myself."

"Yeah, I know."

"Errr... hello?"

Tarris smiled at Asher's obvious attempt to make contact. She knew that Rya didn't speak but emanated a warm fuzzy feeling that would settle Asher's nerves greatly. Asher would understand *"thank you,"* but it would only be in abstract images and thoughts.

Asher looked at her in wonder. "And you live like this every day?"

"Why? Is it bad?" Tarris had never known what it was like to live without her twin. Even when she was on an assignment, Rya was there in her mind. Their connection was unbreakable.

"No. It's..." Instead of an explanation, Asher pulled in Tarris and kissed her long and hard. Emotion welled up as Tarris responded eagerly to her. "Oh my God!" Asher moaned almost painfully.

"What do you feel?" Tarris's insides jumped with giddy glee. Asher's feelings could be read quite easily, but through her own link with Rya, the sensations were magnified. Tarris was barely able to hold in a moan.

"I... ahhh... no... oh God no... it's..." Asher rambled, and it pleased Tarris that she had been able to make her speechless.

Tarris held on tightly to her connection with Rya. She allowed it to fill her mind and stir up images she had never even imagined. Hauntingly erotic images that she knew had not come from her mind. "My, my, Asher. What a dirty mind you have."

A blush spread rapidly up Asher's chest to her hairline. "Oh Lord. You got that? Oh no." Her hands rose to her face as she tried to cover her shame.

"Don't be embarrassed. I just never knew you could do that."

"Oh please, don't rub it in."

"Maybe when I have my legs back we can try that, because I'm not going to hang from the ceiling to satisfy your lewd dreams." Tarris laughed gently as the blush deepened. "Stop it… there's nothing wrong with what you thought. I was just pulling your leg."

"Why you…" Asher wrestled herself onto Tarris and took up residence between her limp legs. Almost immediately all play was forgotten as their bodies touched. Asher tasted every bit of skin she could find while her fingers discovered the body underneath her.

Tarris's mind was awash with sensation. Asher had obviously figured out how to make use of Rya as she sent out a mixture of sensations to her that she had never experienced before. Love, lust, sex, abandon, and adrenaline all merged in her head. It gave her a good idea of what passion was, and it was a heady mixture. She could easily give into its intoxicating allure. And she did. If only this once, she would experience it all.

Tarris was barely aware of what Rya did. She knew her shadow was flying, and like a hungry child she was greedily absorbing all the new sights, sounds, emotions, and thoughts.

Tarris rolled Asher over and clumsily tried to follow. Instead, she rested herself on her elbow. Her other hand explored, and her lips and tongue followed. She took her time as she absorbed both the external and internal indications of what Asher was feeling. It was truly extraordinary. So much pleasure was nearly too much. Her hand slipped down to dark curls, and her gaze rose to meet the dark eyes watching her.

"Touch me." The words were so soft they were nearly

inaudible. As if to illustrate what Asher wanted, an image popped into Tarris's head and she followed. Almost immediately a soft moan floated in the air. She repeated the action again with the same result, this time accompanied by a gentle sway of the hips. Lust swept through her, and an overwhelming urge to reach completion rushed through her mind.

She looked down at Asher and watched her breathing accelerate. Asher's delicate fingers grabbed handfuls of sheet as the sweet torture continued, and her swaying hips picked up momentum as her excitement grew. Tarris could feel it all.

She had been so wrapped up in her own pleasure that she didn't keep track of Rya. The spirit found Asher's soul and gently touched the essence that was her. It was a sweet meeting of souls, a delicate dance of introduction. As Asher reached her peak, her soul burst into a blinding flash, pulsing wildly in response to the passion felt.

Tarris was overcome with Asher's orgasm as she herself twitched uncontrollably. Well, at least the top half of her. It was like a phantom twitch. Her mind knew it was there, even if her body didn't. Her resolve to get her legs back just doubled. If that was what it felt like, there was no way anyone was going to stop her.

An unearthly scream filled the air as Rya tore herself from Asher and flew around the room like a tornado. Glass shattered and electrical equipment exploded. Tarris instinctively threw herself across Asher as glass and hot metal flew everywhere. "What the—" Rya slammed into Tarris at great speed, and her back exploded. "Arrgghhh!"

"What just happened?" Asher asked. "Oh God, I feel like my heart was just ripped out." But Tarris didn't answer. Dark eyes looked up at her. "What? Tarris? Oh God, honey, what's wrong?"

"My…" Tarris's voice was ripped from her throat at the pain "My back. It… it… Christ… it feels like someone stabbed me in the back." She was barely able to breathe with the agony. With difficulty she spoke to Rya, *What's going on?*

It hurts! It hurts!

Talk to me Rya. What happened?

It hurts.

You could say that again. Tarris's mind shifted back to the pain while she tried to make sense of the myriad of images that flooded her mind's eye.

"Can you move at all?"

"I don't know." But she didn't want to try. Any movement was going to hurt. She was barely able to lift herself up for Asher to wriggle out from underneath her before the pain became too unbearable. She collapsed to the bed and mentally tried to dampen the pain she felt.

"Light!" Asher called. "Oh God, Tarris."

"What is it?" She breathed rapidly as shock and adrenaline mixed to hold her in their grasp.

"It… I'm not sure… there's…"

Tarris reached out for Asher's arm. "Wait."

"I've got to do something," Asher said.

"Camera."

"You're injured and you're worried about a damned camera?" Asher whispered.

"Please… check."

The bed dipped as Asher got up and looked for the scanner. "Where is it?" It sat on the table, a smoldering piece of useless equipment. "Damn it!"

"What?" Tarris hadn't moved from her position facedown on the bed.

"It's broken." Asher approached the wall and could see a small wisp of smoke from the tiny hole. She returned to the bed and gently rested her ass on the edge. "It looks like the camera's gone, too."

"Got to check."

"I have to do something about this, Tarris, and to hell with your peeping toms. There's a piece of metal sticking out of your back. It looks like a piece of that ring around your spine." Tarris could hear the concern in Asher's voice.

"My wrist," Tarris whispered. Asher grabbed Tarris's wrist and found the meditab under the skin. She rubbed it briskly to release the medication that would flow through her strongly.

"My equipment. How do I get to it?"

"Cupboard... bottom shelf... emergency switch." The analgesics were finally working and took the edge off the stabbing pain in her back. She had never felt such agony as she did then, even after the accident which caused it. Thank goodness whatever had ruined the scanner and the camera hadn't damaged the circuitry inside her.

Unaware of her nakedness, Asher ran to the bathroom and found the mirror cracked in two. She dropped to the cold floor to find and activate the switch that would release her equipment.

The platform slowly lowered. She grabbed the suitcases before the lift had stopped. What was she doing? She should call for transport to the hospital not look for her own equipment. But secrecy was important to them both at this point. If they knew that Tarris's metal ring was broken, it could change everything. Could she do this? It wasn't a good place to do something this delicate, but she could see no other option.

She dragged her suitcases to the bed and flung them open. She loaded her medispray. "What's that for?" The gentle mumble told her that the meds had started to take effect.

"It's anesthetic. If I'm going to take this out, I need you perfectly still."

"No anesthetic," Tarris said.

"But—"

"Rya was so panicked, I don't know what she would do if I was out cold. No anesthetic."

"How about a local?"

"Fine. Just do it quickly… please." Pale eyes closed as Tarris succumbed to the pain and discomfort. She waited quietly for Asher's ministrations.

"I don't know… maybe we should take this to the hospital." Asher had a sudden stab of indecision. Any operation that involved the spine was tricky, but under these conditions, it was downright stupid.

"No!" Tarris barked. "Oh God… No." She lowered her voice and her anxiety in an effort to take the strain off the injury. "You have to do this, Asher. You…" She blew out a deep breath. Asher could see the strain on Tarris's face as she tried to ride over the back spasm.

Asher gave her the local anesthetic. The medispray absorbed through the skin to deaden the area underneath it. She gave Tarris's hair a gentle stroke before she stood. "Let me get ready." Drug-laden eyes looked up at her. Would she ever be ready to do this?

While the drugs did their work, Asher got out her

instruments and set up a powerful light to illuminate where she was working. She activated a small portable generator on her sterilization unit, which emitted a pulsed UV light to give her a clean environment to work in.

She dug around in her suitcases for what she would need and found a gown to cover her nakedness. How could she forget something like that? It wasn't like she was naked on a regular basis. Idly, she shrugged. It was a thought for another time.

Finally, she was ready. It had been awhile since she had done any surgery. These days her time was committed to her theories. Asher looked to the heavens in a brief prayer, not that she had considered religion in any depth. However, at this point, a little help from above would be appreciated.

She laid out everything she would use under the sterilization unit, giving it the allotted time for proper treatment. "Are you okay?" Her heart went out to Tarris. Life was just not giving her a break.

"Hmmm?" It seemed that the anesthetic had begun to work. "Yeah, I'm still here."

"And what is Rya doing?"

"She..." Tarris's brow creased. "I don't know what you did, but you sure scared her."

Asher thought for a moment as she idly caressed Tarris's strands of hair. Tarris's eyes closed at the touch and a smile crossed her lips.

"Are you okay?" Had she given Tarris too much medication?

"Yeah... that's nice."

Asher felt a tug at her heart as she watched Tarris greedily absorb her attention. The timer went off on the unit, and she withdrew her hand to start the operation. "Try to relax, okay?"

"Any more relaxed and I'd be asleep."

"See? I should have given you the general anesthetic."

"Well, Rya's behaving at the moment. We'll see."

Asher tried to be as gentle as she could, as much for her own sensibilities as for Tarris. Maybe she was too close to Tarris to be doing this. The laser cut through skin to reveal the carnage below. Whatever had happened had shattered the metal ring around the spine. It certainly solved the problem of trying to remove it. She had been worried about how to cut it without damage to the spine below.

Gently, Asher picked away the pieces. She scanned the area with her monitor once or twice to check for errant shards of metal. At one point, she thought Tarris hummed and it brought a smile to her covered lips. Was she humming for herself or for Rya? Did it really matter? Asher turned her attention back to the operation, rechecking a number of times for metal. Satisfied that she had all the pieces, she bathed the area with a liquid solution and sealed the jagged wound with the laser.

"There. I think that's it." Now it was in the hands of a higher power. Tarris's biggest hurdle would be infection.

"What..." Tarris smacked her dry lips. A moment later Asher held a cup to her mouth and dripped a few drops onto her lips. "Thanks. What... was... that you put in my back?" She barely put the words together. Apparently Tarris's drowsiness had caught up with her as the adrenaline wore off.

"It's a concoction of mine. It's a mixture of enzymes, electrolytes, steroids, antibiotics, and anti-inflammatories. It should help to fight infection and stimulate the nerves in your back." Before Asher had finished, a gentle snore came from Tarris. Asher brushed Tarris's face and hair with a slow, gentle motion.

"Rya," she whispered, "I'm sorry for whatever happened. I didn't mean it." Asher thought about those moments before all hell had broken loose. Tarris had... oh God, what a feeling that was. It was... it was... She closed her eyes to feel that rush again. That was when Rya broke away from her. Maybe it was the surge of passion? She would have to ask Tarris in the morning.

Chapter 6

Tarris slowly regained consciousness, but as soon as her senses touched reality, she wanted to crawl back into a blissful comatose state. Rya's escapade had taken every bit of energy she had and left her weak and disoriented.

"How are you feeling?"

It took Tarris a moment to remember who belonged to that voice. She lifted her head off the pillow and rolled it to the other side. Asher lay there in a skimpy shift. A woman she had barely known two days was sleeping in her bed. Had she lost her mind? Was she so intent on self-destruction that she was doing things that were totally out of the ordinary for her?

"Wehrearelmeu mmptutptp." Tarris smacked her dry lips.

"A moment." Asher rose from the bed and moved to the kitchen, seemingly confident in her state of undress and her place in the apartment. She returned with a drink flask and lowered the top to Tarris's waiting lips. "Try again."

"Wehrearelmeu mmptutptp."

"Huh?"

"That's how I feel."

"Oh. Let me take a look at your back."

"Do you have to?" Tarris wasn't ready for Asher's

pushing and prodding, especially first thing after she woke up.

"I'm the mediprac here, Trooper. Don't tell me my job." Asher sounded stern.

Tarris turned her head back to its original position and just lay there.

Asher peeled back the dressing to study the incision. "Considering the carnage that was there last night, it's healing nicely. The wound closed by the laser is clean, and the swelling underneath is only minimal. It looks like the complications that I feared aren't going to happen, and for that I'm grateful. You should stay in bed today."

"No, that's not an option."

"You're not going anywhere."

"Don't tell me what to do. It's my life, dammit." Tarris struggled to roll over and took stock of her body. While the wound site was sore, the rest of her body was in reasonable shape. However, her most fervent wish would not be granted. The lower half of her was still in darkness. She felt as much in her legs today as she had yesterday... nothing. The operation didn't work, and she was shattered. All hope was gone.

"I'm your physician—"

"But not my mother." Tarris touched the button to raise her bed and threw her arm over her eyes. No one, least of all the woman next to her, would witness her dream slowly die. Rya was the only one who truly understood what it meant to her, and the two of them would mourn the failure in silence. When the bed didn't move, Tarris touched the button again. "Damn it!" The circuitry in the bed frame was one of the casualties from Rya's explosive re-entry into her. "Fuck!" Her fist slammed into the mattress in frustration.

"This is foolish." Asher rose from the bed and shook her head.

"This isn't some sort of joke. The operation didn't work," Tarris snapped.

"Were you expecting some sort of miracle? Surely, you know it's not that easy."

"A miracle was all I had left, Asher." She took an unsteady breath before she continued. "Now I don't even have that. Maybe you should just go."

"But..."

"Please." She just wanted to be alone. "I'll arrange to have your luggage delivered to your apartment."

"So that's it, huh?" Asher said flatly. "You do realize that it's only a matter of hours since the operation. Something could still happen, Tarris."

"If it hasn't happened by now..."

"Are you always this impatient? No wonder..." Asher stopped.

"What?" Tarris's eyes bored into Asher. "No wonder what?"

"Nothing. That ring had been in place for a number of years, Tarris. It's not going to repair itself overnight. But if you want me to leave, fine. Just let me get my clothes." Asher turned on her heel and walked toward the bathroom where she had placed her discarded clothes from the night before.

Tarris regretted her harsh words. Asher had been there to help her, and she was prepared to throw her out on her ass the first opportunity she had. Her grief had taken priority over what Asher had revealed to her.

Her mind wandered back to the passion of last night, and Rya shifted around restlessly. Her shadow didn't want to remember, but Tarris needed to know what had caused the sudden explosion in her back. What had scared Rya so badly that she had to slam into her body at such a terrifying speed? Tarris's attention turned outwards as Asher re-entered the room.

"Do someone a favor," Asher said, "and they kick you in the teeth. Of all the ungrateful…" She looked at Tarris. "What? I'm not moving fast enough for you?"

Tarris shook her head. "It's not that. I was trying to remember what happened last night that made Rya scream around the room and cause so much destruction."

"I was meaning to ask you about that."

"Then why didn't you?"

"You wouldn't let me." Asher's voice rose in aggravation. "You were too busy wallowing in self-pity."

"Wait just one minute—"

"No. You wait. You came to me, remember?" Asher's finger jabbed the air in Tarris's direction. "So don't you go blaming me for this."

As soon Asher was within arm's reach, Tarris grabbed her and pulled her down swiftly to meet her. Her lips found the softness of skin and kissed it. The stirrings she had experienced last night resurfaced. What she felt then was no mistake. Tarris pulled back and panted lightly from the contact. Why on earth did she do that?

"Why on earth did you do that?"

Was Asher a mind reader? Considering how tumultuous Tarris's life had been recently, it wouldn't have surprised her. "I have absolutely no idea. I… I'm sorry."

"Don't be sorry. I just wasn't expecting it."

"Me, either." Tarris looked away from the intense stare. She was full of surprises today. "Maybe it's all that emotion rolling around inside me."

"I thought troopers didn't have emotions." Asher shook her head. "A romantic trooper. That's sort of a contradiction in terms, isn't it?"

"Yeah," Tarris said and returned Asher's grin, "but there's always a first time." She sobered. "Look, I'm sorry about before."

"Don't be. I'm sorry I let off a bit of steam."

"And I didn't say thank-you. You were right. I was feeling sorry for myself. I had hoped that after the operation everything would be all right. I guess I was wrong."

Asher perched herself on the edge of the mattress. "To be honest, I don't know what to expect. The wound itself is fine, but what your nerves will do… I don't know. My research covers only patients with recent nerve damage, not damage sustained sixteen years ago. Still, we had some luck with the removal of the ring, so anything's possible."

"You…" Tarris was hesitant to say it. "You don't have to stay if you don't want to."

"Hey. I have to keep an eye on my patient, don't I?" Asher smiled. "But do you really have to get up?"

"Yeah. I don't want them to know I was injured."

"Why?"

"Because it makes me appear vulnerable. Now that I know they've watched my every move, it matters even more." Gingerly she tried her body and eased into the wheelchair next to her bed. As she lifted her legs onto the footpads, she thought back to last night. "Do you remember when Rya jumped out of your body?"

"You didn't feel it?"

"Sure, but it was such an explosion of images that I can't make any sense of it."

"I have a theory about that."

"A theory? That sounds so analytical."

"I'm a mediprac, remember? It's my job." Asher grinned at her. "Rya flew out of my body just as... as... you know." Her hand rolled in the air as if to supply the missing words.

"As what?" Tarris didn't understand.

"When I"—Asher inhaled deeply before she finished the sentence—"climaxed. I was wondering whether that might have had something to do with it."

Was that what that feeling was called? Maybe Tarris should have paid more attention to the conversations going on around her when she was growing up. Before the accident, she was too young to pay attention, and after... Well, immediately after the fall, she had tortured herself with what she would be missing about sex. Besides being counterproductive, her fantasies about sex made her both frustrated and angry. After a while, there was just no point dwelling on what she would never have.

"Maybe," Asher said, "the feeling was too much for her to absorb."

"Maybe. It certainly scared the crap out of her." Tarris searched for her twin who cowered in the deep recesses of her mind. No amount of cajoling was going to bring her out at the moment. "She doesn't want to come out to play."

"Tell her I'm sorry. I didn't mean to scare her."

"We didn't know what would happen. Now we know."

"Yes, now we know."

Asher managed to keep a disgruntled Tarris in the apartment for the morning. She had explained that normally with such surgery, the patient would be on her feet by now, but Tarris had suffered a horrific trauma to her back, which scattered pieces of metal in all directions.

With help from Asher, Tarris had donned her body suit. She walked over to the wall and removed the dead camera, which left a deep gouge as a reminder of what had been there, or more to the point, what they had done to her. Her anger simmered all the while, which lent a certain viciousness to its removal. With that out of the way, she and Asher spent the rest of the day cleaning up the mess from the explosion.

The apartment looked a little different from the night before. In one corner was heaped the remnants of Tarris's electronic lifestyle. A pile of twisted metal and circuitry sat there, formerly a screen, a computer, and a food reconstituter. Fortunately, her wheelchair could be maneuvered manually; otherwise it would be on the junk pile as well.

One of the few things not scrapped was her body suit, and for that she was grateful. Luckily it had been sitting in the spare room with her exercise equipment when Rya freaked out. Her suit was the only thing that made her feel anywhere near normal.

"How are you going to replace all this stuff?"

"I have absolutely no idea." Tarris didn't want to think about it. While she lived comfortably, her finances were not good enough to replace everything. And now that she knew the Council was against her, some of her possible avenues for help were closed. "But I'm going to find out." The brightness of the day was fading to twilight. There wasn't even a sun today, only gray skies, and it pretty much summed up her life at the moment. "I've got to go."

"Where are you going?"

"To see Derille."

"And what do I do? Stay at home like the good little woman?"

"Where on earth do you get these ideas? That sort of thinking hasn't been around for over a hundred years."

"But the sentiment is the same," Asher huffed. "You expect me to wait here for you?"

"Fine. Come with me then."

"Oh, no, no, no. It's safer here." Asher held up her hands in surrender.

Just as Tarris was about to leave, Asher stopped her. "Did you forget something?"

"I don't think so."

Asher held up the tiny box that had been attached to the ring around her spine. "If you're intent on carrying out this charade, you might need this. Turn around."

Tarris reluctantly did so, and Asher taped the tracker to her back. She still had to hide from the world, and it galled her that she just couldn't be herself. Angrily, she left her apartment to venture out into the dangerous, dark world of night.

Tarris strode down a number of streets that led to a place she had visited once before. The two tiny cameras was clutched tightly in her hand and cut into the meaty pad of her palm. Rubbish fluttered as she passed by, stirred up by a light zephyr that wasn't there.

"Give us your code." A disembodied voice cut through the darkness.

"In your dreams." Tarris was in no mood for a mugging.

The assailants stepped into the halo of light and waved

a stunner in her direction. "Come on, your wrist."

"I don't think so," she growled. A simple step would have moved her back into shadow and Rya could help, but her anger needed an outlet and this seemed the ideal opportunity. As she took a step toward her attackers, she reached behind her to release the locking mechanism on her suit. It was not something that she did lightly. One false move would collapse her legs. But at that moment she wasn't working on logic. She was pissed. Really, really pissed.

"Would you look at that?" A broad-shouldered figure moved farther into the light. "She wants to play." He laughed merrily.

Tarris didn't like being underestimated. She lowered her shoulder and rammed herself into the larger of her two assailants. They both fell to the ground, leaving Tarris at their mercy. The servo suit was useless for getting up from the ground.

She looked up at two faces that seemed amused at her helpless state. The whole world was laughing at her, and she let them.

The thinner of the two robbers hunkered down next to her and moved his laser scalpel over her wrist. "Now, this won't hurt a bit. It'll hurt a lot." He chuckled at his own morbid sense of humor.

The first touch of pain pushed her to the limit. Tarris lashed out and knocked the ruffian with the scalpel on his butt. Before the larger man could touch her, she reached behind her neck and massaged the tab under her skin.

She knew what the reaction would be when they realized who, or more to the point, what they had caught. Their smiles dropped and were replaced with fear. They backed away and searched frantically for an unseen force ready to pounce on them.

Tarris smiled, her expression showing a kernel of insanity and a healthy dose of anger. "Get them!" she called. They didn't wait around to see whom she talked to.

She just lay there. Threatening them with who she was wasn't how she wanted to defend herself, but it was effective. She crashed her fist against the ground in frustration. The whole world seemed to be her enemy these days, and she didn't know how to turn it around. The pain in her head pounded against her skull. By instinct, she reached for her wrist and massaged it until the pain slowly subsided.

She sat up and leaned back on her hands. How was she going to get up? The overhead lamp dangled by a thread, the brightness flickering on and off. Her hand fell upon a discarded flask. She latched onto it and threw it in a fit of anger. It flew high into the air and connected with the swaying bulb with a bang. The lamp exploded and threw the area into darkness. She felt the welcoming arms of Rya lifting her to her feet. Automatically, her hand slipped to the locking mechanism to make sure that when Rya let go she was going to stay upright.

She couldn't even protect herself; surely, she had hit rock bottom. There was nothing more she could lose.

†

By the time she reached Administrator Derille's house, Tarris's back reminded her of the abuse it had taken the night before. She pushed the pain and discomfort aside and stopped near the closed gate. The grounds appeared to be deserted, but with Derille's penchant for gadgets, that didn't mean they weren't guarded. It took a great deal of prodding to get Rya to emerge, and it was only the reassurance that Asher was back at her apartment that drew her fighter out.

You are such a wimp... she mentally scolded her.

She scared me, sister.

Tarris stopped. *What did you just say?* While the images were still in her head, Rya had started to verbalize. Their communication had always been on the basest level, and while she knew her shadow could speak a word or two if the need arose, it wasn't something that happened spontaneously.

The light. It was so bright, it hurt. I never felt that before. Only through you, sister, do I know what pain is.

Rya had never strung so many words together before. *The light?*

Within your friend.

Asher.

Yes, Asher. Her light shone brightly. It drew me, and I couldn't look away.

Do you... Tarris was nearly afraid to ask. *Do you feel any different?* She was comfortable with their relationship, because she understood all the nuances that they shared. If Rya had changed somehow, their dynamic had changed also and she wasn't sure she could handle that.

Different? What is different?

Not like before, Rya. Just... just... different.

I don't understand.

Understand? Such a concept would indicate rational thinking, wouldn't it? Tarris swept a hand over her brow. It was all too much. Her anger had been pushed aside, and she wasn't quite ready to let it go. Her righteous indignation was slowly bleeding away, and she needed to focus her attention on the where and why she was here.

Rya, I need to see Derille. Please.

As you wish, sister.

As you wish. This was going to take some getting used to. At least the rush as Rya left her was still the same. She didn't want to experience the contact of last night anytime soon.

While she couldn't see her shadow move toward the house, her mind's eye saw it perfectly, in the eerie glow of Rya's night vision. Indeed there had been the usual assortment of invisible laser beams, but there was the odd new trick added to Derille's arsenal. Not that it slowed down Rya. She effortlessly slid to the front door and barely paused as she slipped through the crack to materialize on the other side like black smoke. Low voices drew Rya away from the door toward the source of the conversation. The shadow found her havens in the room, taking a roundabout route to get across the foyer. The light from the large room cast a muted glow over the floor and stopped Rya from getting closer.

What are they saying?

I can't hear, sister. Rya automatically started to cross the semi-shadowed floor to get closer to the muted conversation. Instead of feeling Rya's essence slip away, Tarris felt the opposite: her shadow sustained her strength with each invisible step. What was going on? Tarris desperately wanted to know what had changed in Rya, but that was a question for another day.

The voices in the room grew louder and became more pronounced.

"She found the camera, sir."

"How did that happen?" The speaker's voice expressed displeasure.

"We're not sure, sir. There was an explosion in the apartment."

Rya edged closer to the half shadows and shifted into the dimness. Her form held true, and she blended into the background. She was invisible.

"So what are you going to do about it?"

"Prime. She knows about us now. What can we do?" Derille pleaded.

"She is not to interfere, you hear me?"

Rya finally had a chance to look into the lit room to observe a man facing a large screen.

Tarris couldn't believe the massive strides Rya had taken. What the hell happened? She wished she had someone to talk to about it, but there was no one she could trust. Rya, her assassin, had stepped into the light, albeit muted light, but light just the same. And she was still whole. This was monumental... and frightening. Had this accident, or whatever it was, made Rya into something more?

The vision before her gave her pause. Tarris saw Derille's back as he addressed the man on the large screen. It was Prime Sholter, but he looked a little different and vaguely familiar. His on-screen persona was much more commanding and charismatic. This side of the Prime was more... she wasn't quite sure what was different. Cold? Scheming? Dangerous? He was all those things and more. She mentally added amoral to that list after what he had done to her.

The conference between the two men wasn't unusual,

after all Derille was part of the Prime's upper cabinet, but their discussion was. They were talking about her and the camera. So Derille knew everything.

Tarris opened the gate and entered, ignoring everything but the front door. It was probably foolish to confront her enemy like this, but betrayal after betrayal had heaped up at her feet and she didn't care about her safety anymore.

She pounded the door with her fist. She allowed the pain to seep into her and take away some of the numbness. Nothing in her life made sense anymore—like she was living in some twilight world full of distortions and mistruths.

The door slid open, revealing the source of her ire. Maken Derille. The man who claimed to be her friend. "Ah, Tarris. Good to see you. Come in. Come in."

As soon as the door closed, Tarris reached for the back of her neck to allow the color tint to drain away and reveal her natural whiteness. She wanted the Administrator to remember what she was.

She followed the portly man to his living room and casually gazed at the silent screen on the wall. The screen was blank, but it wouldn't have surprised her if the Prime was on cloak and would listen to their every word. Not that she cared. Her words were as much for him as for the man standing in front of her.

"This is a surprise. Is it in reference to the unit being suspended?" Derille asked with such sincerity that, if she didn't know the truth, she would have believed him.

"Let's cut out this crap, Maken." She watched him wince at his name with some satisfaction. "This is yours..." The tiny camera fell onto the small side table and clattered as it hit the top.

"What are you talking about?"

Tarris had to give it to him. He kept up the charade despite the evidence. "You tell the Prime to stay out of my life." She turned on her heel and started to walk out, her black coat fanning out like a cloak.

"I don't understand, Tarris. I thought we were friends."

"So did I, you son of a bitch."

"But what happened?"

"That happened!" She pointed at the broken device on the table, "You had my trust I until I found out what you were, Maken." Again he cringed. He obviously didn't like her using his first name. *Screw him.* "You're a lying, cheating, sorry excuse for a human being, Maken. A lousy politician."

He smiled. "Well I am a politician. You got that right."

"Don't play word games with me, Administrator. I've done nothing to deserve this." Tarris strode to her quarry, grabbed a handful of shirt, and pulled Derille toward her. "Why, Maken? Why?"

"I don't know what you're talking about." She could see he was valiantly trying to hold onto the lie.

"I don't care whether you admit it or not, Maken. Tell them to back off." Her fist let go of the material, and she turned to leave.

He didn't respond until she was nearly at the doorway. "Or what?"

Her ice blue eyes stared at him over her broad shoulder, pinning the man in place. "If I find any more evidence that I'm being watched, I walk away." With that she left.

Rya remained where she had been. She had sensed

Tarris's agitation and it took a great deal of strength to stop herself from going to her sister's aid. She had a job to do, and she would remain at her post until Tarris called her home. Long moments after Tarris had gone, the conversation began anew.

"She was just here," Derille said.

"And?"

"She's threatening to walk if we interfere further."

"It seems that your use to her is no longer needed, Maken."

"So it seems, sir. What do we do now?"

"For the moment, we don't want to lose such a valuable asset. Let her think we're acquiescing to her demands, but I want that observation to continue. She may still be useful."

The image faded on the screen, and Derille emerged from the living room. He stepped into the small lift to the upper floors, unaware that he had passed Tarris's warrior. If Rya possessed lips, she would have smiled.

Chapter 7

The return journey was less eventful than the trip to Derille's home. Tarris had waited outside the gate for Rya's return, and she walked home with some purpose, keeping to the shadows. She was in no mood for another confrontation.

By the time she reached her apartment, she was cranky. She scanned her wrist over the infrared and stepped through the doorway as it slid open. Only by instinct did she stop Asher from hitting her.

"Don't scare me like that!" Asher said.

"Relax." Tarris felt it was easier to tell her to relax than it was to do so herself.

"So, how did it go?"

"I found him, we met, and I left. End of story." But Tarris's tight stance told a whole lot more.

"Take off your clothes."

"I beg your pardon?" Heat traveled up Tarris's chest to her face. "Did you say…?"

"Yes, take off your clothes," Asher repeated.

Slowly she complied but waited for some sort of ambush by Asher. "And why am I taking these off?"

"You really need to get out more," Asher said in a teasing tone. "I'll give you a backrub."

"A backrub?"

"Don't you know anything, Trooper?" A hand came up and she stopped. "All right. All right. No more teasing. The backrub will ease your back muscles, and removing your clothes will also give me access to give you another injection."

Tarris hated injections. While she was no stranger to them by any means, she only tolerated them. She eyed Asher and wondered how far she needed to undress to satisfy the woman. When she stopped at her underwear and the suit, a finger wiggled in the air.

"Keep going."

"Everything?"

"Everything." Asher waved her finger at the underwear. "Come on, come on."

Tarris slowly complied. She wasn't quite sure this was all necessary. "I don't know..." Asher disappeared into the bathroom to find her supplies. Since when did a backrub have anything to do with medicine? Sure, it would feel nice, but she had better things to do than indulge Asher's whims.

Tarris was about to tell her to forget it when she spotted Asher standing in the bathroom door, a bottle of lotion in one hand and her injector in the other. But it was the gentle smile on Asher's face that melted Tarris's resolve to be strong.

Tarris dragged her limp body up the bed and clumsily rolled over onto her stomach. She buried her head in her folded arms. She couldn't look at Asher while she moved. Being so vulnerable was not in her nature. After all, she had been pushed and prodded by the best in the medical world. Why was it such a problem now?

Her skin flinched when Asher's soft hands touched her back. Asher slowly kneaded tired and aching muscles into submission. Something cold hit her back and pooled into a small lump. "Wha's that?" Tarris's words slurred as the massage took hold of her.

"Just some lotion." Asher kneaded the cream into Tarris's tight flesh. The tension eased with the warmed cream as it melted into the deeper tissue. Tarris released a sigh.

While Tarris was relaxed and dozing, Asher attended to her medical needs. She administered the medispray and encouraged its dispersal with another quick massage. She applied a special paste to the scar and spread it with her finger until it disappeared. As a final step, she lowered her lips and kissed the spot.

"Why did you do that?"

"You felt it?" Asher asked hopefully.

"Sure, but it's above my break. You can try lower down if you want."

Asher's lips brushed the skin lower down, right on the dimple above Tarris's right ass cheek. "How about that?" she whispered seductively.

"Hmmm…" When Tarris hesitated, Asher wondered whether something had indeed happened. "No, of course not."

"How about this?" Asher moved her lips slowly up Tarris's back and placed kisses along her spine.

"Hmmm…" The sound rumbled deep in Tarris's throat and a dreamy smile crossed her lips. "Much better." When those wandering lips latched onto her earlobe, her eyes flew wide open. "Wow!"

"So, my dear Trooper…"

"You don't have to do this now that the camera's broken."

"I know," Asher whispered, "but I want to."

"You do?" Tarris asked. "Could you just… you know… hold me instead?"

"Sure." Asher smiled. "I can do that." She made herself comfortable on the bed and helped Tarris into her arms.

Tarris swept up a blanket over both of them and immersed herself in the warmth of the woman underneath her. This was what had been missing from her life, the comfort of another human being. Corman would have argued that point, but Tarris had always considered herself human; a special human, sure, but a human nonetheless.

As her soul bathed in the careful attentions, Asher's hand rose to stroke her hair. Memories flooded back to her childhood as she tried to remember such a tender moment as this. But she couldn't. Her mother had been attentive and nurturing, but Tarris never once felt embraced in a loving cuddle.

It was strange, now that she thought about it. She had always just accepted that as part of their relationship. She had known no other loving interaction, so for her that was normal. Asher had now shown her what could be, and Tarris realized that the relationship between her and her mother had been somewhat clinical, almost distant.

Tarris dozed off to sleep in the arms that encircled her.

She awoke later that night, with Asher's steady breath blowing across the top of her head. Her instincts wanted to pull back, but she forced herself to relax and stay where she was. She recognized that her heart cried out for the attention, and she was eager to grant its wish. Here she could let her guard down and be human; she could enjoy those human emotions that had been denied her.

Rya pulsed gently inside her with a new vibrant energy that flowed through her system. Something had changed. Tarris twitched violently as pain shot down one leg.

The motion woke Asher. "What?" She tried to sit up, but Tarris's weight kept her pinned to the mattress. "What's wrong?" Her eyes blinked a few times.

"Pain. Oh! Ahhh!" The violent twinge robbed Tarris of coherent speech. Just as she fumbled around to reach her medipatch, the ache faded away. She slumped against the soft squishy body underneath her. "Sorry," she murmured.

"What's going on?" Asher struggled to slip the dead weight off the top of her.

"Light." Tarris's instruction activated the overhead light. She drew in a great gulp of air and blew it out forcefully. "That hurt."

"Pain? Where?" Asher slipped her hands over Tarris's body.

"My leg." Asher reached for Tarris's left leg. "No, the other one."

"Hmmm, interesting."

"Meanwhile, I'm trying to stop my heart jumping out of my chest, let alone Rya..."

"I get the point. Sorry." Asher showed some concern at Tarris's discomfort. "Is it still hurting?"

"It's stopped, for now." Blood red starbursts exploded behind her eyelids, echoing the eruption of stabbing pain that had ambushed her.

Asher's hand slid down her leg. "Can you feel this?"

Tarris waited some moments before answering in the hope that something would eventually happen. "No." She looked up at Asher. "But that could change... right?"

"Of course, right."

Tarris lay awake the rest of the night in the hope that something would change, but it was uneventful. She wasn't sure whether that was a good thing or not. She would do just about anything to be able to walk again, but the searing agony that shot through her earlier in the night gave her cause for concern. Not that she was afraid. No, she was a member of the Special Black Shadow Corps, and they knew no fear. Justifying it to herself as concern seemed to satisfy her stoic nature.

In the morning, Tarris got a nudge from Asher. "Get dressed and let's go for a walk."

"Are you trying to distract me?" Tarris gazed at her accusingly.

"Am I that transparent?" Asher didn't even try to deny it.

"Yes. But you're right. I can't help but think about my legs. Any idea where you would like to go?"

Asher looked through the window to the outside world. As usual it was overcast and windy. "Somewhere warm."

Tarris got dressed, occasionally glancing at Asher standing by the window. She seemed to be in a world of her own even though her gaze was aimed straight at Tarris. "You ready to go?"

"Hmmm?" Asher returned from wherever her mind had been. "Give me a minute." She hurried to the bathroom to prepare for the day.

Tarris went to the wall and muttered, "Safe." The hidden block revealed itself to her, and she extracted the silencer and the scanner Derille had given her. She wanted to see a man about a bogus piece of equipment. Her eyes swept over the contents of the box, and she made a mental list in case she needed to suddenly disappear. She had accumulated a piece of technology here and there, some of it illegal, that she thought one day would come in handy. Maybe that one day wasn't too far away.

A rustle behind her back caused her to whisper, "Stealth." With some satisfaction, Tarris watched the box fade and become wall again. "So, are you ready now?" Tarris straightened, locked her suit in place and walked toward her companion.

"About as ready as I'll ever be."

"What's wrong?" Tarris watched a range of emotions flow over Asher's face.

"Just wondering what's waiting for us outside. Especially after you stormed over to the Administrator's house like that."

"That thought had crossed my mind. I think we should be safe in public." Still, Rya was useless in the light of day, and they were both vulnerable. Not completely helpless, but her mugging the night before severely dented her confidence.

The door whispered quietly shut as they left the apartment. Tarris turned to face the door and clipped a tiny piece of wire into one of the crevices.

"What are you doing?"

"It's my intruder alert." Her finger pushed the clip under the rim so that it was just out of sight. "If they try to bug my apartment, I'll know it." Tarris tapped the back of her neck. After her hair turned to black, she reached for Asher's hand. "Come on, let's go find some warmth."

†

"I haven't been to this one before." Asher stood next to Tarris outside the metallic monolith. Tarris swept her wrist over the scanner and waited for the door to move aside.

"I practically live here," she said. Tarris really liked this park, maybe as much for the companionship she knew she would find here as for the comforting warmth of the artificial sun. Her companion seemed amused. "What?"

"That doesn't surprise me at all," Asher said.

"What doesn't surprise you?"

"You're not fooling anyone, you know. This place reeks of positive things. Clear blue sky, bright sunlight, clear water, and green grass. You actively seek these out, Tarris. You need them to balance the darkness in your life."

"I think you're mistaken," Tarris said a little too quickly.

"No, I don't think so. You're a trooper, and that requires a certain amount of cool detachment. Am I right?" Tarris gave a slight nod. "Subconsciously, you seek out those things that give you pleasure, in particular this park. It's a balm to your soul."

"But I have no soul, remember?"

"Troopers might not have souls, but you're the exception. You have a troubled soul that's looking for the light."

She's right, my sister. She's the light to my darkness.

So, what does that mean?

I don't know, but I feel it. I feel her.

Tarris felt dazed. She didn't even begin to understand what Rya was trying to say.

"Are you still with me?" Asher asked. "Hello?"

"Sorry. I don't know if I really agree with what you said, but I do like this place. It's..." She searched for the right word. "Comforting."

Tarris found Darmen seated on the ground and leaning against a tree, as she had many times before. He was talking into a small hand-held device, which she assumed to be a video comlink to his main office. It didn't surprise her that Darmen possessed one. He had always jokingly told her that he worked; now she had the proof. "Tarris, my dear." Darmen put down the device. "It's always a pleasure to see you."

"Busy working my friend?" Tarris chuckled. She noticed the curiosity in his eyes as he studied her companion. "What's that in your hand?"

Darmen held up the small device. "A pendric."

"What's a pendric?" Asher asked.

"Darmen, this is Asher Hyrea. Asher, this is Darmen... Sorry, I don't even know your last name."

"Just Darmen. Nice to meet you, Asher." His eyes swept over Asher's face as if trying to gauge their relationship. "Any friend of Tarris's..."

"Don't start." Tarris grinned.

"And you said you didn't have any friends." Asher shook a finger at her.

"Computer programming isn't all it's cracked up to be." It was a subtle hint to Asher not to mention who she was. "It can get lonely sometimes."

"Ah, the nature of the beast," Darmen said. "I know that feeling very well." He held up the small device. "I can't seem to escape it at the moment."

"Shouldn't you be in your office?"

"Probably, but I get more done here than in a sterile office." He smiled. "You won't begrudge an old man his little idiosyncrasy, will you?"

"Of course not." Tarris wasn't one to talk. Her life was one big idiosyncrasy.

"How can that little thing be work?" Asher asked.

"A pendric is a virtual office, my dear. It projects a 3D holographic image of my office desk. It's like I'm there, but I'm not. I can interact with everything on it."

"It sounds like the Anatomatix used by medipracs," Asher said.

"Really? Do tell."

"It's a holographic 3D model of a human. Medipracs use it to practice surgery, without having to worry about killing anyone."

"You seem knowledgeable about this."

Tarris reached into her pocket. "I would like to ask your opinion on something." She didn't like asking for a favor because it usually meant owing one in return, but this was something she had no expertise in. "Someone who I had called a friend gave me these awhile back." In her hand lay the two devices. "I was wondering if they actually do what he claimed they did."

Darmen picked up the two pieces out of her hand. "Interesting. This one looks like the bug detector I gave you. And this..." He pinched the tiny block of metal between his thumb and forefinger and held it up, turning it from side to side to study it. "This looks like it belongs in a computer."

"You were right about the first one." But that wasn't the one that would raise an eyebrow. "The second sets up a 'ghost' communication line."

"A 'ghost' line?"

"Yes, it was supposed to make a safe connection between me and whoever I contacted. One that couldn't be monitored."

"Interesting." Darmen's eyes lit up at the information. "Very interesting. Why do you doubt that they do what this person claimed they did?"

"Because I found out he was lying to me about other things. Would he be lying about these, too?" Tarris didn't want to elaborate and hoped the vague explanation would satisfy Darmen's curiosity. She felt his eyes on her, trying to read her body language.

"How soon do you need to know?"

"There's no hurry. I was just curious, that's all." She tried to appear only mildly interested and tried to hide the subtle signs that would give her away.

"Give me a couple of days."

"Fine. Thank you."

"No. Thank you." He grinned up at her. "It's not often we get a chance to tinker with something new."

"I would prefer if you handled this yourself." Had she tipped her hand?

"Should I ask why?" He looked at her carefully. "Ahh, just as I thought." But that didn't stop him from agreeing to tinker. "Did you get a chance to try the scanner I gave you?"

"Yes I did. That was how I found out about this scanner."

"Good to hear."

"But..."

"But?"

"There was an accident in my apartment, and I'm

afraid your scanner was destroyed."

Darmen sat quietly for a moment. "Don't worry about it, my dear. It was one of many prototypes. As long as you're safe."

"You are too kind, Darmen."

Darmen turned his attention to Tarris's companion. "And what do you do, Asher? Are you also a computer programmer?"

Asher wasn't sure what to say so she deferred to Tarris.

"She's a mediprac."

"A mediprac?" Concern crossed his features. "Is something wrong, my dear?"

"No, everything's fine. We met at the Archives and decided to take a walk in the sunlight." She hating lying to the old man, but her life around him seemed to be made up of a series of lies.

"So you've just met?"

"Yes," Asher said. "I didn't know she was a computer programmer."

"I'm sure she has many secrets to tell, Asher." He cast a quick grin at Tarris. "Go and enjoy yourselves and let this old man get back to his work."

"Work, Darmen? Sleep more like it," Tarris teased. She had rarely seen him work, but considering the position that he held, he must have done so at some point. "So in two days' time, my friend?"

"Two days, Tarris."

She glanced at her chronometer and took note of the time for their next meeting. "Until then."

"Have a drink on me."

Tarris looked up to the bright light above. "Sounds like a good idea. Let's go get a drink."

Asher nodded cordially and followed her to the receptacle. Tarris scanned her wrist and retrieved the insulated bottles.

Asher shook her drink, her thumb brushing the activation point. "So who was that?"

"Just a friend," Tarris said.

"You don't trust anyone, do you?"

"I've been taught not to, Asher. My life has been one big mystery, most of all to myself." But she could see the hurt. They had shared a lot in a very short period of time. "I only know him as Darmen. He's the head of a big corporation but likes to spend his time lazing around the park."

"And you don't think that's suspicious?"

"Suspicious? Maybe. Unusual? Definitely. Do I trust him? Likely. Do I like him? Yes." That was a lot of information she had revealed. She hoped her trust in Asher was also warranted.

"What happens now?" Asher asked.

"He'll let me know—"

"No. What do we do now?"

"Do you mean am I going to tell you to get out now that the ring has been removed?" Tarris studied the ground as she talked.

"You don't mince words, do you?"

"I can't afford to, not in my line of... of..." What could Tarris say?

"Employment? Do the computers fight back?" Asher giggled as Tarris stared at her blandly.

"Do you want to go home?" Tarris tried to gather around her as much dignity as she could muster. She had already shown too much of herself to Asher. She was not

147

going to lower herself to beg. Troopers never ever begged.

"Should I?"

Tarris couldn't tell from the question whether Asher wanted to go or not. She was not one to make the woman stay if she didn't want to. "What about my back?" She congratulated herself for a smart question.

"I could leave all the medication you'll need."

"That sounds like you want to get out as quickly as possible." Tarris knew Asher could see the hurt, despite how much she tried to hide it.

"Not at all, Tarris. But I know you're a loner. I can survive very well by myself if need be."

"But having spent time with me has made you a target, too," Tarris said. "Unless you have some hidden lethal talent, you would be safer with me."

"Is that your way of asking me to stay?" Asher asked with a note of hope in her voice.

"I would never do such a thing. If you wish to stay, then you can stay. I was just pointing out that you're not out of danger yet." Tarris took a long draw on the water bottle and allowed the cool liquid to slide down her dry throat. She had little experience relating to people. Cursing Corman or giving orders were her only real need for conversation, so anything more, at least to her, was unnecessary. While this rule was not a life-saving one, it was one she subconsciously adhered to.

Rule Nine in her Survival Handbook: Conversation is the friend of misconception.

"You just can't say it, can you? You're a coward," Asher said.

"Me? A coward?" Tarris was insulted.

"Why can't you just admit that you want me to stay?" Asher pulled on Tarris's arm and stopped her walking away. "What are you so afraid of? Me?"

"Fine. Will you please stay?" But it was more a statement from Tarris than an invitation. She finished her bottle and returned it to the receptacle for recycling.

Asher followed her and threw in her own bottle. "You make it sound so appealing."

Tarris turned and stepped up to Asher. While they were equal in height, Tarris's personality expanded the visual conception. She reined in her anger and took a deep breath. "Will you please stay?" she said softly.

"Why didn't you say that in the first place?" Asher added a small smile.

†

After they spent the afternoon in the park, Tarris took Asher to the Archive building to catch a late movie. Tarris introduced Asher to the subtleties of classic cinema, and it was nearly a disaster. At first, Asher laughed, but Tarris soon found Asher's head on her shoulder and Asher's hand in her own.

"That movie was certainly different," Asher said as they stood outside Tarris's apartment.

"Did you like it?"

"It was... different," Asher said again.

"Different. As in different awful or different strange?" Tarris joked. Her hand rose to where she had placed the metal clip and found it missing.

"Just different different. It was strange without the

hologram aspect."

Tarris held up her hand, and Asher fell silent.

Tarris opened the door and stepped quietly inside. She uttered no words and motioned for Asher to stay where she was. She assumed Council drones had been there installing devices to monitor her every move. It seemed that Derille didn't take her threat seriously. Now he would pay.

"They were here?" Asher sounded nervous as she looked around the room.

"There's nothing missing, except my trust. Pack your things."

"Everything?" Asher stood as though stunned.

"Only what you can carry." Tarris was already on the move and drew a small sack out of the back of her wardrobe. She filled it with food and water, a small toolkit for her walking frame, and spare medication patches. She threw in a handful of clothes on top.

She turned her attention to the corner of the room and her hidden stash. "Safe." The word revealed the hidden compartment in the wall. Tarris opened the box and looked inside but hesitated when she reached for the contents. Had they found it? Was everything in the box contaminated? This presented another addition to her already growing list of problems.

Asher came up behind her. "What's up?"

"I don't know." Tarris walked into the bathroom to activate the secret switch for the hidden platform in the roof. When the lift had lowered the square of ceiling to the bathroom floor, she searched around in a metallic locker that housed all the bits and pieces she had accumulated over the years from friends and foes. She extracted a small box and slipped it into her pocket. She took out a pair of transparent gloves and slipped them on.

She passed Asher and went back to the wall. The gloves fit like second skin, as they were supposed to, and gave the appearance that she wasn't wearing anything at all. She reached into the box and extracted each piece one at a time, placing them on the floor after she inspected them. "Asher?"

"Hmmm?" Asher leaned out of the bathroom doorway to answer Tarris's call.

"Have you got something like a dye or some sort of infrared light?" It was an old-fashioned method, one that she had no problem using.

Asher disappeared for a moment and emerged with the sterilization unit. "Will this help?"

Tarris looked at the box. "I suppose it couldn't hurt." She stepped back and allowed Asher to set up the unit. The UV light pulsed over the items on the floor, but nothing happened. "Well, that did nothing. Wait." Tarris stopped when she saw a tinge of purple touch the money on the floor. The color spread over the spare scanner and the false barcode ID she had kept for an emergency. On each of the items there was a small black spot, and Tarris knew immediately that they had been tagged. "Damn it."

"What's wrong?" Asher watched as Tarris switched off the unit.

"They got to my emergency funds."

Asher reached for the scanner on the floor. "What's wrong with—"

"Don't touch that! Look." Tarris held up her hand and turned on the UV unit. Her fingers glistened with the purple stain. "My guess is that if I had touched it without protection, my fingers would leave an invisible mark wherever I went." When she switched off the unit, the color faded and her fingers returned to normal.

"And why would they do that? Just who the hell are you?" Asher took a step backwards. After a hesitation, she stepped forward again.

"Someone they are making damned sure doesn't disappear from their sight." Tarris gathered up the tainted items and put them back in the box.

"But isn't that what the box in your back was for? To keep track of you? This is sort of overkill."

Asher had a point. "Unless they wanted to see who I came into contact with." With difficulty, Tarris straightened up and locked her legs in the upright position. A shard of white-hot pain shot through her legs, and she drew a harsh breath.

"Something wrong?" Asher stepped forward and touched Tarris's arm. "You look like you're in pain."

Tarris held herself in check when Asher grabbed her. "Nothing I can't handle." She refused to touch the medipatch in her wrist, because she didn't want to appear vulnerable. When the pain had passed, she reached for the box and put it in her sack.

"What's the point in taking that? Won't they be able to follow you?"

"Will you stop worrying? I have plans for these items." Tarris waited until Asher's back was turned, and she punched her thigh. She wasn't sure what to expect. She knew in her heart what she hoped to find, but it wasn't to be. She felt nothing. The same lack of sensation she had known for the last sixteen years.

She reached for her bag and gave her apartment one last look. It made her angry that they were driving her from her home and she could do nothing to stop them.

"Let's get out of here before they come back." Tarris grabbed Asher's hand. Asher barely had time to pick up her belongings as Tarris pulled her toward the door. Fifteen feet down the corridor in the opposite direction to the exit was a small alcove. Tarris detoured to the niche and pulled out the box. She removed the scanner and the ID barcode and threw them toward the small receptacle there. The items disappeared in a hail of sparks, atomized in the incinerator beam, as did the glove Tarris had been wearing. But she kept the money, at least for now.

"I thought you said the money was useless."

"Come on." Tarris steered Asher back toward the exit. "Not if we spend it." She had considered trying to give her pursuers the slip from her building, but the money she kept would be sending signals of her whereabouts. Instead, she walked out the front door and onto the sidewalk with Asher at her side.

They turned right and walked briskly toward the open-air market. The market was highly illegal, but no one seemed to mind. The vendors bartered openly, and the prices were usually high. Any sort of fresh food from the outside was worth its weight in oil.

They continued along the streets toward the seedier part of the metropolis. The market was forced by necessity into the less-patrolled areas. It wouldn't seem right for the Council to have something so illegal right under their noses in the main square. Tarris wondered who the sellers were paying for the privilege of conducting their illegal businesses. No wonder the goods were costly.

"Where are we going?" Asher panted as she tried to keep up with Tarris's brisk pace. "You know, for someone who can't walk, you sure can move when you want to."

Tarris gave her a dark look before she turned her attention to the surrounding area. "You don't have to remind me," she said, her voice harsh.

"I… I didn't mean to—"

"Sorry," Tarris said. "I don't like being reminded of it."

"Where are we going in such a hurry?"

"Hurry?" Tarris kept up her steady, even pace. "I've had to slow down so you can keep up." Her gaze swept the area to find those who watched her. "We're getting rid of the credits."

"Why didn't you just throw them in the incinerator with the other things?"

"You'll see."

"But—"

Tarris held her hand up to stop any further conversation. She trotted over to a nearby alcove and dragged Asher with her. Before Asher could complain, Tarris grabbed her arm and ran her barcode over the portal. A slot opened below it to dispense a small earpiece and microphone. Tarris placed it over her ear and spoke clearly, "Two seven two three two omega delta five nine nine."

The connection was made, and she heard the familiar voice. "Yeah?"

"It's Tarris."

"Errr… yeah." Tarris smiled as she heard the nervousness in the man's voice. "What do you want?" he asked.

"I need new ID."

"What happened to the other one I gave you?" His anxiety was replaced for a moment by mild annoyance.

"They got to it. I can't be sure."

"How long?"

"One hour." Tarris would have liked it sooner, but even one hour was probably asking too much.

"One hour? Are you crazy?" The voice rose in intensity before it calmed down. "I can't do it in that time."

"You know who I am, P. You really don't want to meet her, do you?" Tarris didn't like solving her problems with Rya, but sometimes a little incentive was needed. "And you have thirty minutes. Stall 27, Jacksters. This time make it a male in his early thirties. And I need some spare credits."

"This is gonna cost me a fortune."

"And you'll pay, buddy, or the Council just might find out about you," Tarris whispered harshly. "Twenty-nine minutes and counting." She ripped the earpiece from her ear, found a nearby incineration bank, and made sure the phone was completely disintegrated and unable to be resurrected.

"What was that all about?" Asher asked.

"Just arranging a new ID barcode and some credits." Tarris walked toward the warzone that was Jacksters.

"Hey!" Asher called after her. When Tarris refused to stop, Asher ran the few extra feet to catch up and slowed down to walk next to her. "Why a new barcode?"

Tarris stopped and looked at Asher. "Are you that stupid?" She took a deep breath and ran her hand over her brow. "Sorry. I'm a bit tense."

"I can feel it," Asher said.

"You can?" Tarris was surprised.

"A little," Asher replied, "in here." She rubbed her chest.

"Huh." Tarris shook her head. "Anyway, the Council

can trace the barcodes on our wrists. If we're trying to disappear, we need a new identity to move around."

"Why this place? What did you call it—Jacksters?"

"You can buy anything illegal there, as long as you've got the credits." Tarris had barely finished the explanation when four young men stepped out and stood in their way. Instinctively, Tarris pushed Asher behind her.

"We don't want trouble, boys," Tarris said.

"Good. Then give us what we want, and there won't be any." The leader of the group looked barely out of his teens.

"And what would that be?" Tarris knew what they wanted.

"Whatever we can sell." The second-in-charge looked at Tarris thoroughly, his gaze starting at her head and finishing at her feet.

"You're not my type," Tarris said.

"Come on, hand it over." The leader pulled out an aging stunner.

"Are you sure that still works?" Tarris taunted him.

"Works well enough for you, lady." He shifted nervously. "Now, come on. Empty your pockets."

Tarris took out the box and handed it over. The second snatched it away greedily and opened the lid.

"Hey! There must be a thousand credits here," he said.

"Just who the fuck are you?" the leader asked.

"Your worst enemy." Tarris raised her hand to the back of her neck. She watched their faces change from menacing smugness to outright fear. She tapped her temple, and her eyes slowly changed from dark brown to the palest hue of blue.

"Crap. Let's get out of here!" The four men ran off as

if the Devil was on their tails which, in a way, she was.

Tarris chuckled as she watched them dash away into the shadows and out of sight. She quickly tapped her skin to restore her disguise.

"Why did you do that?"

"I didn't want anyone to get hurt. They were about to jump us, Asher."

"You don't know that!"

"Calm down." Tarris put her hands on Asher's shoulders. "I won't let anything happen to you."

"Damn my curiosity," Asher said.

"You wanted to know, so I'm telling you." Tarris's gaze scanned the area for any further threats as she talked to Asher.

"No, I mean I should have left you alone in the first place, then I wouldn't be in this mess. It's all because of my stupid medical curiosity." Asher pulled herself out of Tarris's grasp.

"Oh." Tarris stepped away. "Fine. We'll get the credits and ID, and I'll find a safe house for you."

"But—"

"Come." Tarris walked off in the direction they had been heading before the attack.

See? That's what you get for giving a piece of yourself to someone, Tarris snapped in her mind.

But sister, she's our friend.

No, Rya, she's not our friend. She wishes to be free of us. Then so be it.

But we need her.

We didn't need her before, and we don't need her now. She's a liability.

But it's because of you she's in trouble.

Damn... Tarris knew Rya had presented the primary argument for protecting Asher. Tarris had made her a target for the Council by association.

Tarris ignored Asher as they walked deeper and deeper into the forbidden area of the city. The area was a law unto itself, because the peacekeepers refused to enter it. The homeless, thieves, murderers, and all others deemed unworthy by the Council lived here.

The silence had been eerie as they walked the streets to their ultimate destination. Asher moved closer to Tarris's side when their footsteps echoed in the chasms of narrow streets.

At the end of one long, lonely street, a noise built in intensity as they approached it. Around the corner, the street opened up to a large intersection, shadowed by a low bridge nearby. The stalls backed up to the walls of the bridge, and this afforded the vendors safety behind their backs.

The noise dropped for a moment as they were both scrutinized to see if they were friend or foe. No one approached, and Tarris found a shadowed alcove across the road to stand in unobserved. From her vantage point, she studied the terrain in front of her.

"Now what?" Asher asked.

Tarris looked at her timepiece. "Now we wait."

Tarris watched the area carefully, and all seemed normal. The market bustled with business, but there was an uneasy tension in the air. She couldn't see anything out of place, but she knew she wasn't the only one who watched the market. Had the Council tracked the credits that quickly, or was it an intuitive guess on their part? In either case, their representatives were present, and it made her predicament difficult.

"Hey! Kid!" she whispered at a child, perhaps twelve years old, who passed by. "Want to earn five credits?"

He looked at her skeptically. Tarris could read in his eyes what he was thinking. Was she luring him into a trap?

"Well? Five credits or I ask that girl over there." She pointed to a young girl who stood next to her father while he sifted through second-hand clothing. "I'm sure she could use the credits."

"What do you want?" The boy didn't move any closer.

"Go to stall 27 and retrieve a parcel for me."

He eyed her suspiciously. "Why don't you get it yourself?"

"Because someone is watching me," she said matter-of-factly.

"Oh." He looked Tarris up and down and finally made a decision. "Okay."

He was about to run off when Tarris called him back. "Hey! Don't you want to know my name?"

"Why? Is he delivering a package to anyone else?" the kid cheekily replied.

The kid was a smart-ass. "Do it slowly. Don't draw attention to yourself," Tarris said.

"What do you think I am? Some sort of idiot?" He ran off into the crowd and disappeared from sight.

"What do you think?" Asher asked.

"I think that kid will grow up to be on the Council one day. He certainly has the balls for it." Tarris grinned as she watched the boy wander around. He touched merchandise and talked to people whom he obviously knew. "Yep," she said, "he'll go far. That is, if he ever gets out of this dump."

It took a few more minutes for the kid to work his way

slowly to the vendor of stall 27. Whatever he said got him the parcel. Tarris was tempted to recruit him to her cause, but she had dragged enough people into danger with their association to her. He retraced his steps to the alcove and handed over the parcel.

"Where's my money?" he demanded.

Tarris opened the parcel, took out a ten-credit piece, and flipped it toward the waiting child "There you go."

"Gee, thanks." He stared at the coin in his hand.

"Now what," Asher asked.

"Yeah, now what?" the boy mimicked.

"Now, we wait until the place empties." Tarris stepped deeper into the alcove until her back touched the wall. She leaned against it and sought solace within herself.

"Oh, great," Asher said.

"You don't have to do that," the boy called as he ran off.

"Strange kid," Tarris said.

"I could have told you that before you gave him the credits."

"But he got the parcel with no fuss."

"True," Asher said, "but what's to stop him from turning us in?"

"Nothing." Tarris looked for the kid, but he seemed to have disappeared. Out of the shadows, about fifty feet to the left of where they were hiding, emerged a large man in a black, knee-length coat. The kid was next to him and pointed in the direction of the bridge. As she watched, the dark figure swept the boy aside and walked briskly on the course he had been directed to.

The kid returned a minute later, an impish smile on his cherub-like face. "You won't have long before he's back."

Tarris could barely conceal her curiosity. "What did you tell him?"

"He asked me if I'd seen anyone sus-piss-cus. I told him I saw a couple of new people heading off to The Battery." He looked up at Tarris.

"And why didn't you turn us in?" She had to know.

"You paid me. He didn't."

Tarris laughed. "Then you better not be here when he gets back."

"I ain't afraid of him."

"You should be, little man." Tarris looked around. "Where are your parents?"

"Ain't got none. Lost 'em in the Sweeps."

The Sweeps were covert operations where the streets of the poorer sections were "cleansed," as the Council put it. People found on the streets at that time were never heard of again. When the operation was taking place, Tarris's unit talked about it quite freely, even to the point of placing bets as to how the victims were disposed of. Now she cursed herself for allowing such a vulgar and callous ritual to take place.

"We've got to get out of here." Tarris looked at the sky. "It's getting dark and cold."

"Follow me," the kid said.

"What's your name?" she asked the child standing there with a casual air of overconfidence.

"Jerad."

"Well, Jerad, lead the way." Tarris swept her hand to one side in an invitation to the boy.

Jerad ran off down the street and left Tarris and Asher to run as well or lose sight of him. Tarris could see why the boy had stayed alive for so long. He was quick, wiry, and slippery—a good combination for a street urchin. Not that they called kids like him that anymore. Troublemakers, that's what the local authorities called them. They were considered a threat to the common decency of the population as a whole. That's why there was never any outcry over the Sweeps. The Council manipulated the situation and presented the operation as a public service.

Tarris struggled to keep up. Her suit wasn't designed with running in mind. She pushed it as hard as she could, but it took a lot of her energy to do so.

"Are you all right?" Asher asked as she jogged beside her.

Flashes of a forgotten dream came to mind, and Tarris chuckled.

"What's so funny?"

"I'll tell you later." Tarris tried to keep track of Jerad as he led them through the maze of streets and buildings. What would Asher think of her revelation? No, Tarris felt it was something better left alone.

Asher started to fall behind, and Tarris slowed her pursuit of Jerad. This was not the place to leave Asher alone.

The light started to fade, and it grew dark quickly in the tall ruins of a civilization.

"Hold up," Tarris said. She placed a hand on Asher's chest and could feel the rapid heartbeat there. "We'll take a rest."

"But we've lost him."

"It can't be helped. I'm not leaving you alone." Tarris reached into her sack, pulled out a bottle, and handed it to Asher. "Take a drink while I look around." She took a few steps away and studied the surrounding area, looking one way and then the other. There was no way for her to establish their position. One street seemed very much like another. Any landmarks had been destroyed long ago. Tarris looked at her chronometer and decided they needed to find cover.

She moved back to Asher, who was breathing heavily. Tarris took a healthy swallow from the drink bottle handed to her and put it back into her pack. "Over there." She started to walk toward one of the abandoned buildings, her decision made by the fact that the roof was still intact.

"Don't go in there!"

Tarris looked around for the owner of the voice and found Jerad had returned.

"We lost you," Asher said.

"You're too slow. Come on." He waved at them and pointed down the street. This time he moved at a slower pace.

Tarris could feel something building within her. It started as a sensation of rushing blood through her veins, which stimulated her nerves to the point of painful pins and needles. It took her a few moments to realize where the sensation was coming from. She stopped in her tracks.

"What's wrong?" Asher was immediately at her side.

"I... I don't know." Tarris had no idea what was happening to her body, but the elation at feeling something... anything... in her legs was welcome news. She stumbled as her equilibrium faltered.

"Sit," Asher said.

"If I do that, I won't get up." Tarris tried to ignore the painful rippling of constricting pain as she pushed herself to walk. Every footstep drew a wave of numbness followed by her nerves jumping about in pandemonium.

"Use the medipatch," Asher said.

"No. This is too good to miss." Tarris gritted her teeth.

"Too good? Are... are you...?" Asher looked at her. When Tarris nodded, she smiled broadly. "That's great news. Right?"

"Yeah, great and painful," Tarris said.

"Do you two yap all the time?" Jerad had returned and stood a few feet away from them.

"Not really," Tarris said. "Come on, let's get under cover."

They continued the rest of the journey in silence. Just when Tarris thought the boy was running them around in circles, he stopped at the wall of a large building.

"This is it?" Asher looked around for some sort of entrance.

"There," he said and pointed to a large grate set into the wall.

"In there? You're joking, right?"

"Nope. In there."

"I'm not going in there." Asher shook her head.

"Stay out here. I don't care," Jerad said absently. His gaze swept the area.

"Just get in there," Tarris hissed as another wave of pain overtook her.

"What about you?" Asher asked with concern. "You'll never get yourself in there."

"I will. Don't argue." Tarris grabbed Asher's arm and pushed her toward the hole in the wall.

Asher had barely entered the drain when she announced, "Oh God! It stinks in here."

Tarris entered, came up behind her, and pushed her onward. "It's a drain. What did you expect?" But Tarris ignored the smell because all her senses were honed in on her legs. While she was in extreme pain, she was thankful it didn't get any worse.

Jerad followed behind to put the grate back in place. "Keep going," he yelled.

"Remind me again why we aren't home in bed," Asher said.

Despite the pain, Tarris smiled. Asher had said "home" and not "your apartment." "Because I want to leave my profession."

Asher stopped and Tarris head-butted her in the rear. "Is that what this is all about? You resigning?"

"You don't resign from my job, Asher... ever," Tarris said soberly. "Now get moving." The pain increased as her muscles started to cramp. To her, it was pleasure and pain all rolled up into one. They were in complete darkness now and were crawling along a pipe that was barely high enough to house them comfortably.

"Go to the right," Jerad called.

"Right?" Asher said. "I can't see a damned thin—" Tarris heard the thunk when she ran straight into a wall with her head. "Owww!"

"I said right," Jerad yelled.

Tarris followed behind Asher and felt the slight incline as they veered right. There was a sudden gust of wind, which was welcome in the confined space of the drain.

"Stop!" Jerad called out.

Tarris extended her hand to one side and felt the brick wall. On the other side, her hand touched air. There seemed to be a niche in the wall, and she suspected this was Jerad's home. Without instruction, she fell forward onto the platform to allow her legs to extend. The cramping pain was still there, and she was unable to relieve it. Her muscles just wouldn't do what she wanted them to. A moan escaped her lips.

"Hey!" Asher's voice was close by. Tarris heard the rustle of Asher's bag and a moment later something cold brushed the inside of her elbow. There was discomfort for a moment before the pain drifted into the background. "That should help," Asher whispered in her ear.

Tarris couldn't argue. She had been too stubborn to give herself the pain relief, but she didn't begrudge Asher doing it for her. Besides, the injection had been done before she had the chance to argue. With her face squashed into the dirty rock floor, Tarris lay there until the pain slowly slid into the background of her consciousness. A few moments later, there was light. She moved her head to face the source and looked at the flickering flames.

"How did you do that?" Asher asked.

"With these." Jerad held up two rocks. "Haven't you seen fire before?"

"Never had the need to," Tarris mumbled. "We use other energy sources less primitive than this."

"Where are they?" he said with a smug expression.

"A lifetime away," Tarris murmured. Her eyes closed, and she drifted off to sleep for a while.

She woke to the smell of something cooking. The sizzle and pop sounds made by the meat bounced around the enclosed space like a ball. "What's that?" She had spoken the words, but it came out as garble.

"I think I'm going to be sick."

Tarris heard Asher speak, and she slowly opened her eyes. Propped over the fire was something small that had once been alive. A few hairs hadn't been consumed by the fire just yet, but they gave Tarris a fair idea of what was on the spit.

"All the more for me," Jerad said.

"Now you're awake," Asher said, "I'll take a look at your back." She hunkered down next to Tarris and extracted her emergency medical kit from her bag. Tarris undid the top of her jumpsuit and pulled the material down to her waist to expose the metal waistband of her frame. She watched as Asher loaded the infuser with her "special mixture," as she thought of it, which was designed to stimulate the nerves and fight any possible infection or rejection that might take place.

"Why do you wear that thing?" Jerad pointed to the metal frame.

"Because I can't walk."

"Yes, you can. I saw you."

"This helps me to walk. My legs are useless."

"Not for long," Asher murmured as she tended to Tarris's back.

"Yes. Not for long," Tarris repeated.

"What's this?" Asher's voice held a hint of panic.

Tarris reached her hand around to her back and felt it. She had forgotten all about the tiny transmitter that had been taped there.

"Oh crap!" Tarris tried to sit up, but Asher held her in place to give her the drugs. Once the injection was done, she removed her hand.

"Now what?" Asher asked as she put away her kit.

"This. The transmitter. That's how they found us at the market," Tarris said, "and now they know we're here."

Jerad backed away until he was against the wall. "Who are you?"

"You don't want to know, kid." Tarris didn't want to scare him.

"Yes, I do. And don't call me kid."

Tarris glanced at Asher, who nodded. She reached around to the tab at the base of her neck and tapped it. Jerad's expression changed from uncertainty to fear.

"You don't need to be afraid, Jerad."

"You're… you're one of *them.* "

"Yes, I'm one of them," Tarris answered in a sad voice. "But I have no reason to harm you. You're safe from me."

Is this why you hide, sister?

Rya's intonation was more of curiosity than anger or fear.

Yes. I don't want to be one of them anymore. I'm human, despite what Corman says. I want my own life, Rya.

With her?

Tarris looked at Asher again. There was a strange expression on Asher's face, as if she knew she was being talked about.

Yes. No. I don't know. I've been alone so long, I don't know how to interact with someone anymore.

You have me.

Yes, I have you, my sister. Tarris smiled gently. My one and only true friend.

And now you have her.

Yes, and now I have her… too.

"You can tell Rya everything will be all right." As Asher spoke, her hand brushed Tarris's back.

"How did you…?"

Asher answered by placing her hand over her own chest. "It all comes from here."

"Are you two getting all mushy or something?" Jerad spoke up from his position against the far wall.

Tarris lifted herself up onto her elbows and chuckled. "As if…" She reached behind her head and tapped the tab. Jerad's stance relaxed as the dark hair replaced the white.

"Is it true?" he asked.

"Is what true?" Asher helped her sit up. It took great effort for Tarris to move about in the small alcove of rock, made even more difficult because there were no handholds to grab onto to help lift herself.

"About them. Is it true?"

"What have you heard?" Tarris placed her arms in the sleeves of her jumpsuit. The magnetic closers attracted to one another once they were near enough.

"Don't we have to go?" Asher reminded her.

"Yes, we do. Grab your belongings," Tarris said. "Jerad, is there another way out of here?" She didn't want to crawl again, but she didn't want to get caught either.

"There's up there." He pointed to the tiny grate way above their heads. It had been the source of the gentle breeze that had blown through the pipes.

"And there's no way of getting up there unless we climb." Tarris knew for sure she couldn't do that. "What about that way?" She indicated the pipeline they were already in and pointed into the blackness.

"It comes up at another grate two blocks away," Jerad said as he reached for a canister of water.

"And it's sure to be covered by the guards. What about the left fork in the tunnel?"

"It goes down."

"To where?" Tarris fastened her bag closed.

"Don't know. No one's ever been down there. At least,

no one who ever came back to say so," Jerad said it solemnly, as if he were reciting some sort of prophecy.

As Tarris looked upward, a shadow drifted across the grate at the top. Faint sounds traveled along the pipe and echoed down to the tiny cavern they were in. She picked up the transmitter and nicked herself with it to smear her own blood over the outside of the box.

"You are one strange woman," Asher said.

"You're only finding that out now?" Tarris patted herself on the back for her witty repartee. Maybe conversation wasn't as hard as she had always thought it was. Asher reached into her bag and pulled out a small atomizer and sprayed the puncture with synthetic skin.

"This isn't a good place to go around with an open wound."

Tarris knew that it was the mediprac in Asher speaking. "True, but this will make them think I've only just discovered the treachery."

"Oh, yeah, that'll really show them."

"Hey!" Tarris's eyebrows knitted together in annoyance. "I'm doing the best I can. Okay?"

"And your best is great, Tarris." Asher patted her hand.

Tarris dropped the transmitter on the platform and flung the bag over her shoulder. "I think I preferred the anger," she muttered. "We're going down. We've got no choice." She grabbed Asher and pushed her back into the pipeline.

Tarris stopped for a moment and addressed Jerad. "You don't have to come. You might be lucky, and they won't harm you." But Tarris knew it was a lie. The kid was a nobody, and the soldiers wouldn't think twice about killing him on the spot. He would become just another statistic of the Sweeps.

The sound of muffled voices grew steadily closer. They would have to move now or lose their chance to escape. Tarris shifted herself back into the drain and pushed on Asher's ass to urge her down the slight incline to the junction. The area went dark, and she heard the hiss as Jerad poured water on the flames.

"Go! Go!" She pushed Asher harder as they approached the junction. Beams of light bounced off the drain walls farther down the pipe, and while their pursuers hadn't found them yet, it was only a matter of time.

The new passage tilted downwards gently at first, but soon the decline got steeper. The floor was covered with slime, and any sort of purchase was nearly impossible. Suddenly Asher gave out a squeal, and her voice disappeared rapidly as she sped away from Tarris. Tarris was about to call out, when her own grip faltered. Suddenly she found herself on a slippery slide down the passage at an ever-increasing speed. With difficulty, she twisted herself around so she slid feet first.

"Asher!" Tarris tried to call softly as she continued her downward trajectory.

"Tarris!" Asher yelled. "There's a drop off! Help me!"

Tarris dug her heels in and tried to slow her momentum. A rotting smell erupted when her feet dug in and unearthed the slime she slid over. Finally, she began to slow. Asher still called out as Tarris approached her. Asher had somehow stopped but was in trouble. Was she to find herself in the same predicament?

Chapter 8

At the moment, Tarris would have been grateful for the feeling in her legs to disappear. The passage had opened up into a huge underground cavern, barely lit by some unknown source. Her quick descent had stopped just short of a sheer drop to the ground below. The pipe had broken away, and Asher hung by her fingertips from the edge.

Tarris ignored the pain, just as she ignored the putrid goo that covered her hands and ended up under her fingernails as she pulled herself along to the edge. "I'm here. Don't panic," she said soothingly.

"I don't want to die," Asher sobbed.

"And you won't. Give me your hand." Just as she grabbed Asher's wrist, a body slammed into Tarris's back, and she tightened herself to stop the slide. The suit creaked as she forced her legs outwards to brace against the walls. "Good to see you again, Jerad," she spoke over her shoulder.

"Yeah, well. I figured you needed my help," he said in his usual cocky tone.

"We do." Tarris really didn't need his help, but if it made the kid feel good about himself, then who was she to stop him? "I have a job for you. See if you can find another way down from here."

"Sure."

She got a push in the back for her trouble as he tried to retrace his way up the pipe.

"I'm still here, by the way," Asher called.

"And I'm still rescuing you. Geez, woman!" Tarris wrapped a hand around Asher's other wrist. "Can you get your foot up to the pipe?"

"I'm not a contortionist."

Tarris sighed and released one of her hands. She reached for the tabs to her suit and locked her legs in place. She returned her hand to Asher's wrist and pulled. Asher shifted slightly but not enough to be of any help.

Let me help, sister.

If you can. Please. Tarris had never consciously said please to Rya before, but somehow it didn't seem out of place.

She tried again, and this time her strength had doubled. Slowly but surely, Asher started to rise toward her. Her head, then her torso, became visible in the muted light. With a final yank, Tarris used her body weight and fell backwards to pull Asher with her and into her arms. Both lay in the mud, Tarris on the bottom and Asher on top of her.

"Are you okay?" Tarris asked softly.

"I am now. Thank you."

"Thank both of us."

"Really?" Asher looked into Tarris's eyes. "Rya? Thank you."

"She says you're welcome."

"Oh, yuk. You two are at it again." Jerad seemed to have the knack of turning up when the conversation got personal.

"We're just resting," Tarris said.

"If that's what you want to call it. There's a small side passage a few feet up there. It's not easy to get to."

Tarris looked at Asher and sighed. "Come on." She helped Asher steady herself on her hands and knees before she unlocked the legs of her suit and turned around. They crawled precariously back up the passage, but more often than not, they slid backwards part of the distance they had just gained. Jerad, being the smallest and the most energetic, reached the intersection first. While he didn't have the strength to pull the two women up, he did give them a steadying hand to clamber up the rest of the way.

Just as Tarris crossed into the side passage, angry voices could be heard from above.

"They must have gone this way. Follow them!"

Moments later two bodies flew by them and jettisoned off the end of the passage. Their screams echoed around the walls as they fell, until the sudden silence signaled the end of their journey.

"Rich? Are you there? Speak to me!"

Tarris could hear the nervousness in the voice from above. Maybe he thought she had killed them. If it would keep the troopers away from them, she could accept the lie.

"Rich? Come on, buddy. Stop fooling around!"

Tarris held up her hand for silence. A few moments later, a rope appeared and descended the large drain like a snake. Tarris frantically waved her hand for her companions to hide.

"So help me, Rich, if this is some kind of joke, I'm going to kick your ass." The voice steadily grew in volume and finished as if the speaker drew level with Tarris. She was itching to see who it was, but she didn't dare move for fear of being found.

The smaller conduit barely held their bodies, so they had no chance of staying out of sight. Tarris braced herself for the confrontation, undecided whether to resist arrest or surrender. She was so preoccupied with the life-defining decision that she barely noticed the tingle that crossed her skin.

Two soldiers finally came into sight, and they stopped momentarily at the entrance to the smaller drain. Tarris stared directly at them, but they didn't appear to see her. Unless they were blind, which she knew they weren't, there was no way they couldn't see her. She searched within herself and found Rya gone. A wry smile touched her lips. It seemed her shadow warrior had developed a mind of her own and had slipped from her to throw up a deep shadow in front of them.

The soldiers continued downwards, the rope jumping around under their jerky movements. When it stopped, Tarris assumed they had reached the end of the drain.

"Shit!" one of them growled.

"What's going on?" a voice from above asked.

"They're dead, sir. The drain falls away to a fifty-foot drop," the same soldier reported to his commander.

"Come back. We'll send a retrieval team later," the voice from above yelled. There were muffled voices for a minute, and the commander called again. "We found what looks like a transmitter in the upper drain. Haul yourselves back up here to continue the search."

Moments later, the two men struggled up the rope, slipping and sliding on the mud as they tried to get their footing. No one moved until the silence had been present for quite a while.

"Why didn't they see us?" Asher asked.

"Rya." Tarris uttered the one word and expected Asher to understand.

"What's a Rya?" Jerad, of course, didn't.

"Someone you don't ever want to meet, boy," Tarris said solemnly. "Let's get out of here." She sat for a few seconds to wait for the people in front of her to move.

They had only moved forward for a few minutes before Jerad stopped. "What's wrong?" Tarris tried to keep her voice low.

"The pipe gets really narrow," Jerad called back. "I could maybe get though…"

"But we won't." Tarris finished his sentence.

The walls of the drain had been closing in on them steadily since they had left the fork in the broken pipe. The atmosphere was cloying and hot, and the putrid air sat distastefully on their tongues.

"Now what?"

Tarris just knew Asher would bring that up. "We've got no choice. We have to go back."

"And what about the waiting soldiers?" Asher asked all the questions that Tarris asked herself.

"Then I guess we give ourselves up." They were in complete darkness, so Tarris couldn't see Asher's reaction. However, the ensuing silence spoke volumes to her. "What? No 'are you crazy' or 'what's the matter with you'?"

"You've figured all the angles, haven't you?" Asher sounded almost too calm as she spoke.

"I'm open to suggestions."

Sister…

"No? Then start crawling back," Tarris said.

Sister…

"Hey! Where are you going?" Jerad's voice called from a little farther down the drain.

"Can you get out?" Tarris adjusted the tabs on her suit to awkwardly crawl back out.

Sister…

"I think so. Wait…" There was a squelching sound, and a moment later Jerad said, "I'm free."

Sister…

What!

Tarris hadn't meant to snap at Rya, but she was at her wit's end. She was a trooper of the Special Black Shadow Corps, and she had run out of ideas.

Rule Ten in her Survival Handbook: Never, ever, run out of ideas.

She felt the withdrawal inside her. *Please, Rya. I'm sorry.*

Her shadow spread through her and lay over her bruised ego like a blanket, warm and comforting.

Hit your right foot against the wall, sister.

Why? What's there?

The answer to your prayers.

Tarris reached the tabs on her suit once more and locked her leg straight. She kicked out at the wall as Rya had asked and hit the edge with a resounding bang. "That's metallic." She relocked her suit and moved back as best she could. Her hand reached out to where she thought the sound came from. The texture was different, and it was recessed into the wall. She searched for some sort of handle, button, or gap on the plate in the dark.

"What have you found?" Asher moved back and sloshed mud over Tarris's hand. "Sorry."

But Tarris paid no attention to it. She had discovered a way out, or what she hoped was a way out. "I think I've found an exit."

"That's great!"

Tarris smiled to herself. If she was being honest with herself, she wanted to be a hero to Asher. She wasn't sure why it mattered, but it did. Her hand rested on a lever of some sort, and she pulled on it. It refused to budge, which didn't surprise her in the least. It was probably rusted, like so many things of the past were. She leaned back and swung her reinforced boot tip at it.

"Shhh," Asher said into the darkness. "Won't they hear it?"

Even if Asher hadn't pointed out the noise, Tarris wouldn't do that again. Her newly awakened nerves were on edge as the vibration from the kick ran up her legs, through her torso, and finished at the top of her head.

"Come over here and turn around. I need your help."

"You? You need my help, Trooper?" Asher joked. "I thought all you gung-ho types didn't need help."

Tarris reached out to find Asher's hand. Hers landed on something incredibly soft and warm, but it wasn't a hand. "Oh. Sorry." Tarris withdrew her hand abruptly.

"I thought we were past that." Asher's voice was low and soft.

"Not in front of the boy," Tarris whispered.

"He probably understands it better than you," Asher said.

"We'll have to try to push the panel open." Tarris searched around tentatively until she grabbed what she thought was Asher's shoulders.

Asher chuckled. "You got it right this time."

Tarris pulled Asher toward her until she thought Asher was level with her. "On the count of three, we try to shoulder the door open. One, two, three."

Tarris threw her weight behind her shoulder and slammed it into the door.

"Owww!" Asher said. "I hope you're not planning on doing that again anytime soon."

Jerad's smaller body squeezed in between the two of them and sat down. Tarris felt his torso movements against her side, even though she had no idea what he was doing. Within moments, there was a loud squeal as the hatch opened outwards. She didn't need her eyesight to know that Jerad sat there with a smug smile on his face. "Don't get cocky, young man."

"Do you want me to go first?" he asked.

"Are you saying I can't climb down there?" Tarris leaned out of the drain and looked at a large cavern. In the dim light, she saw a metal ladder that ran from their lofty height to the ground below. It wasn't an ideal exit, but it was the only one they had. "Go ahead."

Jerad climbed through and started down the ladder.

"Why didn't you go first?" Asher asked.

"Because I don't know if this damned suit will let me." Tarris watched the boy scamper down safely. "I want you two out of here in case it all goes horribly wrong."

"What could possibly go wrong?"

"Oh, I don't know." Tarris couldn't stop the sarcasm in her voice. "The suit buckles. I get tangled up in the rungs. The ladder gives way and flattens me. They all sound like nice alternatives."

"I'm not leaving you here." Asher touched Tarris's arm.

"Will you two stop that!" Jerad yelled from the ground.

"How does he do that?" Asher looked out the hole at the kid staring up at them with his hands on his hips.

"No argument, okay?" Tarris said softly. "I want you down there and safe."

"Why?" Asher tugged on Tarris's arm.

"You're my responsibility, and I want to make damned sure you're okay."

"Why?" Asher repeated.

"I don't know. I just do." Tarris couldn't look Asher in the eye.

Without another word, Asher prepared to leave.

"One final thing," Tarris said. "If something happens, will you take care of Rya for me?"

"Is that normal?"

"Not really, no. If the host dies, so does the shadow," Tarris said matter-of-factly. "But I don't think that rule applies to Rya and me anymore."

"What are you trying to say?"

"I think when she was in you, and you had… you know." Tarris could feel a blush start. "She connected with you. You gave her something more. You gave me something more. She has her own identity now."

"She didn't have that before?"

"No." Tarris leaned back. "I called, and she would answer that call. Now, she talks to me. She was the one who found this doorway."

"Ah."

"I wanted you to think I had found it," Tarris said sheepishly.

"Are you coming down or what?" Jerad called from below.

Tarris looked out the door and caught a glimpse of Jerad standing there impatiently. "Don't keep the boy waiting."

Asher climbed through the hole and stood on the small ledge. She gave Tarris one final glance, grabbed the railing, and started the climb down the ladder. Two steps down, Asher stopped and looked up. "I will take care of Rya." She continued the journey downward.

When she reached solid ground, Tarris addressed herself. "Come on now. You can do this." But could the suit do it? She had pushed it to its limits, and now she had to ask for more. Sooner or later it would give out. Would she reach the bottom before it did?

Chapter 9

Tarris dragged herself through the hatch to rest precariously on the narrow ledge. She barely had room to move, and her useless legs made her work even more laborious. With effort, she managed to close the hatch behind her, using her shoulder to push hard against it. Finally, she heard a clunk as the lever fell back into place. If they were to be followed, the soldiers would have to find the exit themselves. That same satisfying clunk, however, also caused her heart rate to pick up. Now there was only one way to go. Down.

"Here," Tarris called, "catch this." She let her sack drop toward the ground, watching as Asher caught it and staggered back under the impact.

Sister.

I have to do this, Rya.

I know you do. I will help where I can.

No! Tarris said a little too forcefully. *This is something I have to do on my own.*

Why, when I'm here to help?

How could she explain what she herself didn't understand? She was deliberately putting herself at risk even though her shadow was able to help.

It's a matter of self-worth, Rya. I need to know I'm

capable of doing this on my own.

What is there to prove? To me, you're everything.

Do you understand what you're saying? Had Rya progressed so far as to understand emotions?

Without you, I'm nothing, sister.

Tarris felt deflated. Maybe Rya didn't understand after all.

You're my life, Tarris. You're my friend, my protector, and my home.

Holy shit! Rya had evolved to the point that Tarris suspected her shadow could exist without her. *If something happens, promise me you'll look after Asher.*

But, sister…

No 'buts,' Rya. She'll need your protection.

How will I survive without you? You know that I die when you die.

"*I don't think so… my friend.* Tarris smiled. Yes, Rya was her friend. *You have also become a part of Asher. You're more than you were, my sister. You once were dark, and now you seek the light. If something happens to me, let her help you be all that you can be.*"

"Are you going to sit up there all day?" Asher yelled.

"Just getting my affairs in order," Tarris called back.

"That's not even funny, Trooper."

"Yeah, yeah," Tarris muttered as she shimmied around onto her stomach and let her useless legs hang over the edge. She wasn't a big believer in religious matters, but she offered up a prayer anyway.

Her strong hands grasped the metal handrail on either side as she slowly lowered herself over the edge of the platform. The muscles in her back flexed and burned under the strain of holding her dead weight in the air. She swung her lower half backwards and forwards from the waist in the hope of latching onto one of the rungs of the ladder. The frame had caught on something, and she felt the slight vibration through her legs. Despite the tenuous position she was in, she smiled. If she survived this, she would walk; she was sure of it.

With that thought, she let one of her hands go. She hoped all those years of lifting her own weight would pay off now. She fumbled around for the upright stringer in an effort to move herself past the platform and onto the ladder. Her fingers grasped around blindly as her other hand started to lose its grip. Sweat touched her brow, adding to her already tense situation, but she was unable to brush it away. She needed a miracle, and she needed it now.

As if someone had heard her plea, Tarris's fingers brushed the cool metal. She grabbed on strongly and waited until she had regained her composure.

"Are you all right?"

"Yeah," Tarris answered Asher's concerned question.

This was where she would live or die. Did she have enough faith in herself to bridge the yawning gap between platform and ladder? Without dwelling on it for too long, she took that final step. Her hand let go, and her body swung down and out with the weight, leaving her hanging by her other hand grasping the stringer and her feet resting on a rung. The sweat increased across her brow as she pulled herself toward the ladder, close enough for her other hand to find purchase. She pulled herself in tightly and pressed herself against the rusty metal. Her blood rushed through her, and her heart pumped wildly out of control.

Well done, sister.

Tarris could hear the pride in Rya's voice.

"Thank you," she whispered. "Now the real work begins." She moved one hand to her waist and pressed a small tab to set the suit into a walking motion. She tapped it again to slow down the pace to almost a stop in the hope of using the suit's movement to shift her feet down one rung at a time.

Her legs moved back and forth slowly, imitating a lazy stroll. Tarris held on tightly and waited for one foot to leave the rung in a follow-through of a step. As the suit brought her foot forward for another step, she lowered herself for her foot to make contact with the next rung. It was awkward and dangerous in the extreme. The suit worked independently of her, and her body was left with no choice but to ride with the gait.

Finally, she reached down and switched off the walk. "Enough," she announced to herself. She was getting nowhere fast, and her strength was waning.

"I'm coming!" Asher called from below.

"Stay there," Tarris ordered.

"No! You need help—"

"I said, stay there!" Tarris shouted in a sterner voice. Images filled her mind as she sought a solution to her immediate problem. She needed to get off this ladder, and now. A scene from one of her old movies came to mind. The move was more dangerous than what she was attempting now, but it would certainly get her on solid ground a lot quicker.

Don't do it, sister.

"Do you have another solution, Rya?" Tarris said in a low voice. When nothing was forthcoming she answered, "That's what I thought."

She replayed the scene in her head and tried to imitate

what was being done. The tricky maneuver involved releasing her legs and bracing them on the outside of the stringers. Once the legs were locked in place, she did the same with her hands, grabbing the outside of the stringers and leaving her braced either side of the rungs.

Refusing to think about the outcome and how much it would hurt, Tarris released her tight grip and allowed the uprights to pass through her palms. The descent became too fast, and she tightened her fingers on the metal pipe and slowed herself down. When the rusted and torn pipe dug deeply into her skin, she panted wildly in an effort to control her pain. Rya moved around inside her in discomfort, but there was little she could do about it.

Tarris stared at the ground as it rushed up to meet her. A few feet from the bottom, she grasped the stringers hard and slowed herself down to a mere crawl. When her feet reached the floor, she just stood there. Her feet and hands still gripped the cold metal pipes firmly.

Asher rushed up to her and gently pried her fingers away. "Oh God! Why did you do that?"

Tarris looked at her blankly for a second before she looked at her hands. Blood pooled in her palms, and tiny slivers of metal stuck out of her skin. "Because the other way was going to kill me," she said in a shaky voice.

"Let me look at it."

"Not here," Tarris said. "We're too visible from above. Jerad, get us out of here."

"We have to see to this," Asher insisted.

"And we will... once we're out of sight." Tarris started to shake.

"That's shock. This won't wait."

"It will have to wait!" Tarris shouted.

Jerad set off across the floor of the large cavern. Under Tarris's instruction, Asher activated the suit and Tarris moved forward. Asher shouldered Tarris's bag as well as her own to relieve Tarris of the extra weight.

They made good time across the expanse of floor. On the other side, they entered a semicircular tunnel standing about twenty feet high. Three tracks of steel rails lay on the ground parallel to one another; one rail was slightly smaller and sat between the two larger rails.

The farther they moved into the large tunnel, the more the light faded, until it was pitch black. The rail at their feet became their friend as it guided them until the dark gave way to light. The tunnel opened up into another open space, not as big as the one they had just left, but one that looked more habitable. A platform sat about five feet above where they stood, and they had to climb up to gain access.

Getting Tarris up onto the platform took a great deal of effort by all three. She herself was unable to use her hands, leaving most of the work to Asher and Jerad to hoist her up the five feet. Afterward, they lay exhausted on the hard ground and ignored the discomfort. Light came from above, somehow filtered through a hole from the outside.

"We'll rest here," Tarris said. "Jerad, are you able to get a fire going?"

"Sure thing." He scampered off to search for something to burn.

"Over there," Asher said quietly, and she offered a hand to help Tarris up. Asher once again touched the suit's tabs to move Tarris over to a corner of the platform. "At least we can have a fire here without it being seen."

"Since when did you become so smart?" Tarris smiled weakly as her injuries took over her attention.

"It must be from hanging around you all day," Asher said with a chuckle.

Tarris landed clumsily on the floor, and she couldn't have cared less. Asher helped her lean against a wall and extend her legs out straight. She reached for her backpack and extracted her medical supplies. "You know, I didn't think I'd be using this so soon after we left the apartment."

"I didn't think I would need it either." Tarris looked at Asher with bloodshot eyes. "I had no choice." Tarris silently pleaded for Asher's forgiveness.

"This is going to hurt." Asher waved the small bottle of antiseptic in front of Tarris's face. "You might want to tap the medipatch before I start."

Tarris reached for the spot on her wrist with a bloodied finger. Before she had a chance to remove her finger, Asher tapped her other patch and sent Tarris off into a medicated sleep.

"It'll be over..."

Tarris didn't hear the rest of Asher's sentence.

†

The sound of Asher's voice caught Tarris's attention. Her medicated body woke up before her drug-soaked mind did. She was lying limp in Asher's arms.

"My mom and dad are gone now." Asher's low voice settled over Tarris like a warm friend. "They didn't get to see me become a mediprac, but I know they would have been proud. I really miss them." Tarris could hear the wistfulness in Asher's voice.

"At least you knew them." Tarris shifted to a more comfortable position before she snuggled her head back in between Asher's breasts.

"You're awake." Asher didn't seem surprised.

"Yes. Tell me more."

"I'll make you a deal. If I tell you my story, you tell me yours."

"Sure," Tarris said readily.

"Oh no." Asher tightened her grip on Tarris's waist. "You agreed to that too quickly. I want the whole truth, Tarris. No shortcuts or hidden meanings, or no story."

No one had ever heard the whole story, not even her mother. Rya was the sole possessor of her secrets.

When Tarris didn't answer, Asher said, "Fine. You don't want to share? Then no more bedtime stories."

Tarris felt Asher's breath across the top of her head, large sweeping exhalations that blew down against her scalp. Asher was not a happy woman.

"No, it's not that. I've never told anyone everything before. It's just not that easy."

"Don't you trust me?"

"I'm trusting you with my life. What more do you want?"

"You know," Asher said, "these last couple of days have been a revelation to me. I've met my very first Shadow Ops assassin, been invaded by her shadow, made love to her, and I'm now on the run with her. And you know what?"

"You want to kick the girl when she's down?"

"No. I wouldn't change a minute of it."

"But I seem to recall you cursing your scientific curiosity," Tarris said warily.

"It was in the heat of the moment. I didn't mean it."

But Tarris didn't dismiss it as easily as Asher had. She

decided to change the subject. "Where's Jerad?"

"After he got the fire started, he and I ate some of your rations. He's off trying to find a way out of here."

Tarris looked into the fire burning a few feet away. Its heat was barely felt from where she was, but it took away the slight chill in the air. She closed her eyes and concentrated on whether she could feel the warmth on her legs. Was it too soon to tell? Her patience was wearing thin at her slow recovery. She had already dismissed the fact that she hadn't walked for sixteen years. She wanted her miracle, and she wanted it now.

As she contemplated her life and where she was now, she felt something. Had she imagined the sensation? Was she so desperate to feel something that her mind was playing tricks on her?

"What are you thinking about?" Asher's lips tickled her ear as she spoke.

"I'm wondering whether I felt the warmth on my skin or I'm so damned frustrated and desperate that I'll believe anything my stupid mind wants to tell me." The fire flickered as Tarris ranted, as if some errant gust of wind had passed through the tunnel.

"You'll walk," Asher said with conviction.

"Are you so sure of that?" Tarris tilted her head to look up into Asher's eyes.

"Nothing is certain, Tarris, but I believe you will. I wouldn't be surprised if you bully yourself into making those legs of yours work." Asher chuckled.

Tarris settled back into Asher's arms. "You're probably right."

"What did your mom and dad think of the accident?"

Tarris thought about it for a moment. "I don't know. I

was pretty well out of it for a long time. Mom was there now and then, but we didn't really talk much after that." Tarris let her sight drop to the licking flames. "I never knew my dad."

"Not even after the accident? He didn't show up once? That's pretty cold."

"Mom was part of a government repopulation program."

"Was she like… like…" Asher hesitated.

"Like me? No, she was normal like you."

"Is that what you all are? Part of some government experiment?"

"Hell, no. We were just abominations, that's all," Tarris said bitterly.

Asher grabbed Tarris's chin and pulled so that Tarris had to look at her. "You are not an abomination. Don't you ever say that again in front of me," Asher said angrily.

Tarris smiled. "A few days ago you would have agreed with me."

Asher let go of Tarris's chin. "I suppose I would have. But now I know better."

"And what about now?" Tarris probably should leave the question alone, but she wanted to hear the answer.

"And now? You're a unique person, Tarris Waite. You're part of a covert unit that strikes terror in the citizens of this metropolis, and yet you"—Asher touched a finger to Tarris's nose —"and your spirit, have shown me that you are a contradiction to everything I believed you to be."

"Does that mean I'm not a maniac?" Tarris asked. "Everything you heard about us is true. Every blood-soaked word of it. They want all opposition dead, and given the chance, they'll try to achieve that."

"You said 'they.'"

"The Council. I just want to live a normal life, Asher. I want my legs back and to be left alone."

"And what about love, Tarris? Don't you want to know love?" Asher asked gently.

"Love?" Tarris rubbed her head against Asher's chest. "I haven't needed it so far. Why would I need it now?" She felt Asher's heartbeat pick up.

"So, you'll be quite happy to live the rest of your life alone," Asher said, more as a statement than a question.

"I have so far."

"But that was out of necessity, not choice."

"Oh no. It was by choice."

"What made you this bitter?"

"I never had friends, at least not long enough for them to become long-time friends. I was removed from my home when I was three and placed in a school. Actually, it was an institution. An institution for freaks like me." Tarris felt Asher's reaction to her harsh words. "It's true. The school only housed albinos."

"Did you see your mom?"

"Only on holidays. She was never the same after I started school. She was..." Tarris searched for a word. "Distant."

"That's sad," Asher murmured.

"No, that's pathetic. The school had alienated me from my mother and got what they wanted. They had me reliant on them to look after me." Tarris could feel the bitterness as she talked. Some things she had kept bottled up inside were coming out, and verbalizing them was helping her come to terms with them. It was her past and she needed to know that. "Oh, we learned stuff about ABCs, but the crux of our training was preparing us for our shadow."

"I thought that happened naturally."

"It does, but they wanted us to harness it, use it, and control it. None of us saw it for what it was back then. But being different cost me. A young boy died because he was my friend, and the school wouldn't do anything about it. I was angry. I wanted to kill the boy who did it. Rya was eager to be out and take my revenge." Tarris's voice grew harder.

"So what happened? Did you—"

"No, I told my teacher I was leaving the school. Then I had my accident and fell down a flight of stairs." Oddly, this time the thought of the terrifying journey down the stairs didn't upset her.

"You don't think…" Asher stopped.

"Think what?"

"Never mind."

"No, what were you going to say?"

"It was just a silly thought, that's all."

Tarris forced Asher to continue when she stared at her. "What if they were scared of losing control over you, and they staged the accident?"

"You mentioned that before. Why would they do that?"

"You're a very valuable commodity, Tarris."

"Come to think of it, my teacher did say I was one of the strongest he had ever met."

"Strongest? How?"

"They had a telepath who could sense our shadows. I suppose he graded each of us."

"Nothing like favoritism. One of the best, huh?"

Tarris heard the amusement in Asher's voice. "No, he said one of the strongest. There's a difference."

"Did your mother look after you when you came out of the hospital?"

"She made some sort of deal with them. The school would look after my needs, and she would give up her visiting rights."

"Certainly sounds like they wanted you, and bad," Asher said.

"Despite the color of my eyes."

"What's wrong with your eyes?"

"They're not pure white. You see, I'm a bastard albino, with tainted blood. That's why my eyes are blue." It had always been a bone of contention to her kind. While they saw it as a genetic weakness, she saw it as her touch of humanity. "They said it was because of my twin, that she died because of me."

"A twin?"

"She died at birth. When Rya made herself known to me, I always thought she was my twin, returned to join me in life."

"That's sweet." Asher smiled. "What about the others?"

"I'm the only one who ever came from twins. Maybe that's what made me so special." Tarris closed her hand around a pebble lying next to her. She threw it at the fire. "Well, I don't want to be special. I want to be nobody."

"Tarris, honey," Asher soothingly replied, "you could look as ugly as one of the actors in those films you're so fond of, and you'd still be special."

"To you?" Tarris asked.

At that moment, Jerad returned. He stopped before the fire and added some tinder he had collected to it. "You finished all this lovey-dovey stuff yet?"

"There was no, as you say, 'lovey-dovey' stuff going on," Tarris said. "I only just woke up."

"Uh-huh." He tossed in the last piece of tinder.

"What did you find?"

"There's stairs over there," he said and pointed to the far corner of the platform, "but they're blocked off. The light's coming from a series of grates in the ceiling. The tunnel continues on to another place like this."

Tarris looked toward the other end of the platform and noticed a sign on the tunnel wall, partially obscured by graffiti and posters. Jerad saw where she had looked and ran off toward it. "It says Jame—ee—son Street," he yelled.

"Is it a name?" Tarris shouted.

Jerad studied the wall. "That's all it says." He ran back. "It's in the wall, not something stuck over it."

"Maybe this was a meeting place of some sort." Tarris thought about it. Despite the stairs to the surface, there was a tunnel at either end. Jerad said that the new tunnel led to another platform. She searched her memories, trying to match where they were to something she had seen. A movie came to mind— not one of her favorites, but she did enjoy it. Toward the end of the movie, the police officer chased someone down into something like this and jumped into some sort of conveyance that moved along the tracks. "This was a transportation network... underground," she announced triumphantly.

"How do you know that?" Asher asked.

"Never doubt the power of the motion picture, Asher."

"Huh?" Jerad's confused face nearly made Tarris laugh.

As she thought about their next move, they heard a distant rumbling. Asher went to the edge of the platform and looked one way then the other for the source of the noise. Tarris noticed that the light from the grates had steadily darkened.

"Jerad, can you gather more tinder for the fire? I think we're going to be here for a while."

Asher returned and knelt next to Tarris. "What's going on?"

"A storm's coming. We'll have to stay here until it passes."

"Why? The storm's up there." Asher pointed to the roof.

"Exactly, and the grates are open to the surface. In a little while, there's going to be water… a lot of water. It will run off down to the rails, and we don't want to get caught if it floods."

"And what about food? We don't have a lot left."

"Then we ration it. We don't have a choice here." Tarris was annoyed. Not that Asher was asking all the logical questions she herself would ask. It bothered her that she couldn't give her the right answers. "Can you help Jerad with tinder? It's going to get cold down here."

Asher grabbed her backpack and pulled out a couple of blankets that resembled foil. Tarris remembered the nickname of the emergency blankets from back in the nineteen eighties. Space blankets. The stupid name had always made her laugh. Were they called 'space' blankets because they didn't take up any space?

"You might want to make use of one while I'm away," Asher said.

"Yes, ma'am."

"Ma'am?" Asher's eyebrows rose. "Who are you calling 'ma'am'?"

Tarris looked around pointedly. "Hmmm, I must be talking about you." There was another clap of thunder, a little louder than the one before. "We're running out of time, Asher," Tarris said.

Jerad passed Asher as he trotted back with rubbish and wood. He dumped it unceremoniously on the ground next to the fire and left to scrounge for more. He lowered himself off the platform and disappeared into the darkness of the tunnel. Tarris prayed that he would return before the flood began.

She found herself on the platform alone, and it gave her a chance to take stock of her physical health. She lifted her hands to eye level. They looked how she imagined they would look. Red, raw, and inflamed, and yet she didn't feel a thing. Her hands had a sheen on them, as if they were covered with something. She rubbed her fingertips together, trying to make sense of the contradictory sensations she was feeling. The contact caused a tinge of pain, but it was cushioned by whatever Asher had put on them.

Tarris tried to close her hand into a fist, but she couldn't do it. The pain gradually increased to the point that she stopped the exercise. She opened her hand up slowly and stared intently at it. Once she relaxed the hand, the pain ceased. So she was okay as long as she didn't use her hands.

Asher returned with her hands full. Another clap of thunder preceded the gentle patter of rain that hit the overhead grates. The water fell a drip at a time, at first, and gathered in small puddles under the holes in the roof.

"Are we okay here?" Asher asked.

Tarris looked around. "The ground's slightly sloped, so the water should run off. We're out of the way of it."

Asher dropped the rubbish in her arms onto the small pile of accumulated tinder. Another clap of thunder boomed overhead, and she flinched at the earsplitting sound of it. "Wow! That was close."

"What did you do to my hands?" Tarris held them up. "Is this one of your little tricks?"

"Of course. Who else would I trust with all my secrets?" Asher made a move to collect more rubbish, and Tarris stopped her.

"It's about to pour down. Sit down and make yourself comfortable."

Asher sat next to Tarris. "Whoo. You stink."

"You don't smell so good yourself," Tarris said. "After crawling through all that muck, what do you expect?" The drips of water had turned into wet curtains. "How about a shower?"

Asher looked over her shoulder at the waterfalls. "Are you kidding? That's cold."

"Well, you can be either smelly or cold. Your choice." Tarris had already made up her mind about her own state despite whatever Asher decided to do. She reached for the tab at her waist and released the tension on the suit. Asher stood there and watched her, but didn't offer her help to rise. It was a standoff, and Tarris knew it. Asher wanted to be asked, and Tarris refused to ask for help. Finally Tarris relented.

"I could use some help here... please," she added as an afterthought. She extended her hand, and Asher took it. Despite the layer of synthetic skin between them, Tarris could feel her warmth.

Asher hunkered down, put Tarris's arm around her neck, and pulled upward. "My, my," Asher whispered in

Tarris's ear, "we are a heavy girl."

Tarris scowled at her. Her free hand manipulated the controls of her suit in an effort to get the contraption underneath her. It took some minutes before she was in a position to use the power of the suit to get her upright. The only promising moment of the exercise was a painful pinch of her skin by the suit.

Finally, she was upright. Both leaned against the wall to catch their breath.

"Do you have that problem often?" Asher gulped air between her words.

"No. I don't sit down like that. Too hard to stand back up."

"No kidding."

Tarris pushed herself off the wall and walked toward the water. Her suit made funny noises, a high-pitched wheeze following by a clunk, and she knew she was in trouble. She held up her hands to Asher in a silent question.

"It's waterproof. Go ahead."

Tarris stepped into the shower of water and started to scrub herself. The water was way past cold. It was freezing. But the cold numbed the pain in her hands, and she could use them to wash. She only hoped she would thaw out in front of the fire.

She barely noticed another presence until she felt hands on her back swiping downwards. She looked over her shoulder and saw Asher's beguiling eyes looking directly at her. Asher smiled gently then went back to her work, vigorously rubbing the slime and dirt off Tarris's clothes.

When she felt she was clean enough, Tarris obliged Asher with the same treatment, scooping away the crusted dirt and grime that lay across her back.

The women stepped out of the rain and immediately felt the cool breeze ripple across their skin.

"Geez!" Asher hissed.

Tarris walked toward the fire and struggled to keep an even gait. She could hear the strain on the metal and wondered if she had the expertise to fix it. But for now, her most immediate problem was getting dry.

Asher prodded the fire and added more fuel to it. It burst into life and sent out a wave of heat in their direction. Tarris turned her back toward the heat and welcomed it. Steam rose off them both. It settled around them for a moment like some eerie dense fog, then it curled away to the ceiling and dissipated.

"Where's Jerad?" Asher asked with concern. Water sluiced down the platform and leapt off the edge in a deluge.

"If he can't make it back in time, I'm sure he's smart enough to take refuge somewhere." Or at least Tarris hoped he would. She had no idea why the kid stuck with them. He didn't strike her as clingy. In fact, he seemed more fiercely independent than she was. Maybe he decided to strike out on his own and leave them to fend for themselves. It was a distinct possibility, but something told Tarris he wouldn't do that, at least not without saying goodbye.

She spent the next half an hour drying off, facing the fire then turning away when she felt the heat was too much. She rejoiced in the warmth that touched her legs. The awakening of her nerves had been a long time coming, and she welcomed the tingling that accompanied it.

When she felt dry enough, she moved to the wall. She leaned back against it and looked at Asher who stood by the fire. When Tarris reached for the button on her suit to sit,

Asher moved.

"Wait!" Asher sifted through the collected rubbish and pulled out some of the items. She built a pile with them on the ground, where Tarris was about to sit herself, and spread out the blanket on top of it. "Now you can sit." Tarris just glared at her. "What?" Asher said, "I'm not sleeping on the hard ground."

Asher had a point. Even with the blunted sensation Tarris had in her ass, any length of time she sat was going to be painful. She looked at the ground uncertainly. Should she try to maneuver herself into a comfortable position or just release the tension on the suit and hope that she landed upright?

As if Asher had read her mind, she stepped up beside her. "Here, I think you need a hand," she murmured.

Tarris kept her mouth firmly shut and accepted the help. She put her arm over Asher's shoulder and tapped the tabs in order to have one of her legs partially support her weight as it bent to allow her to descend. Asher's arm wound around her waist, and Tarris jumped when her hand hit a ticklish spot.

"I'll have to keep that in mind," Asher said, then chuckled.

About six inches from the ground, Tarris pushed the final button and the suit collapsed. As Asher straightened out her legs, they could hear the grating from the frame. "I think some of that muck got into the joints," Tarris said, but it wasn't really necessary to say so. She suspected Asher was able to figure that one out by herself.

"Will it take water if I wash it?" Asher unstrapped the frame from around Tarris's legs.

"I've walked in a deluge with it, if that's what you

mean." Tarris was content to let Asher continue. She leaned back on her hands and watched as Asher's hair fell forward, the wet dark strands partially hiding her eyes from view. Suddenly two circles of vibrant blue appeared within the hair, and Tarris realized she was being observed. Her gaze dropped to her legs, and she could feel the heat of an oncoming blush.

The sound of gentle laughter drew her gaze back to Asher. They looked at one another for a moment before Asher pulled the frame from beneath Tarris and walked over to the falling water. She stood outside the waterfall and briskly moved the joints of the suit within the cascading water.

Tarris pushed herself back a foot to take advantage of the wall. While Asher worked on her suit, she looked at her clothed legs. They weren't emaciated like others with her condition, for which she was thankful. The suit had been a Godsend to her. Not only did it give her a certain amount of independence, but it also kept her muscles toned. Now walking was only a matter of regaining strength.

Tarris grinned. Her desire to be whole again had been such a lifelong wish that she had seriously doubted it would ever happen. She touched her leg with her finger. When she felt it, she laughed out loud.

"You seem pretty happy with yourself."

Tarris jumped. She hadn't heard Asher come back. She was breaking another one of her cardinal rules.

Rule Eleven in her Survival Handbook: Always be aware of your surroundings.

"What's wrong?"

"Huh?" Tarris looked up at Asher's confused face.

"You were laughing and now you're scowling. What's the problem?" Asher put the suit down near the fire to dry.

"You're a distraction," Tarris said.

"And that's a bad thing?"

"It could be." Just as Asher was about to sit down, Tarris added, "Can we move the fire a little closer?" Asher stood there and waited, then Tarris spoke again, "Please?"

Asher used a length of wood to scrape the fire a little closer to the wall. Once she was happy with its position, she threw the wood onto the settling flames.

"Where did you find that?"

Asher looked at the wood she had just added. "Jerad told me you use it to make the fire last longer." She retrieved the suit and moved it the extra foot to the heat.

"I didn't think there would be any of that stuff lying around."

"Ah!" Asher reached into her pocket and took out her laser scalpel. "It seems that the rails sit on top of wood, so I just helped myself." She waved her scalpel in the air. "Damn, that stuff is heavy."

"Smart thinking," Tarris said.

Asher's smiled widened, and Tarris came to the conclusion that her statement was more than just words to Asher; it was a compliment.

"If that's all, mistress, may I sit down?" Asher was already in motion when she spoke.

Tarris waited until Asher was seated next to her. "It's too late now to ask for anything."

"What do you want now?" Asher's voice was tinged with annoyance.

"Nothing. I just wanted to see if you would do it."

Tarris wasn't prepared for Asher's body landing on top of hers. She reached blindly to hold onto the squirming body pinning her down, until Asher found the spot she had threatened to remember. "No! Oh no, no, no, no," Tarris pleaded. The urge to throw Asher off herself was enormous, and it took all her self-control not to do so.

Asher stopped for a minute and looked deeply into Tarris's eyes. "Rya? We're just playing, okay?" She then addressed Tarris. "Just so we don't have any confusion here." Asher's finger scraped across the ticklish spot, and she laughed as Tarris responded.

"Do you really want to do that?" Tarris mock threatened her.

Asher leaned in and pressed her lips against her prisoner's. It was long and lingering and spoke of more than just friends. When Asher pulled away, Tarris asked, "Why did you do that?"

"Because I wanted to." Asher slipped her hand from Tarris's side and moved downwards to where there had been no feeling. This was a whole new experience for both of them.

Tarris's breath caught in her throat as Asher's finger blazed a trail across her virgin skin. She could feel it. This was not mental compensation on her part. Her actual nerves felt the touch for the very first time. "What about Jerad?"

"He can get his own girlfriend," Asher joked. "Didn't you say he'd take cover until it was over?"

"That's what I'd do, but then I'm not Jerad."

A large clap of thunder broke overhead to emphasize the continuing storm above ground. "See? Even the sky is agreeing with me," Asher said as her hand continued to wander.

"Why?"

"Don't you want to know? Feel what I feel?"

"You know I do, but why me and why now?" Tarris berated herself for trying to discourage Asher from what she was doing. Asher had offered to answer the burning question that had been haunting her since her accident.

"What if this is the only chance we get? What if something happens, and one of us dies? Do you want to die not knowing what love is?"

"Love? Who said love?" Tarris asked with some trepidation.

"Making love has an element of love and passion, otherwise it's just having sex."

"And this... love." Tarris looked nervously at the woman who hovered over her. "Is that what you feel... for me?"

"Scared that you have to reciprocate, Tarris?" Asher's words held no hint of bitterness. "This experience is something I give to you freely, without any strings attached. I want you to experience it all, before it's too late."

Asher spoke as though she knew what the outcome of their lives would be, and Tarris didn't like it. It was the final rule in her book and one that had gotten her through her tortured life.

Rule Twelve in her Survival Handbook: Pessimism will ensure failure.

She had made up many other rules in her life, but they were passing promises fashioned for the circumstance at the time. These twelve rules she had tried to abide by to ensure her survival. Now she had invited Asher into her life, and she was in danger of laying herself open to attack from those she had so jealousy guarded herself against.

If this love was so inherently dangerous for those concerned, why get caught up in it in the first place? Tarris doubted that love was involved between them, but if it made the experience all the more pleasurable because of it, she could play the game and allow Asher her dreams.

As Tarris's mind contemplated her questions and doubts, Asher hadn't been idle. The clasps down the front of Tarris's jump suit popped one by one, revealing pale flesh a piece at a time to an inquisitive hand. That same hand roamed the unclaimed territory and found an ignored nipple ripe for teasing.

Tarris struggled to make sense of the mixture of emotions Asher stirred within her. Asher's hand continued the downward journey under her suit to the top of her thigh and through her hair. The touch was so light Tarris almost missed it, until Asher found her.

Tarris's hand came down on top of Asher's. "Wait," she said nervously before she looked around. "I... I don't..."

"Shhh." Asher's finger covered Tarris's lips. "It's the right time. Can you sit up?"

Tarris's abdominal muscles stood out in vivid relief as she lifted herself to sit without using her hands. "Now what?"

"Ah... errr..." Asher babbled. She stared at Tarris's impressive six-pack. "Take... errr... Pull down your suit," she finally managed to get out.

Tarris struggled with the suit, and when Asher began to help her, she figured she wasn't undressing fast enough.

She moved her hand to cover her colostomy bag, but Asher pulled it away.

"Don't do that," she whispered. "It's a part of you. It's not ugly." She leaned down and kissed the skin above where the bag sat. "Besides, we'll soon have that removed once we can get your urinary system working again."

"We?"

"It's not really my area of expertise, but I know a few people who will help." Asher moved back up to Tarris's lips and kissed her. "You don't think I'm going to let you go through this all alone, do you?"

"I... I don't know. I thought—"

"I know what you thought, Tarris Waite. You thought as soon as this is all over I'm leaving you. Haven't you got it through your thick head yet? You're stuck with me from now on."

"I am?" A jolt ran through Tarris at the news. The excitement she felt would soon make her dizzy, but she was already dizzy enough from Asher's statement. She wanted to stay.

Tarris grabbed Asher by the hair and dragged her down to kiss her roughly. She was on a high, physically and emotionally, and she wanted more. She put her fear aside and allowed Asher to show her the wonders of making love.

As they kissed, Asher's hand slid down Tarris's torso and through her hair. With gentle insistence, her fingers stimulated Tarris while her mouth latched onto Tarris's throat.

Tarris wasn't quite sure what to make of the feeling. The sensation wasn't unpleasant by any means, but the whole thing was so out of her range of experience that she was afraid she'd make a fool of herself.

Asher's lips found the pulse point at the base of Tarris's throat and laved it constantly until her breathing became labored. Without conscious thought, Tarris moved her legs slightly apart to give Asher more room.

Rya shifted within her restlessly, and Tarris understood that feeling. She wanted to move, to cry, and to beg for the ache within her to go somewhere or do something. She didn't know what she wanted, but she wanted it all.

Asher moved and Tarris nearly cried out when the hand that had been giving her so much pleasure—and frustration—was removed. But it was only for a moment. Asher insinuated her leg between Tarris's, and the hand that had so tormented her returned with increasing pressure.

Tarris placed her hands on either side of Asher's head and pulled her down for another kiss. This time she nipped, she tasted, and she explored. She allowed her instincts to drive her body to find that moment she had experienced earlier through Asher. She wanted her own explosion, and to see the stars behind her own eyelids. She wanted to be so totally consumed that she didn't care if she died a second after it.

The sensation swelled within her, doubled and tripled by Asher's own emotions transmitted to her by Rya. It was different this time, and yet it was the same, made even more tumultuous with her own skin, bone, and muscle finally able to feel what had only been in her head and in her heart. With Rya's help, Tarris felt their two heartbeats go wildly out of control, to mirror the wild abandonment she felt. "Ash," she whispered, "oh, Ash."

Tarris's head spun. Adrenaline flowed through her like a heady synth wine. It was intoxicating in the extreme and stirred feelings that had been long dormant. She had always considered her libido to be her nemesis, a beast to be harnessed and beaten back into the dark recesses of her mind. The beast had no place in her life, and she was better off without it. But Asher had awakened it, breaking the chains that had kept it prisoner all these years, and Tarris didn't want to stop it.

She was unable to deny herself. Her hands were already in motion, skimming over the fevered body lying on top of her. Had she asked for more than Asher was prepared to give?

A warm sigh escaped Asher's lips, and she smiled. Tarris's hands moved with greater purpose to knead the muscle underneath Asher's soft skin. Her passion flared to life demanding more. Tarris raised her head and captured Asher's lips, nipping the skin roughly. Asher responded enthusiastically and stirred the flames of her desire.

Images appeared in her mind, but Tarris wasn't sure of the source. Was it Asher making known her wishes, or was it the dreams from so long ago showing her the way? In either case, she would use the pictures as her map for pleasing Asher. She had been the recipient of Asher's love, and now she wished to give it back.

Tarris paused. Was this what love was? Was it the giving and receiving of this ultimate gift with someone who made that gift so special? She had never associated her secret desires with love before because they came in the night when she was at her most vulnerable. But why were the images the same? Was this all part of her libido's plan to show Asher what her lover was really like? That she harbored thoughts that weren't for the likes of her?

While her mind had one idea, her emotions had another

and had already manipulated Tarris's hands to roll Asher over to the ground. She rested her weight on her left forearm while her right hand snaked down Asher's sweaty body. When Asher's breathing hitched, she said, "This is what you want, huh?"

Asher nodded her head.

"Do you want more?" Tarris was unable to stop the words.

When Asher reached to touch her cheek, Tarris drove her fingers into Asher's warmth to seek that inner sweetness. Asher moaned. When Tarris's thigh replaced her fingers, Asher moaned again. "No," she breathed.

"No?" Tarris laughed and pushed her fingers in once more, this time using her thigh to add force to the intrusion. "No more?"

"No. I mean yes. Yes. More!" Asher pleaded.

This wasn't supposed to happen like this. But Tarris couldn't stop it. She had lost control of her passion. It had filled her mind with scenarios, dreams from long forgotten times when she still screamed at the world about the injustice of her accident. She had wanted to know what she would be missing in the years to come and tortured herself with images of sex in all its forms. Now she was being tormented with the secret fantasies that had stayed with her all these years.

"Do you feel me inside you?" Another image came to mind where her fingers had been substituted for something more appropriate. Tarris couldn't help the surge of passion that flooded her, unaware of her own physical response to the sordid images that flashed across her mind's eye. A deep chuckle escaped her lips as her hand stilled.

Asher shifted underneath her. "God, Tarris! Not now!"

Her fingers dug into Tarris's arm.

"I want to feel that," Tarris whispered as her fingers returned to the warm haven of Asher's body, "to feel you inside sliding against my skin." Asher whimpered again.

Tarris's words invoked a mental image. The sensation was unbelievable, and coupled with the visual image, her libido rose with Asher's anguished gasps. Tarris felt Asher's response down to her very soul.

Tarris could no longer ignore her feelings any more than she could stop breathing. Her thumb circled Asher's small bundle of nerves begging for attention. The scene played out in her head and came to such a tumultuous conclusion that Tarris didn't hear either of them cry out. It took several moments for her to realize where her fingers were or that her hand was wet.

"How... how did you do that?" Asher's voice was filled with wonder. "You've got to remember that move." Asher breathed heavily. She smiled up at Tarris. "You do realize that your legs moved."

"They did?" Tarris looked down at the limbs in question. "But how?"

"Maybe you had some help."

"Maybe."

Asher meant Rya, but Tarris knew better. Her inner urges had flexed their muscle and showed her how much of a slave she really was to her own passion. "Let's get some rest." Tarris shifted her weight to one side and nestled her body next to Asher. She grabbed the blanket and pulled it over their satiated bodies.

"What about Jerad?" Asher mumbled as she relaxed.

"We'll go and find him when the rain stops." Tarris hoped that the search would be enough of a diversion to stop Asher asking questions that she wasn't ready to answer.

Chapter 10

Rya had been restless while her sister's body twisted and turned. She could feel the heat without the need to expand her consciousness. It had a familiar flavor to it, one that she had briefly touched in Asher. After her initial reticence, Rya wanted that experience again. It called to her and demanded her presence, and she couldn't stop herself from answering that call. Her fears were somewhat allayed by the fact that it was Tarris's body that stimulated her need to find the light. Tarris had always been a comfort, a source of joy, and her home. Not that she had been able to articulate those emotions before her exposure to Asher, but now there was eloquence to the pictures and emotions attached to each and every word she thought.

Her sister was lost in the moment, and Rya took the chance to find the need she so desperately wanted to assuage. It gnawed at her, driving her newly awakened senses to distraction until it became an obsession. Once she found what she was looking for, she latched onto it and suckled like a baby, in an effort to slake her thirst with the life-giving power Tarris offered her.

But to Rya it was incomplete. Something was missing in the mixture, something that had to be added to feed the hunger she so desperately wanted to satiate, and she knew where to find it. Without completely leaving Tarris, Rya bled through her sister's skin and muscle and sought out the feverish body above her. This time she entered Asher without fear and quickly found the wellspring that was her nirvana before it burnt out.

She understood that the blazing inferno that existed in these two bodies was fleeting, and she had little time to indulge herself in the heat and passion before its fury died down. She drank it, bathed in it, reveled in the blistering combustion of the two souls, and rose from those ashes like a phoenix. This was meant to be. Or at least that was Rya's opinion. Not that she had ever had an opinion before, but suddenly she felt she needed one.

Wistfully, she withdrew from Asher to settle back within Tarris to find that part of her sister she considered her home. The two women lay wrapped in each other's arms after it was all over.

Rya hadn't hesitated to leave Tarris without her consent, and she had finally made a decision on her own. She would grab their destiny in her own invisible hands.

Gently she extricated herself from the dozing Tarris and hovered momentarily over her before she moved toward the overhead grate and access to street level. She balked at the fading light, but it was more instinctual than any actual blinding on her part. The realization of her new power was still a matter of acceptance, and it took some prodding for her to proceed out into the light of day.

Drifting along the streets was a heady experience. Rya no longer needed to find the darker places of the lanes and byways she knew so well. Citizens were still going about their daily business, oblivious to her presence, and it pleased her. She was now truly free.

She turned her attention to her mission. She had walked this path before, in a different light to be sure, but a path she had touched previously. When her senses detected the familiar trail, she covered the remainder of her journey quickly and with purpose.

This time she entered the house without fear and took up position in a far corner of the room as Derille stood in front of his large communication screen to talk to the Prime. This was something that Tarris needed to know about, so Rya made sure that their connection was active.

"...such incompetence!" Prime Sholter yelled from the vid screen. "How did she escape?"

Derille held up a tiny box. "She found the tracker."

"That's impossible."

"And yet here it is, sir. It was covered in blood."

"If that were the case, she'd be lying next to it." The Prime's gaze flicked from side to side, as if he were silently having a conversation with someone off screen. "Did she go down?"

"The only path down led to a dead end and a drop of fifty feet," Derille said. "We lost two men to find that out."

"No matter," the Prime said and dismissed the loss. "So where did she go?"

"The second path led to an outlet two blocks away."

"Then why are you standing there? Get moving." Prime was about to terminate the connection when Derille spoke.

"Sir, we had that exit covered. She just... disappeared."

"Then find her..." Prime left the sentence unfinished.

"Or?"

"You know what I'm capable of."

Derille's face hardened. "Yes, Prime, I'm well aware of what you're capable of."

"I want her back alive… or dead," the Prime said with finality.

"And the mediprac?"

"No witnesses, Derille."

"But—"

"No witnesses." Prime stared straight ahead. "If she stumbles across the facility, the guards are ordered to shoot to kill. Is that understood?" The Prime leaned forward, and the screen went blank.

"Perfectly," Derille mumbled. He touched the remote, and another person came onto the screen. "Tell the perimeter guards to be on the lookout for two women. They are to be shot on sight."

Rya waited a moment longer to watch the Administrator's reaction after he terminated the call. He inhaled deeply and let the air bleed out between his pursed lips. He was not a happy man.

You are safe for the moment, sister. It pleased Rya that Tarris had some peace, even if it was only for a few hours.

This was foolish, Rya.

This time Rya understood the nuance in Tarris's voice. It was not a remonstration but a show of concern. *But now we know what they know.*

Hmmm. What is this facility the Prime talks of? Rya felt Tarris's confusion and concern. *Never mind. Please come home.*

Please. Rya rejoiced at hearing the word, although she wasn't sure why she should feel the simple satisfaction from a single word. *As you wish, sister.*

With one final glance, Rya left Derille's house to seek

her own safe haven within Tarris.

"What?"

Asher's voice brought Tarris's attention back to the train station. "It seems we're safe, at least for now."

"You seem so sure of that."

"Rya visited one of them, a member of the Council, and caught the end of a conversation about us," Tarris said. "They think we're above ground somewhere." Tarris debated whether to tell Asher everything. It was probably wise not to hide anything at this point. "We have to be extra careful from now on. The guards have orders to shoot to kill."

Asher blinked a couple of times while Tarris waited patiently for her reaction. "So." She popped another piece of freeze-dried fruit into her mouth.

"So," Tarris repeated. She continued to clean her suit. Conversation had been practically nonexistent from the moment they both woke up. Tarris had sat there sullenly and worked diligently to get her suit back to working order, while Asher took some sustenance.

"Now do you wish you'd never met me?" Tarris asked the question again. It seemed like forever since the question had been raised. But their lives were on the line, and Tarris wouldn't blame Asher for leaving the whole mess behind her.

"Imagine the story I'll be able to tell when this is all over."

"That's not an answer," Tarris said.

"Does it matter what the answer is?"

"It's just a matter of saying yes or no. How hard can it be?"

"Harder than you think, my dear Tarris." Asher smiled sweetly at her. She lifted a hand to caress Tarris's cheek. "Some things you're not ready to hear."

"Stop treating me like a child," Tarris said, but she stopped short of slapping Asher's hand away. She leaned into the touch and eagerly absorbed the emotion behind the action.

"But in some ways you are still a child, Tarris. You're only learning things now that the rest of us have known for many years." Asher slid her finger to Tarris's lips. "Now before you speak, listen to me. I'm not pointing out your faults or belittling you. You've been given a gift that none of us can begin to imagine the depth of. Don't be in such a hurry to know it all."

"And you're hijacking the conversation, Asher. You still haven't answered my question. Do wish you had never met me?" Tarris didn't know why she was tormenting herself this way. Why couldn't she let sleeping dogs lie?

"Now? No. And before you ask, I'll tell you why. You have bullied, cajoled, and argued with me to help you. Sometimes you can be a real pain in the ass."

"Geez, thanks."

"But you wormed your way into my heart, Tarris Waite. I care for you, more than you'll ever know." Asher dropped her hand. "And that's all I'll say for now."

"Stop playing word games with me." Tarris put down the frame and lifted herself onto her palms. She winced as she clumsily shifted herself away from Asher. "Nobody ever says what they mean. Derille. Darmen. You." She used her abdominal muscles to steady herself while she reached for her clothes and wrestled with the material. "Shit!" She threw the jumpsuit to the ground in disgust.

"Here, let me." Asher moved next to her and reached for the discarded jumpsuit. Methodically she pulled the sleeves out and reversed the legs before she presented the suit to Tarris. "Do you want me to help you?" she asked tentatively.

"Why? Don't think I can do it myself? Heaven forbid that I've taken care of myself for the last sixteen years without anyone's help."

"Tarris." Asher tapped her shoulder. "What's wrong with you?"

"This is your chance to get as far away from me as possible before I get you killed."

"Is this what it's all about? You're afraid for my life?"

"Of course." But Tarris spoke a little too quickly.

Asher rose to her knees and spread out Tarris's suit, reaching down to feed the material along her legs. She waited for Tarris to lift herself off the ground with her powerful arms before she slid the material over her ass and up to her waist. Asher looked up from her position at Tarris's waist and gazed intently. "And that's it?" When Tarris nodded, Asher continued. "You are such a hypocrite. You're playing word games with me right now."

Tarris snatched her suit out of Asher's hands and shoved her arms into the sleeves roughly. "Everyone who stays with me ends up getting hurt."

"You mean everyone who loves you ends up getting hurt."

"That's what I said," Tarris said defensively.

"No, you didn't. Why is it so hard for you to say 'love'?"

"Because it's not a word in my vocabulary, okay? I can't afford to have someone love me."

"Or for you to love someone back. That's it, isn't it? You're afraid to love me." Asher stood up and reached for her clothes. She dressed quickly in an effort to counter the chill in the air.

"I'm afraid of hurting you, Ash."

"What happened before… it's all right, Tarris. It's what passion is all about, hon. Expressing yourself like that. Don't be afraid of it. Embrace it."

"Not like that," Tarris said. "Not ever like that."

"What' going on inside your head?"

"I was too rough. It's not supposed to happen like that."

"Did you hear me complaining? Passion comes in all forms, Tarris. Don't try to hide from it."

"But I have to. It… it…"

"Scares you? You just can't say it, can you?"

"Fine. It scares me, and it should scare you." Tarris shifted uncomfortably. "We have to get moving."

"We're not moving from here until we sort this out."

"Why is it so important for you to know?" Tarris asked in a defiant tone.

"Because it concerns you." Asher looked at her.

"Something's always been there, hiding away until it sees a chance to make me think things."

"What sort of things?"

"Things I have no use for."

"You mean sexual things." Tarris hung her head. "Things you want to experience and feel. Things that get you excited."

"Yes." Tarris said the word so softly that Asher barely heard it.

"Well, I'd call that a vivid imagination, but it certainly

isn't something to be feared." Tarris didn't look convinced. "Obviously you've been thinking about sex a lot, despite what you told me before. I think you've held yourself in check very well for sixteen years in limbo. If it were me, I'd probably still be ravishing you."

Tarris let out a small chuckle.

"That's better. Tarris, honey, it's nothing to fear, all right? It's just your libido stretching its mental muscles. It wants action, and you're trying to hold it back."

"But—"

"Did you hear me complaining? In fact, I think I did quite the opposite. I look forward to you fulfilling those imaginative thoughts of yours in the future." Asher winked at her and drew another smile from her.

"The future?"

"Unless you don't want me around anymore." The question was tentative, yet Asher said it in a voice that was anything but. She wanted Tarris to see she had made her mind up. She had answered her question. She was with Tarris to the end.

†

The water had receded enough for them to venture farther down the tunnel toward the next station. Tarris held the torch high above her head to light the way.

Asher was right. It would have been simpler to send Rya on this mission, but Tarris had two reasons not to. First, Rya was now at a point where she must be treated as more than a fetch-and-carry service. Rya had developed into a sentient being and had earned the right to be treated as such. Right? Tarris was trying very hard to convince herself that this was the prime reason for this foolish venture into the unknown, because the second reason was even more foolish and fraught with danger. She didn't want to spend any more time alone with Asher than was absolutely necessary, because she was scared of her own feelings toward her. She had seen the essence of her true nature, and despite Asher's assurances to the contrary, she wasn't sure she could handle it.

Tarris amended the word "scared." Scared wasn't a word she used often, and especially not when referring to herself. She was "concerned" or "troubled," but never scared. It implied cowardice, and she never thought of herself as a coward. After what she had gone through in the last sixteen years, she was sure no one else would use that word to describe her either.

Then what was it that concerned her about Asher? Was this ache around her heart Asher's doing? Was this need to protect her something more than just concern?

You rationalize things too much, sister, Rya said.

Tarris sighed. She couldn't even console herself in private.

The darkness receded, and another platform came into view.

"Hello? Jerad?" Asher's voice echoed around the empty space without an answer. "Stay here and I'll check it out." She clambered up onto the platform before Tarris had a chance to even argue the point. While she watched Asher move about the platform, she rested her chin on her forearms and leaned against the platform edge.

"No luck?" Tarris called.

"Well, he's not here." Asher said. There was a rattle of metal. "The exits are all blocked off. He didn't leave this way." Asher reappeared from around a corner. "I did find this, though." She handed over a discarded bottle.

"Someone's been through here recently. This type of bottle heater wasn't invented until about nine years ago."

"Maybe it was Jerad."

"I don't think so. I don't normally carry this type of bottle. Besides..." Tarris hesitated and rummaged through her backpack. "No, I only grabbed two when we left and they're here."

"Then this means..."

"Yes, it does, and all the more reason we need to find Jerad."

Tarris waited for Asher to come and sit down on the edge. She placed her hands around Asher's tiny waist and effortlessly lifted her down to the rail tracks. Asher's stunned expression made her smile. It was one of the few times her body's limitations had caused that reaction. "Come on." She extended her hand in invitation and led Asher back into the darkness at the far end of the platform.

They had passed through another three platform areas with the same result. The exits were blocked, and Jerad was nowhere to be seen.

"What do we do now?"

Tarris could see that Asher was concerned. "We can't go back, and there's no other way out. We have to keep going forward and hope we meet up with Jerad."

"And if we don't?"

Tarris didn't want to think about it because it meant the kid had run out on them and left them to wander around in the dark. Tarris had always thought she was a good judge of character, despite her decision on Derille. She put that down to an aberration. If she was wrong about Jerad, did that also mean he would turn them in? The chance for a big reward would certainly be tempting.

"I just hope he got out and is hiding away somewhere. If they find him, he could end up like his parents."

Tarris felt Asher's shiver through her fingers.

"So for now," Tarris continued, "we go forward and hope to find a way out of here." She led the way and used the light from the torch to pick her way through the debris in the tunnel. In fact, this was their second torch. The first one had burned down to a stump and left Tarris fumbling around for a quick replacement.

"So what does Rya think about this gung-ho attitude of yours?" Asher called from behind.

"She's all for it."

That's not what I said. Rya stated. *My way is a lot safer.*

The conversation echoed along the long empty tunnel. The only other sounds were the dripping of water into a puddle and a low, audible scratching. They carefully stepped along the tunnel, moving from one wooden piece to the next between the metal rails. Tarris pulled up short, and Asher ran into the back of her. "What are you—?" Asher's words were cut short when Tarris held up her hand to signal stop.

Voices could be heard far-off. "Shhh," Tarris whispered.

"Well, d'uh…" Asher followed in Tarris's footsteps. The ground was uneven, and they had to carefully watch where they placed their feet.

The blackness started to fade and turn to gray with every step closer to the voices. Tarris disposed of the torch in a nearby puddle of water. She moved over to one side to hug the tunnel wall. She expected Asher to follow close behind, and she didn't waste her time confirming the fact.

"Is this why Jerad didn't come back?" Asher said in a low voice.

"Uh-huh." Tarris suspected this was the "facility," as the Prime put it. She was about to find out why the facility was so important. At that precise moment, her suit squeaked. This was not good.

"I thought you said you cleaned that thing."

"Shhh," Tarris hissed. She thought she had, too, but Asher had broken her concentration and left her fragmented. No wonder she missed a spot or two.

"What's going on?"

"You just can't stop talking, can you?" Tarris turned and faced Asher and spoke a little louder than she wanted to.

"I'm just asking a question."

"At the wrong time."

A strange voice said, "Oh, I wouldn't say that."

"Shit!" Tarris spat out.

"You got that right." The guard sounded amused. "Now, move it." He waved his weapon in front of them.

Do you want me to take care of him, sister? Rya asked with concern.

Not yet, Rya. Let's see what we can find out first. Tarris would take the opportunity presented to her. She hoped she could get them out of the situation they were in if the need arose.

"Now look what you've done," Asher said.

"Me? I wasn't the one asking all the questions."

"Shut up, both of you." The guard shoved the muzzle of his gun in Asher's back and pushed hard.

But…

It's all part of the plan, Rya.

Tarris, this is either incredibly bold or monumentally stupid.

When did you develop a vocabulary?

Pretty neat, huh?

Yeah, Tarris said. *Neat.*

So you're going ahead with this plan when I can easily solve this for you?

Tarris gulped heavily. She wasn't sure whether it was her guilt that made the statement sound like she was a useless tagalong or whether Rya had developed a case of overconfidence. *Yeah.* Tarris inwardly sighed. *Something like that.*

As they approached the next platform, two guards stood on the edge and peered down at them, their weapons drawn and ready. At the far end, Tarris caught a glimpse of two more guards carrying what looked like a dead body between them. A disintegration booth had been set up in the corner of the back wall. When the guards reached the booth, they tossed the corpse into the beam. It sizzled and crackled for a moment, lighting up the dim space with a blinding flash, before the booth fell silent. No remnant was left. The former human being had been obliterated.

"Who was that?" Asher murmured.

"Some poor homeless person from the Sweeps." Tarris made an educated guess, but she knew she was right.

"Move it." The guard prodded Tarris in the side.

"Which way?"

"Up," he answered and waved his gun in that direction.

"Then I'll need help."

The three guards laughed.

"It's true," Asher said. "She'll need help to get up onto the platform."

"Then you help her," the first guard said with finality.

Tarris laced her fingers together and waited for Asher to put her foot into the stirrup. Once she was safely up, Asher reached down with her hand. "I don't know if this'll work, but I'll try."

Tarris grabbed the offered arm and tried to lift herself. Her arm and back muscles strained as she struggled to lift her own weight by sheer strength. It didn't take long for her to realize that something more was needed.

"What's the matter with you?" the guard on the railway track asked.

"Can't you see she's wearing a walking frame, you idiot!" Asher snapped. "She's not going to get up here anytime soon without some help."

The guard placed his weapon on the platform next to one of the other guards, who kicked it backwards and out of reach. They trained their sights on the two women as the guard lifted Tarris from below, and with Asher's help, she managed to get onto the upper level. Asher moved behind, placed her hands under Tarris's armpits, and lifted until she could get her buckled legs underneath her. The frame protested loudly as Tarris activated it to move into an upright position, the servos grinding against the grains of dirt still within the rods. Asher steadied her as Tarris slowly rose. One of her arms inadvertently brushed against the base of Tarris's scalp and the hidden tab.

Tarris felt the movement before she saw it. The guards took a few steps backward as the color drained from her hair to reveal her true identity. "That's right, fellas," she growled. "Be afraid, very afraid." However, having just fumbled around to get onto the platform had, at least in Tarris's mind, destroyed the myth that surrounded her identity.

Find the boy, Tarris stated.

But—

Just find the boy then return here. I want to make sure he's not in any danger.

As you wish, sister.

There was no gentle exit by Rya this time. In a show of strength to her enemies, Tarris told her to make it dramatic. Discarded waste stirred in the whirlwind of air that traveled along the platform like a mini tornado. *Nice one, sister*, Tarris said as Rya slid off the platform and into the darkness at the other end.

They will not underestimate us again. The thought faded, as did the breeze.

The three guards pointed their shaking guns at the two women, each one glancing at the others, obviously nervous. "D... D... Don't move." But the order was less than authoritative.

Asher looked at Tarris. "What's wrong with this picture?"

She was right. They should have been shot on sight. "I'd say someone issued a new order."

"Control, this is Team Alpha Three D." The third guard spoke in the direction of his shoulder and the implanted microphone in his uniform. "We've caught the two women you were asking about. What do you want us to do with them?"

"Bring them in." The reply could be heard clearly. It gave the guards approval to take them through the border security and into the heart of the operation. As far as Tarris was concerned, everything was going along nicely.

Her hands were manacled behind her back with plastic strips, as were Asher's. Tarris knew they were unbreakable. They were the standard equipment used in law enforcement, and it was another reminder of who the enemy was here. The State. Or at least the Prime. He was the law, and unless someone acted now, he would extend the mandate of his brand of law until no one would be able to stop him.

"Let's move it." A rifle butt waved toward the far end of the platform. "Stay four steps ahead and two feet apart. We want to see both of you at all times."

As they approached their destination, Asher mumbled. "And what's the plan?"

"I'm working on it." Tarris stared forward. The roof slid away to reveal the floor above. It allowed access to above ground and what Tarris suspected was "the facility." The immediate area was flooded with artificial light.

"Well, well, I was beginning to wonder whether you were too stupid to find this place."

Tarris let her head fall back and groaned. This was the last person she wanted to see right now.

Chapter 11

"Corman."

"You're not surprised?" he asked.

"I suppose I'm not." Tarris stumbled up the stairs. Her secured hands made it impossible to make adjustments to the operation of her suit. Corman, as usual, seemed amused by her discomfort.

"And is this the slut you've hooked up with?" he sneered.

"I wouldn't go calling the leader of your group a slut, soldier," Asher retorted, earning a smile from Tarris.

He growled at her, but Asher stood firm. "And I assumed you'd had your distemper shots. Silly me."

This time Tarris laughed out loud. "Where were you when I needed a witty reply?"

"Probably taking out someone's liver," Asher said.

"Stop it, both of you!" Corman yelled.

"Or what, Corman? We're dead one way or the other anyway." In her peripheral vision, Tarris saw Asher cringe when she said the word "dead."

"But how you die is up to me," he said a little bit too happily.

"It's up to the Prime, *Trooper*."

Tarris didn't bother to check who was talking. She

knew that voice. "Maken," she said in a flat tone.

"You should have stayed in your apartment, Tarris," Derille said. "Get out of the way, Corman. Let her step up."

Reluctantly, Corman moved back to give them room to come up the stairs. The guard behind them again prodded them. "Move it."

Tarris continued to the top step, her gait far from smooth.

"You look like one of those pathetic drunks in the Sweeps," Corman muttered as she finally stepped onto the floor above the platform.

"You should know, Corman," Tarris said and earned a punch to the jaw for her trouble. She chuckled at him and absorbed another punch to the cheek.

"Stop it, Corman!" Derille yelled. "You have no right—"

"I have every right! I've had to put up with this bitch for years. I've earned that right, Administrator." Corman's white eyes burned with an inner fire.

"I think he needs a collar, Maken," Tarris said. "If you don't get him under control... he'll destroy you." She could feel the heat from the puffiness around her cheek that she just knew was there.

"Where are we?" Asher asked as she stepped up beside Tarris.

"You've got to be kidding. You expect me to tell you—" Derille rolled his eyes, and Tarris interrupted him.

"What does it matter?" she asked, "We're going to die anyway."

"She's got that right," Corman said. "I'll personally see to that. We're in The Battery."

Tarris looked him squarely in the eye. "You know

what your problem is? You've got a loud mouth." She had heard that name before, but where? Jerad came to mind, and she remembered. At Jacksters, when she was trying to get a new identity, the kid had sent the man in the black coat to The Battery. Somehow they had circled around in the tunnels and ended back where they had entered them.

When Corman's fist lifted for another strike, Derille yelled, "Trooper Corman! If you disobey one more order, I'll see to it personally that you are incarcerated for the rest of your life with the light permanently on. Am I understood?" Corman jerked forward, and Derille again yelled, "Trooper! Stand down!" The volume of his voice rattled a nearby cup.

Begrudgingly, Corman backed up a few steps, his hand still in a fist by his side. Tarris was aware that if he could have killed her with a look, she would already be dead. His glare was pure evil, indicating in one moment of clarity that her life was already forfeit and it was only a matter of time before he would make her pay for his embarrassment.

"I'd tell her everything if I were you, Maken," Tarris said with a smile, "because she won't let the matter drop until she knows."

"I don't—" Asher started to say.

"Oh, yes you do. You pester and pester until you get what you want." But Tarris said it with affection in her voice.

"And what's so funny?" Asher asked.

Tarris knew Asher would stand there with her hands on her hips if her hands weren't tied behind her back. "Nothing. I think it's just too damned cute, that's all."

"Oh, excuse me while I puke," Corman said.

"Go right ahead, Corman. With some luck you'll choke

on it."

"You bitch!" Corman closed the gap of a few feet in an instant, threw himself at Tarris, and knocked her to the ground. He wrapped his fingers around her throat and squeezed her windpipe.

As the guards tried to pull him off her, his grip tightened even more. The contact was only broken when four of them pulled as one to separate them.

"Why do you keep doing that?" Asher asked.

Tarris gasped for air, but it didn't stop a grin on her face. "Because I can." She had held her anger in check for too long. It felt good to finally tell Corman what she really thought of him. Two guards helped her to her feet.

"Trooper," Derille stood in front of her and said, "you live dangerously by taunting him like that. Despite what I say, he is favored by the Prime."

"Figures," Tarris muttered. "And you know what's really scary? Both you and the Prime know your threats are hollow. Corman can do what he likes, and he knows it."

"I do what I can." Derille turned and walked away. "Bring them." She could see he fully expected them to walk with him, because he didn't stop and wait. Instead he continued to walk to a door on the far side of the floor.

Sister, are you all right?

Tarris acknowledged Rya's unspoken words. *I'm fine. Just having some fun.* It wasn't exactly fun, but it was satisfying nonetheless. *What of Jerad?*

He's untouched for now. He resides with others of his kind. Do you wish me to return?

As much as Tarris wanted the comfort of Rya inside her, she stopped her shadow. *Not yet. I want them to think I'm helpless.* Strangely, Rya remained silent. Tarris knew what she would automatically say, but Rya didn't say it. Was her shadow being tactful by not pointing out she was helpless without her? *They don't know about your new abilities. Let's keep it that way for now. Protect Jerad, but keep close in case things change for the worse.*

As you wish, sister.

Suddenly, Tarris had an odd thought. If Rya had said nothing now to save Tarris's feelings, could she trust her implicitly to tell her everything in the future? Had this changed how they interacted from now on? No, that wouldn't change. They had been through too much together for that to change. In things that mattered, there would always be the complete truth.

Then again, maybe she had imagined it all in her head. Maybe she made more out of the omission than need be. It was all blown out of proportion because of the chance of being killed. Or maybe it was the thought that Rya didn't need her anymore.

You've been a good friend, Rya.

The words tumbled around in her head.

And you will always be my home, sister.

Tarris felt a pang of guilt for even thinking such trivial thoughts. How could she doubt Rya's sincerity?

"Take the mediprac and put her with the others," Derille said.

Corman bristled but did as he was told. He signaled to two of the guards to remove Asher. "Say goodbye, bitch," he growled.

"Goodbye, bastard," Asher said to Corman.

He was ready to strike again, but Derille stepped in. "Corman! Just do as you're told."

Corman motioned the guards toward Asher and stood

back. He watched with undisguised glee as she was led away. "I think I'll move her up on the list," he said.

Tarris glared at him but didn't give him the satisfaction of asking the question.

"Not interested in knowing what will happen to her?"

"Why bother?" Tarris said wearily. She was so sick of Corman's mind games.

"Obviously she doesn't mean as much to you as you do to her." He shrugged his shoulders. "Oh well."

"Go harass a little old man, Trooper," Derille ordered. "You've worn out your welcome here." When Corman was gone, he said, "Why do you taunt him like that? Especially in the position you're in?"

"Because I'm damned well sick of his games, Administrator. He's a real pain in the ass and enjoys my discomfort. If I can give a little back then that's a point for me."

"Sit." He extended his hand in invitation for Tarris to perch herself on a nearby chair. "You've really got yourself into deep shit here, Waite."

"No kidding?"

"Stop it! You should have stayed put, and everything would be all right."

"All right? You've been spying on me. Everything you told me was a lie. How can that be all right?"

"I'm sorry about that."

"That's a laugh." Tarris couldn't hide the sarcasm in her voice.

"You saved those most precious to me," Derille said. "I haven't forgotten that."

"And yet that didn't stop you from taking away something very precious to me. My privacy."

Derille paced back and forth. "It was out of my hands, Tarris. The Prime wanted you kept under surveillance. I had no choice."

"There's always a choice, Administrator. I thought I proved that. If it bothered you so much, you could have said no."

"No one says no to the Prime, Tarris. If you had given it time, you would have come to discover that point. But now…"

"Now. Yes now. I suppose that's it then." Tarris hesitated. "So what will happen to Asher?"

"The mediprac? She'll be used for experimentation."

"What experimentation?"

"That shouldn't concern you right now. What you should be worried about is what's going to happen to you."

Derille was right, but Tarris was more interested in Asher's life than her own. She sensed the guards around her shifting nervously, as if they were expecting her to react.

"She's no threat," Derille told them, "at least not while the light's on. Keep your distance and make sure the light remains on at all times."

"Administrator!" a technician yelled from across the room. "Call for you."

"Stay alert," he said as a final order. He walked across the floor to the small office on the far side. He disappeared through the sliding door to the office behind it.

An older man, obviously the leader of the guards, talked to her. "Not one move. We see that shadow of yours, and the others die. Got that?"

Tarris watched his hand lower to a button on his belt and assumed it to be some sort of alarm. She nodded her agreement. Rya couldn't be in two places at one time, so

Tarris was on her own.

Protect Asher and the boy.

But, sister…

No, Rya. This is an order, not a request. Keep them safe for me. Please.

There was another hesitation from her warrior. *All right, sister. If that's your wish.*

That is my wish, my dear friend. I want them safe.

Derille emerged from the room and stood outside the door. A couple of minutes later, Corman joined him and they talked. Both of them approached her, Derille deep in thought and Corman with an evil grin on his lips. It was not promising.

"I'm needed at the Council chambers. Corman will escort you back to the Corps headquarters. One false move on your part, and they will die. Understood?"

Tarris so wanted to answer with a smart-ass comment but instead settled for a nod. For now, she would have to follow their orders.

"Prick," Corman muttered as they both watched the Administrator leave. Tarris kept her mouth shut. She didn't want to agree with her mortal enemy.

Corman removed his weapon and butted her in the chest with it. "Now you're mine," he said and grinned wickedly at her.

"Derille said 'hands off,'" Tarris reminded him.

"That he did," he said enigmatically. "Move it." He waved his pistol toward a far door.

Tarris looked in the direction he indicated then glared at him.

"Don't you want to know what's going to happen to your bitch girlfriend?"

It couldn't be good. Corman took too much enjoyment in tormenting her with the possibilities. "I'm sure you can tell me."

"Aww, come on, Waite. Can you look me in the eye and say you don't care? I'm disappointed." The smile dropped from his face. "Move it."

"I'll need my hands to do that, Corman."

He looked around. Half a dozen armed guards watched her every move, and all the lights were on in the large open space. He nodded at the closest guard. "Do it."

She felt the manacles loosen around her wrists.

"Don't even think about it," Corman said. "One false move from you, and the mediprac dies." His finger hovered over an alarm switch on his belt.

Tarris slowly and carefully moved her arms to the front of her body. As soon as her wrists were close enough together, the manacles were refastened.

"Now, move it."

Whether she liked it or not, Corman was going to show her Asher's fate. She activated the suit and was glad to be able to manipulate it. Trying to climb the stairs without the legs locked down was hard work, and her abdominal muscles ached badly from the strain. Now she knew what it felt like to push the walking aid in a direction it didn't want to go.

Her fingers brushed over the tabs, and her suit smoothly moved her across the floor to the door on the other side. Corman remained a few steps behind her, intent on her every move. She looked over her shoulder at him. He had one hand hooked in his belt, while his ever-present finger hovered over the button that would sign Asher's death warrant.

"Open it," he said. One of the guards obliged him, and the door slid silently into the wall cavity.

Tarris tapped the tab and nimbly stepped through the door to a room that looked suspiciously like a laboratory, or what she imagined to be a laboratory. Strapped to one of the tables was, she assumed, a homeless woman. Her tattered clothes and grimy face gave Tarris the clues to make the assumption. Strapped to the wall was another derelict, a man this time, and a young boy was next to him. Tarris's heartbeat sped up. Was it Jerad? Quick observation allayed her fears. The child was about the same height and age, but it wasn't him.

"So?" she asked without emotion.

"Watch."

The woman on the table was injected with some sort of mixture, and the scientist backed away quickly. Tarris glanced at Corman and saw an almost demonic look in his eyes. Whatever was about to happen would be dramatic and unpleasant.

The woman started to twitch and escalated to what looked like a seizure. She strained and bucked under the restraints, her heaving body trying to break the straps that held her down. She moaned, screamed, growled, and dribbled over and over again as whatever she had been given overtook her senses. Slowly the jerking slowed down. It returned to twitching and finally ended in stillness and death.

The scientist moved to the prone figure and rested his fingers on her neck. "Subject number two seven nine. Failure." There was weariness in his voice as he recorded his findings.

"Two hundred and seventy-nine? You mean to tell me

you've killed two hundred and seventy-nine people with whatever you're trying to do here?"

"And counting." Corman giggled. "After the two on the wall, your mediprac whore will be next."

"That's barbaric."

"They're from the Sweeps. No one will notice they're gone."

Tarris had suspected as much. She tried to hide her abhorrence of the callous disregard for human life that Corman obviously enjoyed so much.

"And it's all your fault," he said.

Tarris bit her tongue. As much as she desperately wanted to know what it was all about, she knew Corman would tell her in good time. For now she wouldn't give him the satisfaction of asking. "Blow it out your ass, Corman," she snarled. "You're wasting your time trying to scare me, so just take me to HQ."

Corman seemed unperturbed with her outburst and sighed. "Come on then. Time's a-wasting." His comlink sounded, and Corman snatched at it. "What?" He fell silent for a moment then cut the connection.

"Is your master calling you?" Tarris didn't see the hand coming and took the brunt of it across her jaw. She lifted her bound hands and wiped away the blood. "Feel better?"

Corman's white eyes blazed at her, and his hands balled into fists. "The Prime wants to see you."

"Oh good."

"I wouldn't be so happy about that if I were you." Corman pushed Tarris hard, and she nearly toppled. "He's going to eat you for breakfast."

Chapter 12

Asher glanced at Tarris as she was led away. Her fate was sealed, and without Tarris's constant presence, she was terrified. Tarris could calm her fears and make her troubles seem a distant memory. While she figured that her life depended on how cooperative Tarris was, she also hoped that it wasn't at the expense of the greater good.

There was a nudge in her back from the guard behind her. "Move it," he growled.

An angry reply sat on her tongue, but she kept it to herself. She needed to stay alive for Tarris's sake. Despite what Tarris said, she knew she had to be there to guide her. Too much had happened between them for her contribution to be dismissed so readily.

Asher trudged after the lead guard, who led her down a long corridor to a side doorway. When she thought she had reached her destination, the door slid aside to reveal yet another corridor. This particular corridor was darker than the one she had just left. It seemed to set the scene for where she was going. Into the darkness to a place from which there was no return.

The third door on the right opened, and Asher was shoved inside. She stumbled over a pair of legs and fell to the floor. The light was gray in the room. Not complete darkness but more a muted light. She rolled over until she was upright and seated on the floor. She looked around at the dull expressions of her co-captives. It was a look of desolation and defeat, and one she was trying very hard not to emulate.

"So you got caught, too, huh?"

Asher knew that voice and was pleased to see that Jerad was still alive. "Yeah. We came looking for you." While that wasn't completely true, Asher wanted the kid to know he was missed.

"I didn't need your help," he said brazenly. "So where is she?"

"The boss has her."

"Who did she piss off?"

Asher scowled at him, but that didn't stop his smirk. "She doesn't want to be one of them anymore, and they don't like it."

"Figures." He sat down next to her.

"What I don't understand is why you're still with us. You got your ten credits and yet you stuck with us. Why?"

Jerad studied the other prisoners around him. "Why?" he repeated. "Maybe I figured I could get more money out of her. I know she's got more, because I saw it in the parcel."

"You could have easily stolen that while we were asleep. No, that's not it," Asher said.

"I know who she is. She would find me and kill me."

"Again, no. She didn't show you who she was until we were in your sleeping hole." She smiled at him. "You've got to do better than that." Jerad sat there and glared at her. "No, you saw her as your chance to get out of that world. She was the key to a better life."

"So?" he said defiantly.

"I'm not saying it was wrong, Jerad. I would have done the same thing. But I'm sure Trooper Waite would like to hear it from you when you see her." *If you see her...* "Do you know what's going on?"

"I dunno. They came and took two or three people, and I didn't see them again."

"Jerad? Honey? Is that you?"

"Momma?" The boy's body stiffened, and his head swiveled from side to side as he looked for the source of the voice.

A woman carrying a ladle and a large pot moved into view, closely followed by two guards. She put the pot on the floor and threw herself at the boy. "Oh God! I thought I wouldn't see you again." She began to cry.

"Momma?"

Asher could hear the dismay in his voice. All this time he had thought himself an orphan, and it was through his connection to Tarris that he found his mother. She would have to make sure to remind Tarris of one more good thing she had done with her life.

"Momma, I thought you were dead." Jerad clutched her tightly, as if she would disappear if he let go.

"Jerad. Honey." His mother looked over her shoulder at one of the guards. He nudged his fellow guard and left the cell. "Why are you here?"

"I came looking for you," he said and pulled away. He straightened up and wiped his face with his sleeve. "I knew I'd find you."

Asher didn't say a word and allowed Jerad to be the heroic boy looking for his mother. Whether that was what he had in mind when he stumbled upon her and Tarris, she might never know, unless Jerad told her the whole truth. Maybe it was all a rescue of circumstance.

"I hate to interrupt, but can we get out of here?" Asher hoped for a miracle.

"No one gets out," Jerad's mother said.

"And yet you're not a prisoner." Asher looked her straight in the eye and saw the shame. "Oh."

"Oh?" Jerad looked from Asher to his mother and back again. "What?"

"Nothing, honey. I made myself useful and saved myself, that's all."

"Would he help us?" Asher asked hopefully.

"Maybe. Maybe not. There's the other guard..." She left the sentence hanging.

"My name is Asher." Asher extended her hand in invitation.

"Calia." She took Asher's hand and shook it. "Thank you for looking after my son."

"It was more like he was looking after us."

"Us?" Calia looked at her son.

"A trooper," he said.

"You let a trooper know who you are? That was foolish, son."

"No! No, she's good, Momma. She'll help us."

"If she can help us," Asher murmured.

"Where is she?"

"The boss has her."

"Then she can't help us."

Asher sensed a stirring in the air. She closed her eyes to focus then smiled. Even in the muted light, Rya was nearby. "Oh, yes, she can," Asher whispered. *We have to get out of here.*

I will see what I can do, sister.

"She's a woman. What can one woman do?" Calia asked.

"She's also a trooper," Asher pointed out.

"That changes nothing. She's one female trooper against the rest of them."

"Don't underestimate her. I did. She is one extraordinary woman." And Asher knew that was true. The more time she spent in Tarris's company, the more she discovered about the woman who wanted to leave her past behind her. She was complicated, unpredictable, and totally unexpected. After her initial reticence, Tarris had totally blindsided her senses.

Asher waited for Rya's response, but there was none. What was she expecting? Rya to come in and wreak havoc? Nothing happened for a few minutes, so Asher sat down on the cold floor.

Jerad stood beside her and leaned against the wall. "Where is she? She hasn't left us behind, has she?"

Asher heard the almost wistful tone of his question. Had he developed a bit of a crush on Tarris? Not that she could blame him. She was pretty sure she had a crush on her as well. "Some things just take a bit of planning, that's all. Help is coming." Asher trusted it wasn't false hope she was selling. "Sit," she said. He slid down the wall to the floor next to her.

"What are you and you mother going to do once you're out of here?"

"Out of here," he said flatly, but Asher picked up the subtle signals Jerad gave. There was excitement, which Asher assumed was finding his mother alive. There was also a bit of doubt mixed with hope about a rescue. She suspected Jerad hadn't given much thought past those two questions.

Asher only had one question. When would she see Tarris again? She had seen a lot of sides to Tarris: a shy friend, a confident trooper, a hero, a lover whose confidence had grown in leaps and bounds and left her breathless, and a woman who had stolen her heart.

"Sure. Don't you think she has a plan?"

He looked silently at her, as if trying to find the lie inside. "Does she?"

"Sure she does. She wouldn't abandon us." Asher smiled.

As if her wish had been granted, the cell door opened. The two guards stepped inside, but their expressions said everything but control. They stumbled farther into the cell. Behind them were armed men, their weapons trained on the guards who had just entered. "This is your rescue, ladies and gentlemen." The voice belonged to a young man, his age estimated by Asher to be in his early twenties.

"You don't fool us." Jerad scowled at the armed men.

Asher thought exactly the same thing until an older man stood in the doorway. "Darmen? What are you doing here?"

He smiled at her. "Asher, my dear. I could ask you the same question."

"Have you found Tarris yet?"

"Tarris is here?" He looked around the cell anxiously.

"Corman has her."

Darmen turned and ordered, "Find where Trooper Waite is, and be quick about it!"

"I don't understand. Aren't you a computer exec or something?"

"Of course. Just like Trooper Waite is a computer programmer."

"Oh." Now she was really confused.

Darmen stepped forward and placed his hand on Asher's shoulder. He steered her to a quiet corner. "We don't have a lot of time. I suppose you could say I'm the leader of the rebels, my dear."

"You were spying on Tarris?" She thought the old man was sweet. Now she was having second thoughts.

"Not at first, no. We weren't spying as such. We just wanted to make sure she was safe."

"Was that why you gave her the bug detector?"

"It was for her protection, Asher, and to show her who her enemy was."

"Once she finds out about you, she might change her mind." No wonder Tarris only trusted herself. Everyone else had a secret agenda, even herself.

One of the rebels stepped up to Darmen and saluted. "Sir. Trooper Waite has been taken to the Prime's residence."

Darmen frowned.

"What?" Asher asked the question and wondered if she would get an answer.

"This is not good." Darmen moved away and gave a command. "Everyone out of here! Now!" His voice was strong and deep, belying his age. He grabbed his second-in-command. "Find the records for this place and collect evidence. We need the proof in order to prosecute." The man stepped away and headed for the door. "Tell the others to free all the prisoners and get them out of here."

"What about us?" Asher asked and moved next to Jerad.

"You come with me," Darmen said as he headed toward the exit.

Chapter 13

"You have turned out to be a big disappointment." Prime Sholter sat down in his large, ornate chair and faced Tarris from across a massive table.

"That's too damn bad." Tarris glared at him to show her defiance. Her hands were firmly restrained, and the room brightly illuminated. He wasn't taking any chances.

"You should have minded your own business, and you'd still be a trooper."

"Maybe I don't want to be a trooper. I'm sick of doing your dirty work."

"And because of that, you're going to die."

"You can try, Roden." His eyebrow rose as Tarris addressed him by his first name. "The people know what you're up to."

"The people? They're sheep, Tarris, and ready to be led wherever I want to take them."

"And what makes you think the Corps can control the people? You can't even control Corman."

"Do you think you're my only asset?" the Prime said easily.

"The Battery," Tarris said.

"We're nearing success."

"It'll never work." Tarris had no idea what the Prime

was attempting to do, but whatever was happening at The Battery didn't look like it was anywhere near completion.

"The problem with the early program was the delay. Waiting sixteen years for the trooper to mature was taking too long."

"So you're experimenting in turning normal humans into troopers."

"And we have an almost limitless supply of volunteers." He laughed.

"But they're not albino."

"We've solved that problem." His lip curled.

"Being albino is a problem?" She had thought she was special. Now she was told that not only was her birth a mistake but that being albino was like having some virulent disease.

"It's rather obvious, don't you think? How can you have a coup with a group of colorless freaks running around? No, we'll soon have an army of normal-looking humans, and you'll no longer be needed."

"I'd love to see Corman's face if you call him a freak."

"Corman is no longer your concern."

"You got that right. Now he's your problem." Tarris leaned heavily on her forearms as she shifted in the chair.

"He serves his purpose."

"And what is the purpose of all this? World domination?"

"One step at a time, Tarris." He chuckled. "Oh, sorry. You can't do that. It's a shame really. You had so much promise, then you had to go and try to leave."

"You bugged my home!"

"Oh no," the Prime said calmly, "long before that. Sixteen years earlier in fact."

"My fall? It was an accident."

"Was it?" The Prime smiled evilly. "We had spent a lot of time and money on your upbringing. We couldn't just let you walk away."

"You crippled me on purpose?" Tarris had already suspected that when they found the tracker, but the Prime confirmed it so casually it made her shiver.

"It was a bit drastic, but it proved far more beneficial than we had ever hoped."

"Beneficial? You ruined my life."

"What life? We gave you life. It was ours." The Prime leaned back in his chair. "You were supposed to be the next step in the evolution of the shadow warrior, Waite. Twins. Can you imagine the possibilities?" He smiled. "We could duplicate twice as many warriors in the same time. Unfortunately, you were the only survivor."

"You were playing with the laws of nature."

"Genetic material, Waite. Nothing more than human building blocks. Haven't you ever played with blocks?"

Tarris could see he was quite mad. "You were tinkering with human beings... with me. What about my mother?"

"And look how well you turned out, eh? You need not worry about your mother. She was merely the vessel for your making. Her right to be your mother expired when you were born, and another took care of you until you entered the Institute. You are an extraordinary experiment, and we have to know how extraordinary. Can we duplicate you in the laboratory?"

The Prime's words confirmed what she had suspected of late. Her relationship with who she thought of as her mother had been distant, even from the beginning. Those times when she needed a mother's love or embrace, it had been casually imparted or not at all. She had always thought it was because of how she looked. Oh, how she wished it were all different. "Are you saying that I'm special?"

"I'm saying you are a rare commodity that we can't let slip through our fingers. Somehow, against all odds, you survived. Why?"

"I don't care why." Her whole life was a lie. Tarris felt a wide range of emotions—anger, despair, confusion, and disbelief—but mostly she felt numb. Her mind couldn't focus on one moment in her life that was real. Even her earliest childhood memories were now tainted with the knowledge that the woman who looked after her wasn't the one who gave birth to her. Any doubts she had about stopping this man instantly evaporated. He had taken away her life, and now she would take away his.

"Don't you want to know why you killed your twin?" The Prime asked the question like he was asking about the weather.

"I did not kill my twin!" Tarris cried defiantly. Had she, by being born, taken away the life of her sister? The thought that she could have been responsible horrified her. She would have gladly given up all she was to have Rya be flesh and blood.

"Maybe that's why you have the power you have. You have hers as well." His fingers met in front of his face, and his forefinger beat rapidly on the pad of his other forefinger. "Maybe the implantation set off a chemical reaction in the mother's body that combined the two fetuses into one. Hmmm. Interesting. It needs further investigation."

Tarris so wanted to show the Prime just how far she had come, but something stopped her. Now was not the time. She would have to save her surprise for when Corman made his move. "You just signed your death warrant," Tarris said. "If it's the last thing I do, I will kill you."

He laughed lightly, as if she had made some sort of joke. "Tell that to someone who doesn't know the truth. You're helpless sitting there, so your threat is hollow. Unless your shadow can walk in the light, you're as impotent as those rebel friends of yours."

Tarris smiled.

"What's so funny?"

"You are, Roden." She said the name deliberately and was rewarded with a furrowed brow. "You have no idea what you're playing with. What's going to stop those people you change into troopers from turning on you?"

"That's what the serum is for."

"Serum? What serum?" Was that what was injected into the woman at The Battery?

"As long as they do as they're told, they get the serum."

"Someone might think it's worth the sacrifice to get rid of you." *Like me.* "It's a very flimsy way of controlling them."

"And, of course, there's the implant."

Tarris was tired of the game. It seemed The Prime had thought of everything. She hoped someone was strong enough to break the conditioning and do what she couldn't. Kill him.

He grinned at her. "In fact, you really are too good to waste. Take her back to The Battery. Tell the mediprac to prep her for surgery in the morning."

"So the implant does work?" Tarris asked.

"We'll find out tomorrow."

She was to be the first. The first in his ultimate army. This changed everything.

Two soldiers trained their weapons on her as the restraints were released. She stood awkwardly and waited for gyros in her suit to compensate for the change of position. She touched her belt, there was a faint hum, and the suit prepared to move her in a casual walk. Her finger hovered over the final button as she stood and stared at the Prime sitting relaxed in his seat. He grinned at her like a man who held all the cards.

She thought about what she would do if Rya were with her. Would she attack him and the world be damned? Would killing the Prime here and now stop the insidious plan going ahead, or would someone else step into his shoes? What about Corman? But Rya was on a more important mission, saving Asher and, hopefully, Jerad, from certain death. Was it at the expense of the greater good? Probably, but she didn't give a damn.

"I'll be seeing you," she said.

"Most likely." The Prime reached for something under the desk, and suddenly, the shutters on all the windows went up, bathing the whole house in a light so bright that she could barely see, let alone a shadow survive in it. Oh yes, he had all the tricks, at least for now.

Her restraints for transport back to The Battery were secured firmly around her upper arms and joined at the back. The guard reached for the switch at her belt, and the suit began to take a step. The guards lifted her up, turned her around, and let go once the legs started moving. All sorts of nasty epithets crossed Tarris's mind that she wanted to say over her shoulder at the Prime, but she would save them for his next visit. Just before she lost her mind, she wanted to curse the man to hell and back.

She took her first step across the Prime's courtyard when Corman came into view. "She's my prisoner," he said in a commanding voice. The guards looked at one another then at the trooper who stood in their way.

"We have orders from the Prime."

"And I'm telling you, she's now my prisoner." He let his shadow ripple under the surface of his skin. "You're not going to argue about it, are you?" His white eyes glared menacingly at his foes. "You can tell Prime Sholter that she's with me at Black Corps Headquarters. We know how to make her comfortable."

Tarris could feel the fear in the air. It wasn't going to be pretty in any sense of the word. Corman had decided it was time for her to pay up, probably with one broken bone at a time.

Corman's two lieutenants, Jackton and Luton, took their places behind him to reinforce his order. Corman smiled and waved off the guards. "Shoo!" His smile dissolved into a laugh as the men scurried off in the opposite direction. "Sheep."

The Prime had said the same thing, but their meanings were far apart. To the Prime, sheep were the masses that could be swayed by his rhetoric. To Corman, his kind were the lions, and the masses were the sheep, ripe for devouring.

At some point, Tarris would have to face Corman, but with events happening so fast, the time and place wouldn't be of her choosing. She hoped she and Rya were up to the fight.

†

"It seems the bitch here was nothing more than a fake," Corman announced to the troopers in the room, his cold eyes gleaming in the bright light. "And now," he continued as he stepped toward the chair holding Tarris, "she'll finally get what's coming to her."

Tarris was propped up in a chair, her body suit removed and her arms tied securely to the armrests. She looked defiantly at her approaching adversary. "And who's going to stop me? You?" She laughed out loud. "You're nothing but a little pissant wannabe, Corman." It was probably foolish to taunt the beast, but Tarris wanted to vent her anger at the arrogant son of a bitch.

"You're not so special anymore, Waite. You're just like the rest of us now." Corman started to move around Tarris, and his cohorts followed, circling her like a pack of wolves preparing to take down a buck. "Those little experiments back at The Battery were about making us like you."

"You were never like me, Corman." Whatever Corman thought went on at The Battery was not what the Prime had told her. For now she let Corman think he was right.

"And who would want to be, woman? But you no longer scare us." He stopped in front of her and lifted his fist. He let fly with a punch to her mouth.

Tarris's head snapped back with the force, and she felt warmth on her chin. She laughed again. "So, little man, you can only attack me when I'm tied up?" Tarris stared him in the eye and saw his moment of indecision as he looked from one trooper to another. "Losing your grip, Corman?"

"Losing your life, Waite?" He nodded at the troopers surrounding her. "Get her." His two closest associates moved forward, but the rest of the unit hesitated. "She no longer has any power. Now, get her!" he yelled.

"And this is what it's come to, huh? They have you turning on your own kind." She looked each member of the unit in the eye in turn to make sure that they stared long and hard into her pale, pale eyes. All this time she had denied her heritage, but now it was necessary to use it to make them see reason.

She was on her own, and her survival depended on turning one or more of the unit against Corman. Rya couldn't help her with this one; not that she regretted for one minute asking Rya to protect Asher.

The young one called Shark backed away to the wall.

"Get back here, Trooper!" Corman bellowed. "It is your duty to eliminate this enemy of the State."

"An enemy of the State?" Tarris said. "I've never done any disservice to the State."

"You did by walking away, woman."

"I have a name, Corman."

"Oh, no you don't, *woman.*" Then he laughed. "If you could be called that."

Tarris refused to ask the question, even though she desperately wanted to know the answer, but she knew Corman would tell her anyway. He was in the mood to gloat. "You don't know shit, Corman."

"You're nothing more than a scientific experiment, Waite," Corman said. Tarris glared at him. "You're not surprised? I'm impressed." He waited for some sort of response from Tarris but got none. "Everything in your life has been to my"—he stopped and corrected himself—*"our* benefit." Still Tarris remained silent. "You're better than I gave you credit for. If it were me, I'd be ranting and raving by now."

"Well, that's the difference between you and me, Corman. I have a thing called a brain." Corman's fist was lightning quick as he hit her again. "And self-control," she added, earning her another hit, this time in the stomach.

"Everything in your life, woman, was planned. In fact, you had no life, which I think is kind of funny." He illustrated his point with a large belly laugh. He sobered.

Tarris grew tired of his jibes. "All right, Corman, let's cut to the chase. What's the bottom line?"

"What? I thought you were enjoying this little story."

"Not as much as you, little man." Tarris wanted it to be all over. Her life had been crap, and now Corman would reveal to her fellow troopers in detail what that crap was.

"You were being watched every minute of every day, Waite. I even know about that little mole at the base of your butt. But the funniest thing was you trying to have sex with that mediprac slut." He grinned. "Floundering around like a fish out of water. Pathetic."

Tarris could feel her anger rise, and her head pounded.

"I have to admit I found the tape of you falling down the stairs quite amusing."

That was it. Tarris had reached that point where stepping over it would see her lose control. She had approached that point a few times, but she had never stepped over it. Corman had finally signed his death warrant.

"So the bottom line, Waite, is that you were made to study, to dissect, and to extract. Your blood was meant for me."

Shark made a move toward the door. "Stand your post, Trooper!" Corman yelled.

"Who put you in charge?" one of the older troopers asked.

"Me," Corman growled as he stared down his opponent. "And the Prime."

Tarris barely acknowledged Corman's words. Her mind had found that place where her rage lived, and it was growing. She had never had such a reaction before.

Tarris looked at Shark and stared deep into his eyes. Shark said nervously, "I'm getting out of here." All but Corman's two lieutenants hurried from the building, which left Tarris to face three.

"You're losing control, Corman. He's just the—" A heavy metal baton smacked Tarris across her back and knocked the wind out of her. She winced as the pain lanced through her body, but she refused to allow a sound to pass her lips. A second baton pounded her legs, and she saw stars. There was a copper taste in her mouth, and she knew her teeth were now tinged red with blood. She had bitten her tongue when the bar connected with her newly awakened nerves, and she added this injury as kindling to the fire.

"You better not make me mad, Corman." Tarris narrowed her eyes at her opponent so he could see the venom there.

"Or you'll do what? Bite me?" He seemed to be taking immense enjoyment out of her predicament.

The door slid open, and a man filled the doorway.

"What are you doing here?" Corman said.

"Prime tried to call you, but you ignored it. He's not happy. Hello, Tarris."

"Why am I not surprised?" she muttered. "Everyone has come to see me suffer. Hello, Maken."

"And you came all the way over to tell me this?" Corman said crankily.

"You seem to forget who's in charge here, Trooper." Derille moved into the room and approached Corman. The air was still for a moment before all hell broke loose. Corman swung a baton against Derille's unprotected body, pounding him to the ground into semiconsciousness.

"Me, you moron!" Corman spat at the body. "It looks like the fun is about to begin." He moved smoothly toward the door, and his two buddies followed dutifully a step behind him. He called over his shoulder, "Oh, don't worry, *woman*, we'll get back to you soon. I've got some unfinished business to take care of with the Council first."

Tarris took a moment to calm down and take stock of her body. While the soreness remained, there didn't seem to be any lasting damage, and for her legs' sake she was grateful. But she had to get free and stop an out-of-control Corman. Suddenly, images of fleeting scenery played across her mind's eye. Rya was coming.

Chapter 14

"Tarris." Her name came out of Derille's mouth more as a moan than a word.

"Are you the babysitter while Corman destroys everything?" Tarris said in an accusing tone.

"I..." Derille pulled himself slowly up until he was sitting on the floor. He reached for the back of his head and rubbed it. "I came here... to rescue you."

"Rescue me? Oh, please." Tarris didn't believe one word of it. "Isn't the Prime sick of playing games with me yet?"

"No... Prime. Darmen."

"Who?" Tarris hid her surprise.

Derille looked at her for a moment. "No... time for games." He struggled to stand, and a moan escaped his lips as he put weight on his legs. "That son of a bitch." He slowly moved to the side of Tarris's chair and undid the wrist braces that held her firmly in place.

Tarris looked warily sideways at Derille and waited for the betrayal. She sat there and watched him circle around her to finally stand in front of her. "You need to get going."

"And what? The troops are waiting outside to bring me down?" Tarris weighed her options. She was now free, but without her frame and without Rya, she was little more than an observer in any confrontation.

"Where's your walker?" Derille looked around the room.

"Outside somewhere," Tarris said. "Why bother?"

"Because you're our only hope to stop Corman," Derille said seriously. He disappeared for a few moments and returned with her suit. He knelt before her and started to fiddle with the straps. Tarris braced herself on the armrests and lifted herself up, standing unsteadily on her two feet. She nearly laughed out loud when she saw Derille's shocked expression.

"You better hurry up before I fall down." Tarris felt her strength rapidly wane. It had taken a lot to stand, and it wasn't going to last long. Derille quickly fitted the rest of the suit around her waist.

"Your legs... but... but... how?"

"The mediprac, Maken. You should have kept her away from me." Tarris touched the tab and stood, braced by the metal rods of the suit.

"I'm sorry about what has happened," he said.

"That's a little late, don't you think?" Tarris moved swiftly and grabbed Derille's lapels. She pulled him forward violently. "You should have left me tied up."

"I'm telling you—"

"And I'm telling you. I don't believe a word that comes out of your slimy mouth."

"But I let you go."

"Another one of your tricks, Maken." Tarris tightened her fist on his clothing, and the material creased across his throat and pressed into the flesh. "What is Prime up to?"

"He..." Maken gasped. "He's..." Tarris eased up on her hold, and Derille breathed a little easier. "He's about to eliminate all opposition on Council."

"And he's using Corman to do it." Tarris's statement was confirmed by a nod from Derille. "But Corman's got other ideas."

"You're the only one who can take him on."

"And why would I do that? All of you used me like some lab rat. I owe you nothing." She felt her anger rise again.

"But some of us are worth saving. What about the mediprac and the young boy? Don't they deserve a chance to live? If Corman succeeds, he's going to destroy us all."

"Now, there's the dilemma. Why did the Council use Corman when they knew how dangerous he is?"

"Prime felt he had things under control," Derille said.

"And he doesn't. So I'm supposed to clean up your mess."

"It's not my mess, Tarris." Derille lifted his hands and pulled Tarris's fist away from his coat. "I'm not with them."

"So you say."

"You don't believe me, I know that. I'm a spy for the resistance."

"And I'm really six foot two with four arms," Tarris said.

"Prime found out I had lied about my family." Derille sat down in the vacant chair and slid his fingers through his lush, slightly graying hair. "They died six months after you came to visit me. That was my punishment for lying to him."

Tarris stood there and took in his words. Was this another lie to add to the mountain of lies he had already told her? She saw a lone tear slide down his face and felt herself soften. Tarris allowed Derille to continue. She ignored his vulnerability as his hand rose to wipe away the moisture.

"Anyway, not long afterward, Darmen recruited me to be their spy inside Prime's empire. But the time has now come to reveal ourselves in order to stop him."

"And who is this Darmen," Tarris asked.

Derille looked up at her and a wry smile touched his lips. "You know him as Darmen, CEO of Computronics. What you may not know is his real name is Garven Sholter."

"Sholter?" Tarris knew that name, at least the surname.

"That's right. He's the brother of Roden Sholter, the Prime."

Suddenly the vague familiarity of Darmen came sharply into focus for Tarris. She hadn't been able to place his face before, but now she knew. There was a slight family resemblance between the two brothers, and while not striking, one could see that they were related.

Tarris felt a sharp jolt to her heart. She had really liked the old man and had considered him a friend. Immediately, her conscience berated her and reminded her of one of her cardinal rules. She had fallen into Darmen's trap, and now she was about to pay.

"So?"

"So… Garven is trying to stop his brother from destroying the metropolis."

"And why should I believe you?" Tarris didn't know whom to believe anymore. At least with Corman she knew where she stood.

"Because if you don't do something, you'll never be free to live the life you so desperately want."

"I can just walk away."

"You tried that before, and look where that's gotten you. Living in the sewer."

"How can I trust you?"

"You can use me as a hostage until we get outside, then you're on your own."

Tarris felt a tingling in her chest, a sensation that was as familiar to her as breathing. Rya was nearby and approaching fast. While she was happy to have her twin back, she hoped her return hadn't left Asher exposed to danger.

"Maken, why? Why couldn't they just leave me alone?" It was the most important question in her life right now.

"You were one of twins, Tarris. It had never been done before. That made you invaluable."

"And my mother? What did she say about all of this?"

Derille's silence was not comforting in the least.

"Don't make me hurt you, Maken."

"You have no mother." That was all he said. Four little words that ripped her heart out.

"So my life was just one big scientific experiment." She had hoped Corman had lied to hurt her. Now she knew. She had no family. She had been alone, and it was the best place to be.

"They've been trying to find out what genetic structure made you so special. They've made some advances in this area and given them to your fellow troopers. Defeating Corman won't be easy."

If Tarris knew that the Prime would also suffer the fate of the others, she was tempted to let Corman have his way. But her conscience spoke again, and despite her obvious hatred for the Prime and his followers, she would have to save him from Corman.

Tarris knew something Derille didn't. She hadn't given any blood since meeting Asher. The genes they had found hadn't evolved into what she and Rya were now.

The door vibrated slightly before a gust of wind blew through the room. Tarris accepted the rush through her body and found comfort in her sister residing within her. She still had to get used to the idea that Rya was invisible now and able to travel through both light and dark without being seen. Tarris suspected there was more to Rya still to be uncovered, and Rya would need every bit of that extra power to win against Corman.

"What was that?" Derille shivered.

"Your salvation." Tarris sidestepped Derille and made her way to the door. The suit still wheezed from the aftereffects of her time in the drains. That, as well as her bruises from the assault, made her gait a little unsteady. But she paid it no mind. Her focus was on the job at hand. Stop Prime. Stop Corman. Save Asher. And not necessarily in that order.

Rare sunshine greeted her as she left the building. Derille followed a few steps behind. Tarris stepped out onto the road and stopped a passing motorist. "I'm commandeering your car, citizen."

The man jumped out of the vehicle and ran for his life, not once looking back at her.

Tarris yelled at him, "You can pick up your vehicle at the Council Assembly building." She lowered herself inside and studied the dashboard.

"Move over," Derille said. "I'll drive."

She did as he asked. "If this is a trick—"

"Yeah, I know. You'll rip my head off." He put the vehicle back into hover and sped off in the direction of the Assembly building.

Tarris sat in the passenger seat and looked out the window at the passing scenery. Life was going on as normal, as if nothing monumentally catastrophic was going to happen. If they only knew...

"Where's Darmen?" Tarris said.

"With the mediprac and the boy." When Tarris made a move toward him, he added, "Don't fear, they're not in danger... at least not from Darmen."

"And where are they?"

"They're at the Assembly observing the Council in session."

"When we get there, you get them out of the building... and fast." Corman would need darkness to be a threat, and once that happened, chaos would erupt. "I want them in broad daylight and on the concourse with other people."

"Fine. And what about you?"

"I do my best work in the dark."

And in the light, sister, Rya added in her mind. *I'm no longer restricted to day or night.*

Tarris could feel Rya's strength within her, and she was barely able to contain it. If she hadn't grown with her, Tarris doubted that her body would have been able to hold her twin. *You could be your own person, Rya.*

You... you do not want me within you?

Tarris immediately regretted the thought. *No! No, please, Rya. You misunderstand. You are the other half of me. That will never change. All I was saying was that if you wished to exist outside of me, you have my blessing. I will always love you.*

She felt the massive knot of tension within her release. Rya was appeased. *But now we have work to do.* Tarris was forced to ignore the pain across her back and thigh where the batons had whipped her, even though she wanted nothing more than to find a quiet bed to crawl into and snuggle up to Asher.

Tarris snickered at the thought. It seemed that her plans for the future now included the mediprac. What did that mean? She liked Asher, there was no doubt about that, but was she thinking about a time after this was all over that included Asher in it? She didn't want to be alone anymore, but did Asher mean more to her than mere companionship?

Why don't you just admit it?

Have you been eavesdropping on my thoughts, Rya?

Sister, it's hard not to hear them. Just tell her you need her.

Need? I've never needed anyone in my life. Derille told me I'm an experiment, just like you. We are bastards of a political system hell-bent on death and destruction.

But Asher has shown us more. She cares for you.

Tarris was annoyed that her shadow had suddenly become her mother. *Now is not the time—*

If not now, when? You can't be sure that I'll win.

You will *win.* Tarris thought with conviction.

Tell her how you feel.

I... I don't know how I feel.

Of course you do, sister, but you won't admit it.

Rya had nailed the problem. Tarris did feel something more than friendship for Asher, but she didn't know how or what it was. Expressing it to Asher, however, was something else altogether.

Both of you walk in the dark.

What?

You and she deny yourselves, because you're afraid.

And how you do know what she thinks? Tarris was confused.

I've heard her thoughts, as I've heard yours. You are both so blind.

Tarris lifted her hand to her mouth and rested her chin in her palm as she placed her elbow on the car door. A smile crossed her lips, hidden by her hand, as the conversation bounced around in her head. Not long ago, Rya could converse in nothing more than vague images. In the short time that Asher had been in her life, Rya had evolved in leaps and bounds. Now Tarris's shadow was her equal and giving her advice on her nonexistent love life. It was all so ludicrous.

"Hello?"

Tarris drew herself out of her reverie. "Huh?" She turned her attention to Derille.

"We're here."

Tarris looked around. Derille was right. Not only were they at their destination, but also the hover car had been parked and closed down.

"We've been here for two minutes now."

"Why didn't you tell me?"

"I have been," he said quietly, "for the last two minutes. I wasn't going to interrupt whatever you were thinking about in case you made good on the threat to take my head off."

"Let's go." Tarris opened the door and allowed it to push out about nine inches before it swung upward. She didn't let Derille see the smile on her face as she stepped out of the vehicle. Sometimes it was good to be dangerous.

Before Derille had a chance to lock up, Tarris was already in motion, her ungainly walk forgotten as she strode across the open plaza to where a crowd had gathered. They were watching the Assembly meeting on a large outdoor screen and milled around slowly as they waited for the debate to finish.

No one seemed surprised to see her, but they did part to give her clear passage to the front steps. So Corman had already arrived before her. Her keen gaze swept the gathered crowd in the hope that she would find Asher, but she was out of luck.

She ascended the staircase and entered the low building. A number of guards were scattered through the large foyer, standing at their posts apparently undisturbed. If Corman was here, he was keeping a low profile, at least for now. She headed for the moving walkway that led to the upper gallery. From there, she would have a full view of the Assembly. Maybe she would get lucky and find Corman before he found her.

Her ascent was too slow for her liking, but she was bound to the speed of the travelator and what the suit would allow her to do. In the silence of the large winding walkway, the metal squeaked and she winced at its loudness. Any chance she had of arriving unannounced was gone.

On the uppermost level, Tarris approached the doorway with some trepidation. What would she find? Deathly silence and foreboding darkness? The door slid open quietly, and she moved just inside to allow it to close. She moved into the shadows to observe the scene. Her hand rose to the back of her neck, and she tapped the tab gently.

Her true guise would bring a reaction, and at this point, she needed to be just one of many in the crowd.

After she felt the tingle cross her scalp, she lifted her finger to her temple and tapped the second tab under her skin. Her gaze scanned the Assembly. Someone addressed the members in a lone drone, and she thought she heard someone snore. As far as she could see, there was nothing out of the ordinary except for some middle-aged politician boring the audience to death. She chuckled to herself. If the Prime let this man talk for an hour or two, he wouldn't need Corman to eliminate his opposition.

She scanned the audience seated in front of her but couldn't find the familiar head of hair she was looking for. Maybe Asher had already left the building and was in the relative safety of the plaza with its sunshine.

Tarris remained at her post in the shadows to observe the proceedings. She looked intently for the Prime and Corman.

I will look.

Rya said what Tarris had been thinking.

Don't be afraid to ask, sister.

Things are different, Rya. I no longer control you.

It was never like that to me, Tarris. Tarris was taken aback by her name being spoken by her shadow. *But we can work together, can't we?*

Yes, Tarris thought, *we can work together... as partners.*

Yes, Rya replied, *as partners.* It seemed that Rya's evolution was now complete.

The politician had completed his rhetoric, and the Prime stepped onto the podium. "It has come to my attention that the enemies of the State are at the front gate

271

and looking for our destruction." He paused for a moment for effect. A murmur swept over the assembled crowd.

It's time, Tarris thought. A hand touched her shoulder, and she jumped, She lifted her fists to defend herself.

"What the hell are you doing here?" she said in a harsh whisper.

Asher looked at her. "I couldn't leave you here to fight them alone."

"I don't need your help." Tarris tried to verbally push Asher away in the hope that she would leave the building.

"Maybe not, but I think Rya does." Asher stepped closer and looked deeply into her eyes. "I think that now, more than ever, she needs both of us." Tarris refused to answer. "I'm right, aren't I?"

"And where's Jerad? Did you leave him all alone?"

"What are you talking about? I'm not his mother."

"You're the next best thing he's got."

"Stop worrying about him, okay? While we were locked up, he found his mother."

The odds of that happening were astronomical. Tarris certainly hoped there was more to the story than Jerad found his mother. "And?"

"It seems one of the guards took a liking to her, and in exchange for a favor or two, he put her on cooking duty."

"A favor? What sort of favor?" Did she really want to know?

"You know, one of those favors that men seem to think all women are good at."

"You mean—"

"Yes, she had to be his whore in exchange for her life. Pretty nasty, if you ask me."

Nasty didn't begin to describe it, and Tarris's anger

simmered.

"Hey," Asher said quietly, "it kept her alive and she found Jerad. She'd probably think it was a good deal."

"And the father?" The fact that Asher hadn't made mention of him didn't bode well.

"Didn't make it."

"And how's Jerad?"

"He's over the moon, but as far as he's concerned, he doesn't know how she survived, okay?"

"Where is he now?" Tarris hoped he was far away from the danger.

"He and his mother were going home to get reacquainted. I told him you'd visit when this was all over."

"Why did you tell him that?"

"I also told him you'd give him fifty credits," Asher said.

"Fifty!" Tarris whispered harshly.

"Yeah, I told him it should help a lot with the whole bonding with his mother experience."

"But fifty—"

"Listen to me, Tarris Waite." Tarris winced at the harsh pinch of her arm. "He took us in and rescued us from the guards. Or have you forgotten? If you can't afford fifty, I'll give you some of it."

"No, no. I can do it," Tarris said. "It just took me by surprise."

"Don't turn out to be a cheapskate, just when I was starting to like you."

Tarris's conversation with Asher was interrupted when the Prime spoke from the stage. "The Party has declared a state of emergency. A curfew will be enforced by the Council's militia. Anyone caught out on the streets after dark without proper identification will be arrested…"

Tarris turned her attention back to Asher. Her hand rose and touched Asher's cheek. "Please, get out of here while you can."

"I walk out of here with you, or not at all."

"Why?"

"You have to ask?"

"Yes, I do. I have to know."

"You've gotten under my skin, Trooper." Asher smiled gently. "And after this is all over, I'd like to get to know you even better."

"Yeah?"

Suddenly the lights went out.

Chapter 15

"This is it," Tarris breathed. She internalized to talk to Rya and found that her warrior was elsewhere, lovingly cupping that part of her that pulsed vibrantly with life. But it was only part of her.

"Is Rya with you?"

There was silence from Asher for a moment. "I think she is. I have this warm fuzzy feeling in my chest."

Rya's presence was in both of them. "I need you, Asher." Tarris wasn't sure where that came from, but her emotions burst into life within her. The warmth that had been there now glowed white-hot. This was the first time she had reached out to someone and didn't have it thrown back in her face, or at least she hoped not. Asher hadn't responded.

"And I need you, Tarris," came the whispered reply. "Why do you think I'm here?"

"For Rya's sake?" Tarris still couldn't believe someone would actually want to be with her.

"For your sake, my dear woman." Maybe Asher heard her harsh intake of breath, she didn't know, but Asher continued, "And yes, you are a woman and not an abomination." She said the last word with emphasis.

Tarris pulled her into a fierce hug and felt her own

heart thumping in her chest. She had never felt so alive as she did at that moment. Despite the dire situation, Tarris sought out Asher's lips in the dark and imprinted on them all the emotion she felt. At that precise moment, she felt Rya move and her shadow swelled both in power and size. When she could no longer contain her, Tarris let her go.

"Everyone stay calm," the Prime announced, almost a little too smoothly. "The lights will be back on in a minute."

There was uneasiness in the air, and Tarris suspected it was as much from the nervous spectators as it was from the shadow warriors she knew were out there somewhere.

It pleases me to see you happy, sister.

Rya had passed her message from outside Tarris's body. As if answering her question, Rya said, *Your love for each other has made me strong.*

"And we give it freely, my friend," Asher said for both of them.

Tarris trembled. Her whole life had turned upside down in the blink of an eye, and she was speechless.

May your love grow, my sisters. Then Rya was gone.

"Did she say 'sisters'?" Asher whispered.

"She certainly did. She's now become her own person and no longer needs my protection." Tarris was heartbroken that Rya was independent, but she couldn't begrudge her the freedom she now had.

"Of course she needs you, just like I do. We're a family."

"Family?" Tarris thought about that and decided it sounded right. "Yes, a family." She grinned into the darkness. "But that's for later. We have business to attend to."

Using Rya's sight, Tarris navigated the obstacles to the large doors to the outside auditorium and caught glimpses of people stumbling about in the dark. Someone was already at the door trying to open it. "Here, let me try," Tarris said in a low tone. But the door wouldn't budge despite all her efforts to activate the electronic eye. She tried brute power to force the doors open, but someone had jammed them shut. "It won't open." It was a stupid thing to say. Even though it was dark, everyone around her knew she hadn't succeeded. If she had, the area would be flooded with light.

"Everyone return to their seats," the Prime said, "or find somewhere comfortable to sit until the lights come back on." But Tarris knew better. There would be no one alive when the lights returned. A twinge hit her in the gut, and she reached out for Asher. "It's begun," she murmured into Asher's ear.

"What do we do now?"

Tarris hated what she was about to say, but there was no other choice. "Hide."

†

When Tarris had made her declaration to Asher, Rya felt the surge. She enveloped the two souls who were reaching out for one another and brought them together, binding one to the other for the rest of their lives. The two soft balls of pulsing white light exploded like an atomic bomb; their touch expanded exponentially and sent out white-hot shards of energy that Rya eagerly lapped up.

This was what was missing from her existence. Her sister's well-being was her own, and it pleased her that

Tarris had finally found some peace. It was something she would jealously guard from any attack. She now understood what an enemy was, and who it was, and she wouldn't allow them to destroy what had happened to her sister.

When the rush of expectation and fulfillment had subsided, Rya left their bodies clinging to each other in the dark. She rested there to observe the two women as they sought solace with one another.

It pleases me to see you happy, sister. Rya knew that was true, despite her sadness that things had now changed forever. *Your love for each other has made me strong.*

"And we give it freely, my friend."

Rya smiled. Her sister had chosen wisely. *May your love grow, my sisters,* she replied then left. Rya's newfound self-awareness meant that now, instead of obeying Tarris's commands, she had decisions to make on her own. She didn't object to that or feel any resentment for it; she was only too aware of what her place was. Whether a trick of fate or an extraordinary twist on natural evolution had led her to what she was now wasn't something to dwell upon. She was capable of something none of her kind had ever reached before: she could survive without her host. Not that she would want to test that theory anytime soon.

She moved with purpose to the blocked door and slid herself under it. The foyer she entered was lit with muted sunlight from outside. The power had been cut throughout the building, which affected not only the lights but also the doors and moving walkways.

She shifted her molecular structure and became denser to give her a three-dimensional form. There was little time and even less energy she could waste to open the door, but she had to try. She was only too aware of the importance of darkness to her enemies. Even a little light, and a chance of possible escape, was something worth expending some energy on.

This particular set of doors had been jammed with a metal rod shoved into the overhead sliding joint, and it stopped any possible forcing of the door. It took several precious minutes to wriggle the object free, and Rya let it drop to the floor with a loud clatter.

She resumed her ethereal form and hurried down the walkway toward the main auditorium. She wasted no time to search for the light. These cowards would be in the shadows, preparing to attack their hapless victims without remorse.

But she had something they would never have. She had a soul of her own, earned in the storm of battle and the heat of passion. A soul that let her make her own decisions about what was right and what was wrong. And most important, a soul that allowed her to live in both light and dark.

Rya slid under the main door easily to enter the darkened auditorium. She resumed her preferred form on the other side. It wouldn't take long to find them. Their distinctive ethereal signatures were easily recognizable in the blackness. Their numbers, however, concerned her.

She stopped for a moment and examined that emotion. Was this what fear felt like? A dread of impending doom that made her hesitate? It was a strange sensation, but there was no time to study it or be guided by it. She had a job to do, and much was at stake. Her ghostly lips curved upwards at the thought. It had been so much easier when she wasn't self-aware. Tarris spoke and she obeyed. There was no reasoning or understanding about it.

She moved boldly into full view of the chamber. Her adversaries were out among the gathered crowd, and she wouldn't waste time by covertly looking for them. If they wanted her, they could come and get her. Of course, her fellow shadows couldn't reason that, while their focus was on her, they weren't elsewhere killing humans.

Take me if you dare, Rya cried out to those who could hear her. She had thrown down the gauntlet and waited patiently for their response. Not that she expected a fair fight from those who would scurry around in the dark to hide their actions. She felt the emotion deep within her and understood its message.

It was more a sensation than actually seeing them that caught her attention. Whispered shadows flitted in and out of her peripheral vision, moving toward her with stealth. But it did little to confuse or intimidate her.

They hovered nearby, content to be seen by her but not attacking. What was the plan? In the past, the shadows accomplished their mission and returned to their hosts. This time they were waiting, but for what?

†

"What's going on?" Asher whispered from the dark.

Tarris had seen everything and was just as confused as Rya was. "I don't know," she murmured. "The shadows have surrounded Rya, but they're not attacking. What are they waiting for?"

"They're waiting for my signal." Corman's voice cut through the blackness. "Lucky for me, Jackton saw you slink into the building. Why won't you just lie down and die?"

"Why don't you do the same?" Tarris looked up into the dimness and saw the muted white of Corman's hair.

"How did you get away?" he asked.

"Unlike you, I have friends."

"And you're with your bitch girlfriend, I see."

She could barely see him, so how could he see Asher? "Like I said, I have friends."

"This time, there's no getting away."

The auditorium door slid open, and the outside light illuminated part of the upper floor. Tarris counted the troopers facing her. Six. Six to one. The odds weren't good, especially when Rya was busy elsewhere.

Corman moved forward, as did his lieutenants, and Tarris braced herself for a fight. In her peripheral vision, she caught swift movement heading for him. A small body landed on Corman's back. It was Jerad. His tiny fists pounded Corman's head. Jackton and Luton grabbed the boy and threw him to the floor.

"I'm not afraid of you," Jerad said.

"Well, little man, you should be." Corman leaned over Jerad and scowled at him.

"What are you doing here?" Tarris asked. Jerad's presence made the confrontation more dangerous.

"You were in trouble, so I'm here to help."

"I don't need your help."

Corman laughed. "You need all the help you can get." He grabbed Jerad's shirt and shook him.

"Leave him alone. It's me you want."

"Why do you care what happens to him?" Corman had a look of disinterest in the boy.

"I'd try to explain, but you wouldn't understand."

"Hear this? She's gone all sentimental on the humans."

"There's your first mistake," Tarris said. "They're not merely humans, Corman. Who do you think you work for, huh? He's merely human, yet he's got your number."

"Not for long. He's just an inconvenience."

"Funny, that's what he said about you." Tarris glanced from Corman to Jerad. "Let him go, or are you so scared of me that you have to hide behind a kid?"

Corman looked around at the others and studied each trooper in turn.

"Or don't you think you can beat a disabled woman?" Tarris continued to taunt him.

"Leave the kid alone," Shark muttered.

"Have you become a human-lover?" Corman said with a sneer.

"I don't hate them as much as you." Shark looked at him uneasily.

"Or maybe you want to join Waite. Is that it? You're taking her side?"

"Are you going to make me wait all day while you bicker?" Tarris didn't want a fight, but her priority was to keep her charges safe.

Corman turned his attention to Tarris. "Are you so eager to die?"

"Are you hesitating because you don't want to get your butt kicked by a woman?" Tarris felt her hand taken by Asher and squeezed gently in support.

Without warning, Corman let go of Jerad and charged. His arms wrapped around Tarris's waist and carried her backward. Her hand was wrenched from Asher's, and the suit shuddered at the impact. She didn't fight the suit's motion. Her back slammed into the wall, and she felt the pain down to her toes. At any other time, she would have welcomed the feeling, but for now her main concern was staying alive.

She locked her fingers together and brought her hands down on the back of Corman's neck. She struck again and again until he let go and dropped to his knees. A quick jab to her belt activated the knee joint in her suit, which swung her foot upwards and hit him under the chin.

"Asher, you and Jerad get out of here."

"But—"

"No arguments. Out. Now." Tarris glanced quickly at Asher and hoped, for once, she would just do as she was told. Would any of the troopers try to stop them? Jackton and Luton were about to move, but Shark stood in their way.

Corman scrambled forward, wrapped his arms around her legs, and rolled sideways to take her feet from underneath her. Tarris was unable to stop the lunge and slammed painfully onto the floor. She hit the buttons on her belt repeatedly to make the suit buck and shift as he vainly tried to hold her legs.

Tarris laughed out loud before muttering, "Oh, the irony."

Corman screamed at her and crawled his way up her body. He used his weight to pin her down while he reached for her neck. As his fingers closed around her windpipe, Tarris lashed out. Her fingers jabbed into his throat and forced him to let go. As he clawed at his injured throat, she pushed him off and dragged herself to the wall.

Tarris quickly glanced around the area. Thankfully, Asher and Jerad were gone. She was alone with Corman and his crew.

"Legs, I need you now," she whispered. She switched off the suit and grabbed the handrail above her head. Using her upper body strength, she lifted her body off the ground. For a moment, she let one hand go to push her legs underneath her while she used the other hand to hold herself in place. Slowly, she rose, unsteady at first. With a great deal of concentration and strength, she willed herself to stand. She faltered once or twice, but she refused to allow herself to fall. This was her moment of truth.

"How…" Shark stood there open-mouthed.

"Nothing is as it seems, Shark."

"This is some trick," Corman said.

"No, no trick."

"But you're too late to stop the massacre."

"Now there's a trick," Tarris said. "You have no idea what my shadow has become capable of."

"What are you talking about?" Corman slowly rose to his feet. He coughed to clear his throat.

"She can now walk in the light."

"Impossible. And even if that were true, which it's not, killing the woman will kill the shadow." Corman reached for his weapon.

"I wouldn't do that if I were you," a third voice said.

Corman looked over his shoulder. Half a dozen men were aiming rifles at them.

"No, I wouldn't do that," Tarris said. "That would only make my shadow very angry."

"Are you crazy?" Corman's eyes shifted back and forth from Tarris to the weapons trained on him.

"She doesn't need me anymore, Corman. If you kill me, she'll rip you apart."

"You're lying."

"Do you really want to know?" Tarris said. Corman kept silent. "I didn't think so."

Darmen stepped into view. "I have men working to restore the lights. Can we stop this?"

"It's impossible to make them stop if they don't want to withdraw their shadows willingly. It's all up to Rya now."

"Rya?"

"My shadow."

Rya had been aware of everything that had happened to her sister, and she was ready to leave the scene at a moment's notice. Tarris might have been willing to bet her life, but Rya wasn't willing to let her die.

She could see the ghostly trails of the hunters as they circled the auditorium. They were sizing up their prey and looking for the deeper shadows where they would be the strongest.

They hunted in a pack now. Corman had them in disarray—Tarris's fight had left his shadow to flounder. But the others regrouped and moved within the darker regions of the hall.

Was she afraid? Concerned maybe. She didn't want to let Tarris down.

Rya moved into the center of the meeting hall to draw her kind. Would they ignore her or attack? With her new awareness, she realized Tarris wouldn't answer this one. She would have to figure it out on her own.

Rya was like a magnet to them. They moved toward her with speed. She rushed to find the less dark areas to travel in and hoped they would follow. There was precious little light to draw her enemies to, so it would only be a matter of time before they corralled her into a dark corner.

But could one shadow kill another? As far as she was aware, through her sister, it had never been done. The shadow could be blinded but not killed outside the host's body. "Kill the trooper to kill the shadow." That was the unwritten law, and it was a law that her enemies would surely test to the limit.

Rya wouldn't let them touch Tarris. Her sister had been her home, her mentor, and her friend, and Rya would protect her with her last speck of darkness. She found a quiet corner where the battle would play out, devoid of humans who could be killed in the fray. *Come to me.*

One by one, the specters moved in her direction. One peeled off from the group and left. Had one trooper had a change of mind? Rya looked at the aura signatures of those present. Shark's shadow had left, leaving five shadows hovering in front of her.

They spread out their darkness like a blanket and slowly moved inward toward Rya. What would happen, no one knew. At best, they could contain her, and at worst…

Rya felt her sister's pain as Tarris hit the wall. Tarris didn't call for her, but Rya felt the need to respond.

They fear the light. It was a mantra that Rya repeated over and over. She could walk in the light now, and she held no fear of it, so why did they? What made her different from her fellow shadows? It all began with Asher's inner glow. That first touch hurt so much, but Rya had survived and grown.

The darkness tightened around her. *I love you, my sisters.* Rya felt the warmth flow through her. *May you grow old together.* The decision was made, and it pleased her. She manifested as a burst of light, burning white hot and blinding. She would leave her conscious self behind to save her family. The light was like looking into the sun, and the shadows had nowhere to hide. Slowly they dissipated, shredded like tissue paper. They had faced the light and lost.

As her strength waned, Rya sought out the man who was responsible. He would know what it was like to live in the dark.

The brightness was blinding, lighting up the auditorium with the full force of a sun. Tarris turned away, and held her hand in front of her to partially obstruct the whiteness. Corman cried out and staggered back, while his lieutenants reached for their eyes.

"I can't see! I can't see!" Corman screamed the three words over and over again.

Shark stood warily to one side as the rest of his platoon reacted to the flash. "What happened?"

"Rya's revenge," Tarris said quietly. "You saved yourself because you withdrew." She searched within herself for Rya's warmth but found only a cold and empty place. "I love you, my beloved sister," she whispered. She raised a hand to her eyes and hid the tears that gathered there. She wasn't complete anymore.

Tarris activated the suit and was once more upright. She felt a hand on her arm. The lights in the auditorium came on. Darmen's men escorted the troopers out into the light of day, lending a hand to guide them. Tarris held Asher back as they approached the doorway.

"Are you all right?" Asher asked.

Tarris looked at Asher's shadowed face. The blinding brightness of daylight behind Asher's right shoulder reminded her of the dream she had experienced in what seemed like a lifetime ago. Rya had disappeared with the sunlight, and Tarris was left to look into the eyes of the woman who had turned out to be her savior.

"What happened?"

"Rya. She's gone."

"Are you sure?" Asher moved closer.

"I've searched within myself. I feel nothing," Tarris said flatly.

"Let's get out of here." Asher's hand moved to Tarris's elbow.

"Yeah." Tarris felt gutted.

"Get that thought out of your head right now." Asher shook her arm. "Everything will be fine."

"What are you talking about?" Tarris blinked rapidly as she walked.

"If something happened to Rya, you won't be alone. You got that?"

Could Tarris survive without Rya? Would she want to? She could feel the coldness even now, as though her soul had shattered into a million pieces and scattered to the cosmos. There was nothing. No warmth. No light. Nothing.

Tarris hung her head and allowed a single tear to escape. As if confirming her anguish, the drop sat on her skin and hung precariously from the top of her cheek. She had a hollow feeling inside, unlike anything she had ever experienced. Was this how normal humans felt? She felt sorry for their miserable existence without the joy of ever knowing the special part of them that lived inside.

"I'm so sorry." Asher placed her hand on Tarris's shoulder. "I'm still here. I won't leave you."

Tarris looked her in the eye. "You won't?"

"No. How could I ever leave you?" Asher's voice was sweet and low.

"Why would you stay? Everything that made me special is gone."

"And yet you wanted to be normal like the rest of us."

"I suppose I did, but not at the expense of losing Rya. Without her, I'm nothing."

"I don't think you're nothing. I always thought you were pretty special."

"Yeah?" Tarris asked, the word tinged with wonder.

"Yeah, you big dope. I love you."

Tarris's jaw dropped.

"Shocking, isn't it?"

"I... I..." Tarris hesitated. She wasn't sure what she felt was what Asher felt. "I think I love you, too." She thought about that statement for a moment. "No, I know I love you, too." While that declaration didn't heal the hole in her soul, Tarris understood she would survive Rya's loss and go on.

They walked down the travelator to the foyer and stepped outside to the concourse hand-in-hand. They observed the slow exit of the audience from the council building. The first few members of the Assembly audience began to filter out of the building, still blinking rapidly from the harsh light of the auditorium.

Among the exiting citizens were Corman and his SBSC followers, shackled together and guarded by the police. They stumbled in their blindness, making their departure slow and conspicuous.

"Is this the end of it?" Asher asked.

"I certainly hope so," Tarris said. "Rya's power far exceeded anything I had anticipated. She not only blinded the shadows but also blinded the hosts."

"That's powerful."

"Hmmm." Tarris caught sight of Shark and gestured toward him. "Shark saved himself and his shadow because he withdrew."

"What will they do with him? I suppose he's the only one with a shadow warrior now."

Tarris felt Asher squeeze her hand. "I don't know."

Prime Sholter was finally escorted from the building, his eyes white and vacant like Corman's.

"Let's hope the rebels work quickly to restore order," Tarris said.

"And dismantle that abomination under the city," Asher added.

"Sholter told me he had succeeded with his experiments."

"Oh God!" Asher's hand jerked.

"But I think he lied."

"What makes you think that?"

"If he had, why would he still need me?" Tarris hoped this was the end of it all because she no longer had the power of Rya. Hell, she could barely walk. She had always said she wanted to be like everyone else. Now she was.

Tarris and Asher walked toward a waiting Darmen. Jerad stood by his side, fidgeting impatiently.

"Jerad! Just what did you think you were doing?" Tarris punched him lightly in the arm. "Glad to see you're safe."

The boy stepped back and blinked a couple of times, and Tarris chuckled at his stunned expression. "I... I... knew you needed my help." He looked at the ground and scuffed his feet.

"Jerad found his mother at The Battery," Asher said.

"Really? That's good news."

"Yeah. I gotta go. She's waiting…"

"Wait!" Tarris stopped him. "Darmen, give the boy fifty credits."

"Fifty?"

"Don't tell me a CEO is complaining about fifty credits?"

"Not at all, I… errr. Son, hold out your wrist." Darmen reached into his pocket and extracted a small rectangle of metal. He pressed a "5" and a "0" into the small numerical keyboard on one side of it. He held Jerad's wrist still while he placed the scanner over the boy's barcode. Two seconds later, there was a tiny beeping sound. "Go to any credit exchange and scan your wrist."

Jerad looked at his wrist and then at Darmen. "Gee, thanks!"

Darmen's expression softened, and he repeated the motion to give Jerad another fifty credits. "Maybe that'll keep you out of trouble." He waved the boy off. "Go find your mother and take her home."

Jerad was about to leave when he stopped and looked at Tarris. "Thanks for letting me come along. I knew you could do it."

"Letting you?" Tarris's eyebrow rose. "You foisted yourself on us. I couldn't have stopped you if I wanted to." She lifted her hand and ruffled his hair. "You're a good kid. Don't let anyone tell you otherwise. I couldn't have done this without you, Jerad. Your mother should be proud of you." Tarris allowed a smile to pass her lips. She watched the reunion between mother and son and felt the sadness return, not only for losing Rya, but also for her own dysfunctional relationship with her so-called mother.

Derille stepped up to Darmen. "We need to issue a statement to the populace."

"You're right." Tarris made a move to leave. "You're leaving?" Darmen asked.

Tarris stopped and looked at him. "You wanted me to stop the Prime. Well, it's done. The rest is up to you."

"But—"

"No! I've done my job, now you do yours," Tarris said as she walked away.

"Where are you going?" Darmen called after her.

"I'm going back to my home and forget I was ever a trooper."

"It's not that easy."

"Oh, yes it is. All I ever wanted was to be left alone."

"Alone?" Asher asked.

"Not by you. I've done my duty. Let someone else keep the peace." Tarris felt the time was right to step aside. She was ready for a life where day was day and night was night, and not the other way around, especially when that kind of life would remind her of who was missing.

"Come and see me," Darmen said.

Tarris could see the plea in the old man's eyes. "At the park?"

"I don't think that's a possibility anymore. Maken will be in contact with you."

"Fine. He knows my number." Tarris smiled grimly. She turned and didn't look back. Asher's finger brushed the pulse point at her wrist and manipulated the analgesic patch there. "What's that for?"

"I know you. You get the crap knocked out of you, and heaven forbid you let anyone see you're in pain."

"You've been with me all of what? Two weeks? And you think you know me?"

Asher smiled. "Prove me wrong."

But Tarris couldn't. All she wanted was to crawl into bed and forget the world for a while. Her body was one big bruise from head to toe. She could feel every aching inch of it even down her legs. "Let's go home."

Chapter 16

Tarris had slept for two days as easily as if she had slept for four hours. Over those two days, whenever her consciousness resurfaced, Asher touched her sleep patch and she would once more sink into oblivion. Whether she liked it or not, Asher made sure she recovered.

On the morning of the third day after losing Rya, Tarris began to wake. Someone was talking.

"...known as The Battery. The abandoned turbine station had been turned into a secret laboratory for human experimentation. Evidence has been collected and The Battery destroyed. The government has designated this site as a memorial to the hundreds of citizens who lost their lives."

Tarris lay there with her eyes closed and listened to the broadcast.

"The election of a new government will take place shortly. In the meantime a provisional government has been set up, headed by the Prime's brother, Garven Sholter. Until the transition is finished, there will be a curfew from sundown to dawn.

"The trial of Roden Sholter and his ministers will commence in six months. From what this reporter has been told, the evidence collected concerning the Prime's secret experiments and his manifesto is likely to bring about the death penalty."

"I see you're awake."

Tarris's eyes had been firmly shut until that point. How did Asher know?

"Your legs have stopped twitching. They do that when you sleep. You won't need the suit for much longer," Asher said.

"You think so?" Tarris opened her eyes and looked at her with a burst of hope.

Asher moved to the bed and sat on the mattress next to her. "With a bit of corrective surgery and a few months of intensive therapy, yeah, I know so." Asher stared right into her eyes, and Tarris could see the truth of it. To emphasize her point, Asher poked her in the leg.

With some joy, Tarris said, "Ow!" Even though her stomach churned with the thought of the life-changing events to come, she smiled. What she had always dreamed of was now within her reach. She made a move to get up.

"Stay put."

"I've been in bed how long?"

"Two days."

"Two days? You let me sleep for two days?"

"If you could see what I'm looking at right now, you'd have let you sleep for two days, too."

"Why? What happened?" Had she missed something?

"Oh, I don't know. Maybe the beating you received made me do it."

"Oh. That."

"Yes, that." Asher chuckled. "You don't have to be a big tough girl around me. I know better."

After what they had been through, Tarris knew she was

right. Her toughness was not a façade, but Asher was different. She had nothing to prove in Asher's eyes. She relaxed and let her head lower to the pillow.

"How are you feeling otherwise?" Asher asked.

"The bruises will disappear—"

"No, not that." Asher covered Tarris's hand with her own. "How are you... inside?"

Tarris had tried to avoid searching that part of her. It had been cold there two days ago, and she suspected that feeling hadn't changed. "I don't know."

Maybe her expression said it all, because Asher changed the subject. "I've made a few calls, and your first surgery will be in a week."

"How am I going to pay for this?"

"I called in a favor or two. We should be able to scrape the money together."

"We?" If Tarris had any doubts about Asher, this put the matter to rest.

"Sure. You're not going through this alone."

"I need to get up. My back's sore from sleeping so long."

"Is that wise?"

"I'm fine. Honest." Tarris threw off the blanket and used the overhead handle to pull herself to a seated position. She saw Asher move then stop. "Can you help me with the wheelchair?" She didn't really need help, but Asher had held herself back the moment before, despite wanting to help.

Asher squinted at her in annoyance. "Don't patronize me."

"Well, if you don't want to help—"

"I didn't say that." Asher's expression softened. "This

296

is going to take some getting used to, isn't it?"

"It sure is. I'm used to living alone."

Tarris's front door alarm rang. She glanced at Asher. "Are we expecting someone?"

"I got a call yesterday. You might want to slip something on." Asher's gaze swept over Tarris's underwear.

As tempting as it was to stay as she was, Tarris maneuvered her chair to the bathroom. Asher followed silently behind her and tossed in her clothes before closing the door. Tarris dressed quickly. She could hear the sound of familiar voices as the door slid open.

"Ah, there you are."

Darmen and Derille stood in her living room.

"I told you I'm not a trooper anymore."

"I don't think I was asking you to be one. Was I, Maken?"

"Not that I recall, sir."

Tarris looked from Darmen to Derille and back again. "Then why are you here?"

"The Council has a proposition for you."

"I told you—"

"It's not a trooper position, believe me," Darmen said. "We were reviewing the trooper program and came across one division that needs someone to direct it."

"You're still running the program?" Tarris asked with incredulity. "I thought you were closing it down." She cast a suspicious glare at the man she had come to consider as a friend.

"This particular division can't be closed down without consequences. We need your sensitivity in this area."

"Sensitivity? Me?" Tarris had never associated that

word with herself.

"For this, yes," Darmen said.

"What can be so important that you need my help?"

"There are children still at the Institute, Tarris. Children who need your guidance and experience."

"Tarris has her first operation next week," Asher told them.

"We're prepared to wait if she agrees to take up the position."

"It could be a few months before she's fully functional."

Tarris frowned. "You make me sound like an android." The door alarm went off again. "No one visits me, now I'm Miss Popularity." Asher answered the door.

"Excuse me, ma'am." An officer of the law stood in the corridor, holding a woman's arm. "I found this young woman wandering around the concourse. She kept asking for Tarris Waite."

"That's me, Officer." Tarris moved her wheelchair to the door.

"Do you know her?" he asked.

At first glance, Tarris wasn't sure. Her dark hair and petite size were rather appealing, and something about the woman's face struck a chord within her.

"Hello, sister."

Those two words said everything. The hint of familiarity Tarris had experienced now came into vivid relief. "Come in." She moved her chair aside and allowed the woman to come into her apartment. "Thank you, Officer."

"Errr, she has my coat," he said. "I found her naked on the concourse."

"Allow me." Asher steered the woman to the bathroom. They disappeared inside, and a moment later, Asher emerged and handed the coat back to the officer. Without another word, she walked to the spare bedroom, returned with an armful of clothes, and handed them into the bathroom.

The young officer in the corridor saw Tarris's visitors and snapped to attention. "Prime! Sir!" He saluted briskly.

"Thank you, Officer. That will be all." Darmen chuckled as the young man turned on his heel and left, the sound of his retreating footsteps steadily becoming faster.

Tarris raised an eyebrow. "Prime?"

"Only temporarily. I have another job to return to."

"You mean the one under the tree?"

"Shhh. Everyone thinks I work hard." Darmen smiled as Tarris relaxed. "I hope you'll consider my offer."

"I heard the broadcast concerning your predecessor." Tarris wanted to find out what Darmen was going to do.

His sad gaze met hers, and he sighed deeply. "My hands are tied in this. His crimes against the State override any feelings I have about the matter."

"But—"

"No, Tarris. I can't begin to understand what he thought. As much as it grieves me, he'll have to stand trial. Besides, I'll be behind my old desk by the time it comes to that. The next Prime will have to deal with it."

Tarris glanced at the bathroom door. Speaking of family, could this woman really be her sister? But that was impossible.

Tarris hadn't given much thought to life after being a trooper. She didn't have a lot of options, even after getting her mobility back. While the Institute held very few good memories for her, there were kids like her that needed help to cope with who, and what, they were. Could she make a difference? "What's your policy on these children?"

Darmen thought for a moment. "That's up to you. We'd like to stop the threat of this ever happening again. We don't want another Corman in our midst. While we need to integrate them into society, these children have to learn what their limitations and expectations are."

"Tarris." Asher's voice distracted Tarris from the conversation.

"What?" Tarris looked in the direction Asher nodded and caught a glimpse of the young woman as she stepped out from the bathroom. "You called me 'sister.'"

"Have you forgotten me so soon?" Her low voice resonated through Tarris.

"Rya?" Tarris said it automatically, but the idea was too ludicrous to consider seriously.

"Yes, sister."

"How… how is it possible?"

"Your sister? Oh my," Darmen said in surprise.

"The bright light consumed me. What happened next, I don't know, but here I am."

"Two days later," Tarris murmured. "You succeeded, Rya. Corman and the others are blind. Their shadows are gone."

"Ahh." Rya smiled.

"It looks like you'll be needing a bigger place to live," Darmen said. "The position at the Institute includes a residence big enough for three people."

Tarris wavered. "You're making it hard for me to say no."

"That's because I don't want you to say no. Look, you

can use the residence now while you have your corrective surgery. Take that time to think about the job."

The offer was more than generous on Darmen's part.

"In fact, I think we can help with the costs of the surgery and the rehabilitation, don't you agree, Maken? After all, Tarris's predicament was caused by the government."

As far as Tarris could see, Darmen had covered every possible reason she might use to turn the offer down.

"Thank you, sir," Asher answered. "Your help is most appreciated." Tarris glared at her. "What? You would be stubborn enough to say no."

Asher was right. Tarris's independent streak badgered her to refuse any help, however innocent it was.

"Now," Darmen said, "I have things to attend to and you, I'm sure, have a lot to talk about." He patted Tarris's shoulder in an almost fatherly fashion.

Asher escorted the two men to the door.

Derille looked back at Tarris. "Well, Tarris, you got your wish."

Tarris blinked blankly before she focused on him. "I did?"

"Family, Tarris. You now have a family of your own." He gave her a smile, and the men walked out, leaving the women alone in the apartment.

Tarris sat in her chair and stared at Rya. She searched inside herself for any answering resonance that would confirm that the woman standing in front of her was, indeed, her lost sister. There had been no gut reaction, but the empty hole didn't feel so cold anymore.

"I don't understand this," she said, shaking her head. "How did this happen?"

"The last thing I remember thinking was that I wouldn't allow them to hurt any innocents. The light was so bright it hurt."

Tarris listened keenly with interest. "Could your sacrifice have been rewarded?"

"Do you believe that such a thing is possible?" Asher asked. She sat on the bed and listened.

"How do I know? How do you explain this?" Tarris pointed at Rya, whose face showed a mixture of confusion and amusement. "What's so funny?"

"Nothing. I am... glad... to be alive."

"You did something no one else could. You stopped the Prime, at least long enough for sanity to prevail."

"Is that good?"

"The Prime's blindness gave the rebels the chance to upset Sholter's plans. Derille rallied the Administrators to the rebels' side and stopped all work at The Battery. So yes, Rya. Very good. Very good indeed. We're both very proud of you," Asher said.

"Proud? This is a good thing?" Despite the question, Tarris saw a glint in Rya's eye. It seemed her praise had meant something.

"This is going to take some getting used to." Tarris reached out for her. "Come here." When Rya was a step away from her wheelchair, Tarris pulled her in for a hug. The contact filled her body with warmth. It was like coming home. "Oh God!" Tarris tightened her grip and drew a groan from her sister.

"Hey! Don't squash her. You just got her back." Asher's voice was full of joy.

"You're real," Tarris whispered into Rya's ear. "You're really real."

"I missed you too, sister." Tarris felt Rya's strength in her hug.

"I..." Tarris faltered. She could feel the tears and tried not to shed them.

"I know," Rya whispered.

Asher disappeared into the kitchen alcove.

"What is this liquid in my eyes?" Rya asked.

"That's tears." Tarris pulled back to show her own tears. "Sometimes we cry when we're happy."

"Is it dangerous?"

Tarris laughed. "Only if you get caught doing it."

Asher returned with two flasks. She handed one to Tarris and the other to Rya. Rya looked at it in confusion.

"It's coffee," Asher said.

"Coffee? What is coffee?"

"I drink it all the time," Tarris said. "You know that. You'll have to get used to drinking and eating and bathing and... oh boy. You have a lot to learn."

"It was easier when I was in you. I only existed."

"But I wouldn't change what has happened for anything in the universe."

"I wouldn't either, my sister."

Tarris and Asher watched as Rya took her first tentative sip of coffee. She winced and they laughed. "Swallow before you choke." Rya made the move awkwardly. They were content to drink in companionable silence for a while.

"How did you defeat them?" Tarris asked.

"It was you, sister. You and Asher. Together. Your love burned bright inside me. I let it out for them to see. They couldn't stand up to the light and were torn asunder by the shards."

"Blinded?"

"They won't return. Their masters suffered the fate of their shadows in light."

"We saw that. They were blind and helpless."

"If I get this right," Tarris said slowly, "you gathered up our love and passion and used it as a weapon. Then you were going to sacrifice yourself to protect the innocents, and now suddenly, you've taken an evolutionary leap and become human. Not born human, but materialized as a full-grown woman, no less. Does that about cover it?" Even as Tarris said it, it seemed too improbable.

"That sounds about right," Asher said. "Except for the twins part at the beginning. Don't forget that."

"Hell, why not toss that in? It sounds so unbelievable now, what's another impossible fact added to the story?" Tarris giggled. She didn't normally giggle, but the truth of the story was too unbelievable even for her, and she was at the heart of the whole matter.

"Do you think the twin part has a lot to do with it?" Asher asked.

"It has to. That's what made me different from the others. I was an experiment. How would they know what would happen?"

"That's highly irresponsible. How could they have such total disregard for life?"

"But that total disregard gave me you... and Rya. Their tinkering with the laws of nature caused a number of extraordinary events that led to their eventual downfall."

"Of course there's also the sex," Asher said.

"Sex?" Tarris could feel a blush coming on.

"Yeah, maybe she's our love child."

"Where on earth do you get these ideas?" Their

discussion was interrupted by a giggle. Rya laughed. It was a strange sound, but pleasing to hear. "So you think it's funny, huh?"

"Of course. If I am the child, does that make you my mother?" It may have been an innocent question, but Rya's smile was anything but that.

"Don't get cheeky, young lady." Tarris tried to scold her, but she couldn't keep up the scowl. "Besides, I am definitely not your mother. Mothers are old."

Rya and Asher exchanged glances.

"Are you trying to say that I'm old?"

"Battered and worn, maybe," Asher said, "but not old. Oh no, I'd never call you old."

Tarris knew Asher's tongue was firmly planted in her cheek. "Careful, woman. I know where you live."

"But don't you see? We gave her the energy to take that next step." Asher seemed rather proud of her deduction. "She is a child of our spirit... our love... whatever."

Tarris looked at Rya as Asher spoke. She was dark as Tarris was light, like two opposite sides of one entity split down the middle. Rya's eyes shone with a rich blue blaze, and her dark hair gleamed in the light of the apartment. She didn't look identical to Tarris, but something recognizable about the features marked her as family. Was she still dangerous? Possibly. Right now, she was more in a childlike state in her new surroundings. Was she a killer because Tarris made her that way? Probably. Would she kill again? Tarris couldn't answer that one. Only time would tell.

"What do we do now?" Asher said.

Tarris looked from her to Rya and back again. "It looks

like I don't have a lot of choice. I'll have to take that job."

"You do have a choice. We can make do with what we have."

Tarris knew she couldn't. Things had changed. She now had a family. "But I don't want to make do. I want to live, my family. I want to live *with* my family."

She was finally happy.

About the Author

Erica Lawson

Erica Lawson is a "dinky di" Aussie, born and raised in Sydney, Australia, 58 years ago. She has worked as a secretary for most of her working life in a variety of interesting fields from a government scientific organization, the fire brigade, the film industry and finally, for the last 20 years, with a psychiatrist. Many of her friends will attest to the fact that she finally found her niche in the last job, gaining many helpful hints for her own state of mind.

Her first book, "Possessing Morgan", was released in December 2009. It is a winner of the 2010 GCLS award for best thriller/mystery novel. Her second book "The Chronicles of Ratha: The Children Of The Noorthi", a science fiction adventure, was released in December 2010 and a finalist in the 2012 GCLS Awards. Erica's third novel, "Soulwalker", released in 2012, won both the Rainbow A ward for Best Sci-Fi of 2012 and GCLS Best Speculative Fiction in 2013. Her fourth novel, "Reflected Passion" won Best Historical Fiction at GCLS in 2014.

Erica has two novels published with Affinity eBooks. "Miss-Match", co-written with A.C. Henley, in April 2013.

Her first solo effort for Affinity, "Out Of Retirement", came out in April 2014.

Erica now writes solely for Affinity eBooks and her previous novels, first released through Blue Feather Books, are being reissued by Affinity. They are available through Affinity eBooks website, Amazon, Barnes and Noble, and Bella Books.

Romance type: Lesbian romance. I qualify that with adventure, thriller, science fiction and historical settings.

Erica Lawson also writes under the name "Aurelia" on online fan fiction.

Website Link: http://www.ericalawson.com
Yahoo Group: Aurelia's Musings
http://groups.yahoo.com/group/aurelia_fan
Publisher: Affinity eBook Press
http://www.affinityebooks.com

Other Books from Affinity eBook Press

Confined Spaces—Renee MacKenzie   Andie Waters
spends her days pulling waste samples for environmental
testing and at night, she tends bar at The Cave, a popular
hangout for straights in a small Georgia town. Serial
monogamy has grown stale for her, so she's content
working to pay off her debts and hanging out with her old
hound dog. Or so she thinks, until a beautiful lesbian drops
by The Cave.Andie suspects her involvement with the
woman will be only temporary. Little does she know no
part of her life will be left untouched. Kara Travis likewise
anticipates nothing more than a brief fling upon meeting
Andie, especially given her reputation as both a personal
ice princess and a corporate hatchet wielder for Royal
Environmental. What luck to find a hot lesbian bartender in
nowhere rural Georgia. Andie and Kara spend a passionate
weekend together and find that their notions of no strings
attached are far from accurate. Their supposed short-term
ideal diversion of a commitment-free romp hits a major
complication when they come face-to-face with one another
at Royal Environmental's offices Monday morning. While
carrying out her duties, Kara discovers crimes being
committed by and against Royal Environmental employees.
Will Kara be forced to shut down the Georgia Division of
the company? If she does, Andie will lose her job. Worse
yet, Kara may lose Andie before she's really even sure she's
got her. Corporate politics, complicated romance, and long

distances conspire to keep Andie and Kara all boxed in. Can love triumph despite the Confined Spaces?

Reece's Star—TJ Vertigo Reece Corbett watches over the dancers in her gentleman's club with the blue, razor sharp eyes of The Animal. Few know that resting comfortably in her office is her newest love, a tiny MinPin named Smudge. What happened to The Animal, known for her rapacious appetite for women and danger? Faith Ashford is what happened to The Animal. Faith and Reece have been together a while now and they have settled into something resembling domestic bliss. This bliss alarms Reece. It's one thing for Faith to see her softer side, that's vulnerability enough, but to let her friends see it…no. Not the best plan. Under Faith's guiding, loving hand, will Reece successfully traverse the rocky road of emotion and embrace the positive changes in her life? Or will she panic and be unable to control that Animal part of herself? Will she take that next step to declare herself fully capable of love and devotion? This third installment in the popular series that began with *Private Dancer* continues the passionate and often hilarious romance of Reece and Faith as they both grow in love and in trust.

Flight—Renee Mackenzie It's 1983 and Kate Hunter is a student at a small, private college in Virginia. When Lana coaxes her onto the back of her beat-up scooter one night, Kate's education starts to encompass more than just her pre-vet studies. Kate has always done as expected of her, so when she starts staying away from home on weekends to spend time with her new lover it's way out of character for her. Lana is secretive, but Kate accepts things as they are and gives Lana her space. When she feels the sting of betrayal, will she be able to continue giving Lana her privacy? Kate's sister April is a high school student playing with fire as she parties with her older boyfriend, Boyd. After finding someone overdosed the morning after a big party, April grows weary of all the drugs and alcohol. Will she be able to convince Boyd that they should slow down? Will she be able to pull it together before it's too late? Kate and April are forced to face up to events from their younger years, their mother's desertion, and their long-deteriorating relationship with one another. Some lives will be lost and others changed forever when the sisters' lives intersect. Will they be consumed by the wreckage, or will they be able to pick themselves up and take flight?

Reflected Passion—Erica Lawson   Where passion, reality, and destiny combine.
Dale Wincott is a 27-year-old woman born into Bostonian wealth and groomed to marry into the social hierarchy. Her mother is a hard-hearted society matriarch, but her father feels for his daughter and helps Dale find a life on her own as a furniture restorer. Françoise Marie Aurélie de Villerey is a 28-year-old Countess, born into the French aristocracy and forced to marry a count much older than herself. For ten years, she was his trophy wife, forced to endure his perverted desires, until the day he finally died. He had broken her emotionally and she no longer cared for what life had to offer, slipping from one sexual partner to another as often as she changed her clothes. Until... that one night when Françoise looked up during a sexual encounter and saw Dale watching her from the mirror. A veritable angel, full of innocence and curiosity, who touched her very soul.

Through the mirror, Françoise embraces life anew, while for Dale it is a powerful awakening, forcing her to discover not only her sensual nature, but the inner strength she possesses.

The One—JM Dragon Phil (Philomena) Casters loves her work as a pilot, above everything else in her life except Ming, her married lover. Phil needs to enhance her status in the community before asking Ming to leave behind her wealthy husband. Rosa Moran a teacher, raised by missionaries in China after the death of her parents. She loves the country of her birth and the people. Her English grandfather desperately wants her to live with him to atone for the guilt he feels about the death of her parents. He sends her a letter requesting her to come home. When Phil flies to the mission to deliver the letter to Rosa, neither can envisage the chain of events about to take place. It starts as a collaboration to save four children, leading them to the surreal private paradise of Langshow. Could this be the perfect place for the children and Rosa to settle? Phil is not so sure. Chang, an old friend from Rosa's childhood lives in Langshow and makes no bones about the fact that he wants Rosa. All thoughts of Ming disappear as Phil tries to fight her attraction to Rosa. However there is the little matter of an innocent misunderstanding—Rosa thinks Phil is a man. *The One* is a romance with everything, love, intrigue, misunderstandings with a happy conclusion—the only question—who gets the girl?

The Chronicles of Ratha: Book 2 A Lion Among the Lambs—Erica Lawson It has been three years since Jordana Laren's path first crossed the Noorthi's - three years since she's had a drink, had sex and a life of her own. Her only excitement has been spent keeping up with her two year-old daughter, Rice, who is definitely a chip off the old block. All has been peaceful until one of the colonists becomes sick. Bad news shifts to worse news when the disease spreads through their community. Unable to get proper medicine, Jordana is forced to rely on the Noorthi healers to come up with a cure. Soon the herbs run out, leaving her with no choice but to search for more on the Noorthi home planet. What is supposed to be a simple pick-up flight turns into a nightmare. Can Jordana believe in herself like her Noorthi sisters do? Only then can she fulfill her destiny as The Chosen One. Follow the colorful cast of characters in this action-packed adventure sequel as they traverse the galaxy. Of course, nothing ever goes smoothly when Jordana is involved.

Cowgirl Up—Ali Spooner   When the new ranch hand, Coal Bryan, arrives at the MC2, the last thing she's looking for is love. Her co-workers are surprised when Coal turns out to be female. Coal, used to the reaction, quickly earns the respect of the crew with her work ethic and skill with horses. Coal uses the strenuous work and friendship of the ranch hands to try and forget her broken past. Melissa Conway, owner of MC2, offers Coal a place to live in her home. They both are shocked to find they are linked in a way neither of them imagined. Mary Leah, Melissa's sister, arrives at the ranch to recover from a recent tragedy. The attraction between Mary Leah and Coal is instant and mutual. Can the three women survive their personal dilemmas? The love and friendship they develop certainly helps but will it be enough to bring them together. Ride along with the MC2, for boot scootin', butt kickin', dirt eatin', rodeo adventures, with a love story thrown into the mix.

If I Were a Boy—Erin O'Reilly Katie McGuire appears to have it all. A devoted husband, a job she loved, and a comfortable lifestyle. Helen Swenson is a successful financial director of a prominent investment firm, with an unfaithful husband, and few friends. Their husbands' annual trip to Padre Island National Seashore to reunite with their air force pilot squad becomes a pivotal point for the two women. Their lives take on a completely new meaning when an undeniable magnetism between them draws them together. Passion and secrecy becomes the norm, as they have no choice but to succumb to their attraction. Can the vacation love affair continue? When they leave for their respective homes, will they regret what happened? Life is not that easy to change and the people around them are the hardest to convince. There is no more powerful motivation than love. Except hate and there are plenty of people who want to see their relationship destroyed. Will Katie and Helen be able to make a life together work or succumb to doubts and the pressures of family? This story will fill you with the thrill of passion and the tenderness of love.

Nesting—Renee MacKenzie Macy Stokes, a divorced mother who is struggling with her sexual identity, jumps at a once-in-a-lifetime opportunity to help her friends. She doesn't foresee it will put her in jeopardy of losing her son, Jeremiah. Fresh out of high school, Cam Webber travels to Augusta, Georgia, to reconcile with her aunt. When she learns that's impossible, she determines to gain acceptance from her aunt's partner, Sharon. Meanwhile, Cam sets her sights on Macy, but Macy has other ideas. Kenny Brewer is a good old boy who loves his wife, Dorianne, even when he thinks she's gone totally off her rocker. Dorianne gets it in her head that a local woman is her long-lost half-sister. But soon, her obsession with that is eclipsed by medical problems that involve them all. Set in Augusta, Georgia, *Nesting* explores the age-old issues of guilt, regret, and redemption, and the part they play in driving people to create and protect family-at any cost.

Reece's Faith—TJ Vertigo In the return of the main characters from the bestselling novel *Private Dancer*, we see the blossoming relationship of bar owner, Reece Corbett and actress, Faith Ashford. The two women explore new, uncertain territory together, using sexual intimacy as a glue of comfort, helping them become strong and whole. A trusting Reece shares with Faith the sordid tale of how she became *The Animal* and Faith finds herself newly empowered by Reece's ongoing trust and support. Jealousy arises when Faith has to kiss a man on her TV show and two amorous women stalk Reece. When Faith is outed on her television show, things get crazy. With the arrival of her parents on the scene, the craziness escalates. As Faith tries to justify her lifestyle and defend her love for Reece, she discovers that nothing about her parents is as she once believed. This, not to be missed passionate and erotic romance, will have you begging for more.

Starting Over—Jen Silver Ellie Winters, a successful potter, is living on a remote hilltop farm inherited from her

315

parents. Her well-ordered life is shaken apart when her past meets her present. Robin Fanshawe, Ellie's philandering long-term lover, has a fragile truce with Ellie. The arrival of women from Robin's present threatens to break that tentative pact. Charming Dr. Kathryn Moss, an archaeologist and an old lover of Ellie's, arrives on the farm searching for a new site to dig. When she discovers a previously unknown Roman settlement and ancient burial site on Ellie's farm, Ellie allows her to start an archaeological dig of the area. Will Ellie also allow the rekindling of an old romance or will she stay with Robin? Can that long term relationship, albeit tentative, recover from this collision or will an old romance trump everything she knows? Will Robin, seeing the interaction between Ellie and Kathryn, leave her womanising ways behind? Will she take a chance on giving herself wholly to the woman she loves? These questions and the mystery of whose royal resting place is disturbed at Starling Hill are answered in this classic romance of simmering passions, anguished loss, and the wonder of love.

Twisted Lives—Ali Spooner A twist of fate leaves Bet and her daughter Kylie stranded at the entrance of the home of Alex Graves, as she flees the control of an abusive husband. When custom–homebuilder Alex arrives to find steam boiling from Bet's car and a beautiful child asleep in the passenger seat, her heart goes out to them. Alex offers shelter to the pair setting off a chain of events that bring both mother and daughter close to her heart and danger to her door. A heartwarming story of true love that will keep you smiling long after you've finished the book.

E-Books, Print, Free e-books

Visit our website for more publications available online.

www.affinityebooks.com

Published by Affinity E-Book Press NZ LTD
Canterbury, New Zealand

Registered Company 2517228